MR CAMPION'S FARTHING

Inglewood Turrets, an expensive anachronism in the leafy outskirts of North London is a cross between St Pancras Station and Holloway Gaol, and the house where the formidable Miss Charlotte Cambric recreates Victorian elegance for foreign culture-vultures. Vassily Kopeck, the half-Russian, half-Polish physicist and an 'attaché of sorts', disappears as effectively as a cat who turns a corner in a London fog after a visit to the Turrets – and thereby becomes a wanted man. Then Felix Perdreau, the flamboyant rare book dealer and friend of Kopeck also goes missing. Making a case for Albert Campion, who cannot resist a mystery?

MR CAMPION'S FARTHING

MR CAMPION'S FARTHING

by

Youngman Carter

Magna Large Print Books
Long Preston, North Yorkshire,
BD23 4ND, England.

British Library Cataloguing in Publication Data.

Carter, Youngman
    Mr Campion's farthing.

    A catalogue record of this book is
    available from the British Library

    ISBN   978-0-7505-3955-5

First published in Great Britain in 1969

Copyright © Trustees of Margery Allingham Society, 2013

Cover illustration by arrangement with Ostara Publishing

The moral right of the author has been asserted

Published in Large Print 2014 by arrangement with
Ostara Publishing

Magna Large Print is an imprint of Library Magna Books Ltd.

Printed and bound in Great Britain by
T.J. (International) Ltd., Cornwall, PL28 8RW

Author's Note

This story is based on an idea originated by my wife, Margery Allingham, who died in 1966.

She and I collaborated in many of her books over a period of forty years, particularly in the working out of details of the plots.

It had been her original intention to write *Mr Campion's Farthing* before her last book, *Cargo of Eagles,* but she changed her mind, largely I think because *'Cargo'* involves events which could only have taken place twenty years after the end of the last war.

Before she died she charged me specifically to continue with the stories which she and I used to devise together. The unfinished *Cargo of Eagles* I completed in her name but the present work is hers only in as much she inspired it and the memory of her last request provided the essential spur.

Editor's Note

The working title of this novel was initially *The Kopeck Enquiry* though by the first draft manuscript this had become *The Kopeck Enigma,* a kopeck being a small Russian copper coin roughly the equivalent of the British farthing. Worth one-quarter of a pre-decimal penny (i.e. there were 960 farthings in a £), the farthing ceased to be legal tender in 1960.

Youngman Carter's original typescript now forms part of the Margery Allingham Archive held at the Albert Sloman Library, University of Essex.

1

Variation on a Theme

The man who stood like a block of grey stone at the edge of a belt of elm trees was looking down a gentle slope towards his intended victim. For several minutes he had not moved, partly to make sure that he was quite alone but also because he was absorbed by the technical side of the problem.

There was the possibility of incidental death, which would be rated as murder, but this was no longer a deciding factor. He had already balanced risk against precaution, penalty against reward, and now after days of waiting the odds were in his favour.

The night wind was blowing in gusts from the South East, the perfect direction for his purpose. It made the evergreens in the garden below him chatter together; they and the outhouse doors nagging at their latches would conceal any betraying footfall.

To his left a bolster of cloud reflected the sodium street lights of London whose fringe began only five miles away and stretched for another forty. Below and ahead of him the motorway cut a deep swathe through the fields, proclaiming its presence by a procession of headlights which glowed and waned as they streamed eastwards to the coast.

The house, four hundred yards distant, presented its unlikely silhouette as each vehicle entered the arc of the by-pass, only to vanish as it drew level. In this theatrical lighting the black shape suggested a toy fort built for a giant's child or a Bavarian castle lifted from its mountain top by Disney for the entertainment of Londoners in the green belt which surrounds the city with half-urbanized grassland.

Inglewood Turrets has been described by cynics as a mongrel by St Pancras Station out of Holloway Gaol and this is not unjust. It is of whitish stucco, crenellated and illogical with occasional cones of steely slate projecting from assorted roofs. The walls are pierced by gothic windows, whose diamond panes, tormented by borders of coloured glass, dye the surrounding trees alternately heliotrope and puce. But the most remarkable thing about the house is that it should have survived for over ninety years.

At its creation it was hailed as 'Cambric's Folly', for Sir Edwin had disagreed with several architects and finished by drawing his own plans and getting, as he generally did, his own way. He was of Huguenot blood, a textile prince who saw only one side of the coin: that which showed his own image and superscription. He had immortal longings and did not recognize opposition.

At the Turrets he had entertained most of the intellectual lions of his day and many who came to scoff remained to prey upon his patronage. He was an excellent host who kept a fine cellar and understood the art of promoting and listening to good gossip.

Though he bought royally from academicians, in literary matters he was more discriminating and helped more than one poet from obscurity to fame. Nearly every celebrity of the age had enjoyed his friendship and his table. Some have even paid tribute in forgotten memoirs. There are many references to him in the *Greenaway Diaries*, the *Letters of Lord Mountfitchet*, and Mrs St John Gregory has described a Christmas week of the late '90s in nostalgic detail.

The host himself was painted by Millais, Solomon J. Solomon, Hubert von Herkomer and John Sargent, his whiskers changing from chestnut to white as canvas succeeded canvas over the baroque mantelpiece of Italian marble in the dining hall.

Sir Edwin may have been a pompous unimportant eccentric, as Mountfitchet, who survived his hospitality for twenty graceless years, observed; but he had a glorious time making an ass of himself, did no man harm, and enjoyed every moment of it.

Sir William Gilbert, who had often part-
nered him at golf, was deeply moved by his
death, and Sir Arthur Sullivan's 'Lost
Chord' was played as an organ voluntary at
the memorial service. Royalty, in the person
of a retired Major-General, was represented
and Max Beerbohm shed an overt tear into
his remarkable top hat.

In a sense the house died in 1904 along
with its first master, but it was embalmed intact. Not a stick was sold; every picture, curtain, trophy and nicknack remained where
the owner had decreed it should be placed,
for Lucian his son was a professional soldier,
a colonel in Prince Albert's Very Own, who
preferred Poona and Polo to obsolescent
culture. The gardens dwindled but remained
trim, the furniture was polished and dusted,
but much of the park land, including the
private golf course, was sold to farmers and
speculative builders. Commerce encroached
on the Turrets but did not devour it. In later
years enlightened legislators, though they
made no preservation orders, forbade further
development except for the by-pass which
cut deep into the approach, destroying the
rustic lodge, the ornamental lake and the
wrought-iron gates.

The present owner, Miss Charlotte Cambric, a great-niece of Sir Edwin, had very
clear ideas on the subject of running an expensive anachronism which was also a Vic-

torian treasure house. It was her life and her livelihood.

The man watching the house was not concerned with history or aesthetics. He was making a final check before the first trespass.

His appearance was exactly as he intended it to be, totally unremarkable from his shapeless green felt hat to his grey suit and his rubber-soled shoes. The anonymity went deeper; not a tailor's label or a laundry mark remained to betray him and his brown gloves were designed to leave no print on anything he touched. An empty envelope picked up in the street and addressed to a total stranger was an insurance in case he was required to produce proof of identity. He carried an old army haversack slung over one shoulder and this, for the moment, was incriminating; but the contents were essential and he would soon be rid of them.

A square of light in one of the servants' rooms above the coach house, now the garage, died abruptly, leaving only three glimmering needles to mark the galleried chamber called the Music Room. He gave himself ten minutes by the mass-produced wristwatch as impersonal as his muffler and began to walk deliberately down the hedge leading to the garden wall and the new approach which replaced the road wiped away by the by-pass. No point in behaving suspiciously: if he was questioned he was bringing a message for a non-existent chauffeur. Miss Cambric did not admit to owning a telephone.

He walked steadily down the tradesmen's drive, keeping to the grass verge by the laurels, and halted at last in the protection they offered. The moon looked unexpectedly through the scudding clouds and the final yards had to be made without cover. The entrance to the low-level courtyard lay beneath a gothic archway which suggested a portcullis. Once down the cobbled slope and into the lee of the walls and he would be safe. He crossed the open space in the moment of complete darkness which followed as the clouds closed in.

The situation was better than he had hoped, for a large American car, too long for its allotted space, squatted half-way between the open doors of a garage and at the back of this lay a door into the house itself. It was not secured, which meant that he had ten minutes in hand, valuable extra time to ensure perfection. In unbroken silence he reached the semi-basement level of the wood store which had apparently been designed as the interior of a wood-cutter's cottage for 'Hansel and Gretel'. He paused to unpack his haversack, pick out a torch and find the tools he needed to deal with the door to the wine cellar.

The lock presented no problem; it was

decorated in tortured iron but had not been made to provide serious opposition to an intruder. It yielded without a creak and he found himself standing on the cool stone floor of the vault, cluttered with discarded crates and the straw wrappings of bottles which had been stacked in the racks lining the walls. Here the architecture suggested a dungeon – and, indeed, Sir Edwin had called the service lift beside the spiral staircase the Oubliette.

The intruder made six separate piles of logs, straw and broken boxes, constructing each with unhurried care. To each he added three small white square firelighters, and a sprinkling of paraffin from the bottle he had brought. The door at the top of the stone steps leading up to the ground floor was slightly ajar and he considered this carefully for a minute, calculating the flow of air. It would be wiser to close it and rely on the gratings at ground level to provide a through draught. The smoke must not get into the house before the oak beams of the ceiling were well ablaze, or the alarm might be given too soon. He pushed the latch home and wedged the foot of the frame with a wooden peg from a barrel.

If the big car, which might contain more than a dozen gallons of petrol, could be successfully fired, it would block the outer entrance and leave the centre of the house defenceless to burn as fiercely as an incinerator.

He made a final survey of his work, re-siting one of the heaps to ensure that the main wood stack could be caught on three sides, and as an afterthought dropped his haversack amongst the logs. Six matches and the job would be complete.

Half an hour after midnight: zero.

With a box in one hand and the first match in the other he froze, listening intently, aware of a trickle of sweat running down his neck from his hatband.

Far off in a room above him a woman was singing.

Back through sixty odd years came the plummy contralto of Madam Kirkby Lunn's recorded ghost, wailing faintly through the enormous brass horn of an instrument called a Senior Monarch Phonograph.

'He – e – e shall fe – e – e – ed his flock like a shepherd...'

Another sound, close behind him, came too swiftly for reaction, and the blow caught him off balance. He pitched head forward on to the flagstones into oblivion. The matches which had been in his hand spun in the air to fall in a cascade on his neck. The box rested for a moment on his shoulder and then slid to the ground.

The unbroken torch beside his body threw a long shaft of light on to the piles of kindling and the eddying dust.

The voice, faint as pot-pourri, flowed on.

'And he shall ga – a – ther the lambs...'

There was often music at the Turrets on a Sunday night.

2

Overture and Beginners

The Small Drawing-Room at Inglewood, large in everything but name, was the only public apartment to show a feminine influence. It had been furnished once and for all by Sir Edwin on the advice of his sister and was based upon the style then prevailing at Balmoral, lightened with touches suggested by photographs of Sarah Bernhardt's salon. Pink velvet drapes, bobbled at the edges, decorated the windows, the fireplace and the cosy corner; occasional tables stood by each chaise-longue and the walls carried a burden of sunsets, highland livestock and autumnal glory by Farquharson, Yeend King, and Landseer.

It was not at its best in mid morning for it had been designed for statuesque ladies seen by shaded lamps against a background of gentlemen in black with expanses of stiff white linen, making small talk about croquet and the Empire.

The young man who opened the curtained door and held it wide was dressed in sharply cut whipcord trousers and his jacket suggested a section of tartan seen under a magnifying glass.

His bright chestnut hair set off the delicacy of the complexion which sometimes goes with it. His voice was solemn and resonant.

'My Lords, Ladies and Gentlemen, dinner is served.'

Silence greeted the announcement and after a pause he added: 'How was that?'

His only audience, a girl who was sitting on the edge of a gilded settee by the fireplace, surveyed him thoughtfully.

'Rotten,' she said at last. 'No good at all. In the first place the words have to be "Miss Charlotte, dinner is served", and in the second place, your accent is hopeless.'

The young man got very near to blushing and his forehead puckered. 'Character part? They didn't tell me that. How do you want it played? Wodehouse butler? Ancient retainer? Or do I go back to Pinero?'

His mentor wrinkled a ridiculously snub nose. 'You're not getting the picture at all, are you? Didn't anyone at your Academy tell you what it's all about? No? Well, if you haven't been properly briefed I'll have to go right through the whole rigmarole because

22

it's too late to get a replacement. Shut the door and sit down.'

He did as he was told, perching himself on an overstuffed rococo armchair. The girl had a small, precise voice and she spoke like a governess trying to explain a point of etiquette to an intelligent child.

'Our weekend guests,' she said, 'come here to get a rather offbeat brand of culture and half of them don't understand what it's all about anyway. We give them a vision of literary and artistic England as it was seventy odd years ago. It has to be done completely dead pan as far as the staff are concerned. *Don't ever forget that.* Mr 'Mbonga 'Mbonga, the cultural attaché from Uravia, may not have a clue about what is going on and the Peruvian Minister of Fine Arts may be a bit adrift, but the Dutch and the Swedes take it all very seriously and some of the Germans are terrifyingly up on the period. We have to be pretty careful. The Americans are the keenest – they have the whole thing taped. They've read all the memoirs and can re-member all the dates. They know it's not quite for real but they are paying for an ex-pensive illusion and they want it kept that way.'

For the first time the young man smiled.

'I suppose I couldn't play it black-face? I have very good ole Virginny "you-all" act which might go–'

She was shocked.

'Certainly not. I don't care if you were a riot at drama school as Othello or Time-Honoured Lancaster or even Captain Shotover – get it into your flaming head that this is a bit-part, only a shade better than a walk-on. No scene stealing at all – right?'

'Just a butler.'

'Just *the* butler. Lottie – Aunt Charlotte – likes it played absolutely straight. A very slight off-white accent, in case anyone has an ear for it, and that's as far as you can go. A suggestion of the lower orders puts them at ease, but keep your aitches in the right place. Respectful deference is the line as from an upper servant who's been in good service all his life and expects to retire on a pension eked out by pocketing plenty of handsome tips. I'll give you the rules about them later on, if you weren't told before you came down.'

'I was told to treat the job like a "special week". That means joining a repertory company for just one part, if you don't know. Martin Halliday who takes us for mime told me I could do it on my head.'

The girl frowned. 'Martin may be an old friend of Lottie's, but he's sometimes as stupid as an ox. The last boy he sent us was Timothy Brain, who's playing a juvenile lead in town now. He was a total disaster. After I'd drilled him for two whole days he turned up at dinner on the first evening wearing side whiskers and a false bald top to his head, using a quavering voice as if he was over ninety and had no roof to his mouth. The Arts Advisory Circle from Pakistan who were staying here saw through him in ten seconds and were bitterly offended. We had been hoping to flog them an autographed set of Swinburne first editions and the whole weekend was a dead loss. *Now* do you get the message? There's only one star in this show and that's Lottie Cambric. She puts a year or two on to her age so that she can trot out stories of Sir Edwin as if she had heard them at first hand, but otherwise she doesn't cheat at all. Our guests pay through the nose for their two days of Victorian culture and luxury – they expect value for money. If you're not prepared to behave you can pack up now and I can save my breath about the work that has to be done. And, of course, the tipping system.'

The young man nodded contritely. He had, he decided, been mistaken in his first impression: the girl had much more to her than he had supposed. Her blonde curls were gathered in a bang over her forehead and her blue eyes were very large and round. But the prim baby face was deceptive: there was power and intelligence behind the mask which called for respect. He surveyed her thoughtfully from her frilled white blouse with its high collar held by a cameo brooch to the closely fitting scarlet trousers which did justice to the curves they encased. The mixture of old and new puzzled him, for although it was not deliberately shocking it was certainly unlikely. She followed his thoughts.

'This rig-out,' she said. 'The top is a fixture for the day. I have to slip into a long skirt in a minute or two because a party of tourists from the Middle West are arriving at eleven. We do quite a big business like that. I'm the guide. They see the main rooms, the library, the manuscripts, the paintings and pay six shillings extra for coffee and seed cake. Sherry is free to avoid licensing trouble. It's hard work.'

Suddenly he felt at ease, safe enough to give a smile which acknowledged the common ground of age and interest.

'I'll be good,' he said. 'What do I call you in business hours?'

'Miss Perdita. My name's Perdita Louise Browning. Lottie always says "She's one of the Brownings, you know", in a sort of throwaway line and never explains. In fact, I'm no relation of the poet, not even an illegit. descendant, which is what she implies. You'll be called "Mr Rupert" by the rest of the staff and "Burbage" by me and Lottie.'

'But it's not my name,' he protested. 'At least, Burbage isn't.'

'All the butlers here are called Burbage. It's partly to save trouble and partly because Sir Edward's man had that name and it appears in several memoirs. You're generally supposed to be a grandson or a great-nephew; we don't labour the point. If you're asked, you say you understand there's some connection and leave it at that.'

'What about tips, Miss Perdita? Martin Halliday said they were very good.'

She laughed. 'The tipping system is very important because we get a share and it really pays most of our wages. This is the drill: I spot the likely house guests when they arrive for the weekend and tell them the secret of comfort here is to give Burbage a fiver straight away and then they'll really be looked after. Lottie's rather mean with drinks after dinner and you explain discreetly that you can fix a bottle of whisky or whatever else they happen to want, in their bedrooms. You imply that it is your own private supply and has to be smuggled in, though in fact it is all house property and part of the service. After that you play it by ear. Some of the Embassy people have fabulous expense accounts – the Benelux people are the best – but you'll be expected to come clean about the takings. The same applies to sin.'

'Sin?'

'Bedroom frolics.'

Her practical approach made it clear that

she was not abashed.

'The occasional spot of nooky after hours. We put the likely couples in the west wing where rooms on each floor are connected by a private spiral staircase in one of the turrets. You or Babette – she's permanent here, her name's Beatrix Faversham, an ex-rep. actress who does the French maid and arranges the hip baths and copper hot-water jugs – explain the layout if the need arises. Most of our regulars, the cultural attaché lot, know all about it, but it is as well to keep your eyes open. They have to do something, poor darlings, because it can get dreadfully drear if they've been bear-leading a very serious-minded party who don't speak the English so good. Lottie's small talk is pretty splendid and we generally have a minor literary lion or a professor of something or other – who gets paid – to help out. But if you cop for a real gaggle of culture vultures it can be crackingly dull if you've heard it all before.

'After dinner, the ladies assemble for cards or conversation in the Big Drawing-Room or the Music Room, which is off it. When the gentlemen join them a nip of brandy is served with the coffee. You bid Lottie a ceremonial and very pointed good night at ten o'clock sharp. "Will you be requiring anything further from the decanters tonight, madam?" "Thank you, Burbage, nothing more. You may retire." "Good-night, madam." That usually shuts them up and leaves you free to make as much hay as you can by discreet upstairs service. Some of the bedrooms have ante-rooms and you can serve as much as you like. By the way, this is the only time ice is allowed except for cooling. You must imply that it's all strictly illegal and you're risking a great deal to oblige your guests. If you play the scene properly, it's foolproof. Remember, it is tax free and represents a lot of the profit we make, so use your loaf. I'll be there to help out if necessary, certainly until you get the hang of it.'

'What about my uniform? I was told that the job was "all found". Do I wear a livery with crested buttons?'

She shook her head. 'No trouble at all. I can fit you from the wardrobe. Tails and black waistcoat for evening. Striped waistcoat and green baize apron or an alpaca housecoat for token appearances in the morning. The real cleaning and polishing is done by real staff during the week but vacuum cleaners are not allowed in front of guests or visiting parties. There's a genuine 1900 Bissel sweeper which is purely ornamental and a lot more props in the way of feather dusters and so on. As Burbage, you only supervise the working staff when you're "on stage", so to speak, and keep right out of their way all the rest of the time. They're paid extra for dressing up in caps and aprons and long black skirts but even so very strict trades union rules apply, so don't...'

She stopped abruptly, listening.

'Lottie's on her way. I hope she takes to you. Good luck.'

The door opened and Miss Charlotte Cambric made, as she always did, a perfect entrance.

She was plump and petite with a mass of white curls piled high above a face dominated by very dark eyes under acutely arched eyebrows. The young man's first impression was that her rustling grey silks came straight from a Du Maurier cartoon in *Punch* and that only a monstrous quirk of fate had prevented her from being a duchess of the period. Instinctively he stood to his full height and regretted the virulence of his jacket.

She paused at the doorway, surveyed him with unconcealed appraisal and allowed a moment to pass before she produced a conquering smile of welcome.

'So you are Rupert,' she said. 'You have your mother's hair.' Her voice was clear and infinitely modulated, giving each sentence a quality which suggested that it might conceal an epigram. 'I hope Perdita has told you all you need to know, because repetitions are devastatingly tedious.'

'She's been very easy to understand, so

far. I hope I'll give satisfaction, ma'am.'

Her laugh had an embrace which was inescapable.

'I hope so, too. We've had some terrifying Burbages lately. Young men trained, if that's the word, as Method actors. They got all their moves wrong and one wonders if they could ever hold a real part, even carrying a spear for Henry Irving.'

She took his arm. 'Now come over here, because your first task is nothing to do with playing a butler.'

She propelled him gently towards one of the windows, a gothic needle heavy with leaded glass. The room was on the first floor and looked towards the rising ground behind the house. An avenue of poplars and laurels led the eye to the focal point of view, a rounded grass mound on the top of which was an oblong stone structure heavily orna-mented and surmounted by a marble urn too large for its plinth.

'Sir Edwin's tomb,' she explained. 'He designed it himself. Not that he's buried there, poor man. He died very conveniently in India and saved us a lot of complications. Now, look carefully just below it and to your left – do you see anything?'

Rupert took his time before answering. The September morning promised heat, but the sun had not broken through and the still air was misty.

'Yes,' he said at last. 'Yes, I do. There's a man hiding in the bushes.'

Miss Cambric snorted. 'Whoever he is, he's up to no good or he'd have gone to the servants' entrance. He's been hanging round the house for the last half hour. This is strictly a job for a gardener but poor old Colt is too deaf to deal with interlopers. Rupert, do you think you could see him off the grounds? Perhaps it would be best if you gave him a lee-etle bit of a fright.'

'Strong-arm stuff?'

She shook her dancing curls. 'Bless you, no, boy. There's a much better way than that if he's the sort of trespasser I think he is. I hate getting out of period but sometimes one has to be modern. Perdita, I sneaked into your room just now and borrowed your camera. It's on the table outside, looking atrociously out of place. Would you be very kind and lend it to our new Burbage?'

The girl had been watching the garden from behind the curtains of the larger window. She let the heavy drapes fall back and turned wide-eyed.

'Of course. Only it isn't loaded. I've run out of film.'

The thought did not disturb Miss Cambric. 'That's of no importance. All I want Burbage – you must get used to the name, Rupert – to do is to take a snap of the creature, or pretend to, and then ask him his business. If he's a policeman – which heaven forbid – he won't mind in the least. If he's some other sort of official, who's come to examine the drains or the rateable value he'll stand his ground and Perdita will see him if he makes an appointment in writing. If he's what I'm afraid he might be, he'll make a dash for it and we must all hope that we won't see him again. Surprise, as Uncle Edwin used to say, is nine points of attack. Go down the Grand Staircase, through the kitchens and the courtyard, sneak along the wall by the herb garden and you'll be right on him before he can move.'

The Small Drawing-Room provided a dress-circle view of the entire episode. In two minutes the young man emerged at the top of the laurel-lined slope and began edging cautiously towards his quarry.

'He's getting warm,' said Perdita. 'The man's just by the Tomb. I saw him move.'

At that distance the thin mist was beginning to blur details but as the young man halted and raised the camera his shout came clearly to the waiting women.

The laurels parted to reveal broad shoulders beneath a dark square-cut head and for a moment the two men confronted each other. Very slowly the stranger extracted himself from the bushes and took a couple of paces forward. Then he bent from the waist and charged like a bull. Rupert, with the camera at eye level, was knocked completely off balance by the assault.

He staggered and tripped backwards on to the rising ground. The attack was undignified but remarkably successful. The heavy man kicked almost casually at the figure on the ground, giving the blow just enough force to prevent retaliation, snatched at the fallen camera and flung it viciously against the wall of the Tomb. Almost before it smashed he began to run and within seconds he had vanished into the dim shrubberies beyond.

'Good grief,' said Miss Cambric. 'That poor boy. He's not seriously hurt – just winded, I think. Yes, he's standing up. I do hope he doesn't form an unfavourable impression of us. I rather took to him, despite his hair. So much more suitable on a woman. He reminds me...'

She broke off, realizing that she was alone.

Perdita was half-way down the Grand Staircase.

3

Under the Rose

The two men who were lying on long garden chairs on the lawn of a Sussex country house were luxuriously relaxed. They had every reason to be, for the view on the clear September afternoon covered the whole sweep of the South Downs from Beachy Head to the great fold which concealed Rottingdean and the drifting cloud shadow varied the shades of green, bringing new compositions as details faded to give place to fresh patterns in the flawless panorama. The lunch had been one of those civilized bachelor events which the English, when they give their minds to it, do better than any other nation. Now the smoke from Romeo y Julietas hung gently in the air and silence underlined the sweetness of the moment.

They were men of the same generation and background but Mr Albert Campion was taller and thinner than his companion. Very large horn-rimmed spectacles gave him a distant inoffensive air, that of a man who might be thinking deeply of a chess problem or alternatively considering the possibility of going to sleep. It was a deliberate deception, well understood by his friends but sometimes unfortunate for those less amiably disposed.

His host on the other hand looked precisely what he was, a retired Army officer. At first glance his clipped moustache and crisp white hair suggested a good cavalry general but he too had cultivated an air of anonymity so that his prim academic voice conveyed that perhaps after all he could be dismissed as a handsome but unimportant mouse. His name was L.C. Corkran, irreverently reduced to Elsie by his friends, and he had recently ceased to be head of what he called 'The Department', a government office whose function was vaguely defined as Security.

He savoured the cigar until its virtue finally waned and brushed it out in a tray on the wrought-iron table by his side.

'You didn't come down here for the Montrachet alone, I take it. You mentioned some other interest, or was that simply a polite fiction?'

Mr Campion sighed. 'I came with two aims in mind,' he admitted. 'The first has been accomplished with no difficulty at all. The second could be more troublesome. I need enlightenment about a little matter which I feel in my bones comes from the area which you've just quitted. It concerns an old mutual friend or I wouldn't have disturbed your rustic idyll. This is the question, and if your lips are sealed you'll have to forgive me. Does the Department still use Inglewood Turrets?'

'Lottie Cambric's place?' Corkran sat up, arching his head forward and considering his guest from under raised eyebrows. 'You know all about it from your own time with us. A very useful cover for unlikely people to meet without questions being asked. The 1897 Society, for example – you're a member, I believe – can talk to the odd chap from a so-called Cultural Mission, the diplomatic fringe and so on. Oh yes, it still has its uses. I don't suppose quite so many people are deceived these days but the advantages are still there. In fact, they're rather improved. A guest can walk down to the new by-pass, pick up a car waiting in a lay-by and get to London and back before he's noticed. Lottie still doesn't confess that she has a telephone. No trouble there, I hope?'

The thin man hesitated before answering. 'There might be,' he said at last. 'I think I'd better show you what's bothering me. After all, it's my excuse for disturbing the peace.' He took out a wallet and produced a double sheet of printed paper. 'This came to me recently – posted from Inglewood.'

His host unfolded the document, smoothed it out on the table, glanced at it and began to laugh.

'This is Lottie's advertising brochure,' he

said. 'It contains every cliché in the English language. She has hardly altered it since it was first written close on forty years ago.

'This remarkable edifice represents the monumental peak of Victorian baroque architecture... It is without doubt among the most important cultural survivals of an age of taste and elegance which remains unsurpassed... Suffice it to say ... this national heritage ... John Betjeman has described it as...'

He paused. 'Is there anything remarkable about this particular copy? The Betjeman quotation has been added, I notice, since it first appeared. Something I've missed?'

'Nothing, except the word "Bert" inscribed in pencil in the top right-hand corner. That doesn't suggest our Lottie at all – she's far too much in period to call me by a nickname suggesting the common man. But somebody put it there to attract my attention. The plot succeeded. At least I kept it on my desk until the following morning, when *this* arrived in a typewritten envelope, postmarked Cambridge.'

Mr Campion held out a sheet of tracing paper of the same size as the original folder. It had been heavily scored by disjointed black parallel lines evidently made by a felt-nibbed pen of the type used for lettering notices.

'I wasn't altogether speedy on the uptake,' he confessed. 'But the word "Bert" appears

38

again in the same corner. Try placing them one above the other and you'll get a very odd result. "Intriguing" is the word that springs too readily to mind, especially after reading the first handout. In a minute or two, unless you're very careful, your imagination will start boggling in its own inimitable style.'

Corkran stood up and placed the two sheets on the table, holding them flat with the tips of his fingers. The words surviving between the gaps in the black ruling were legible beneath the transparent paper and he began to read aloud.

'*Inglewood Turrets. Miss Charlotte Cambric and others … in great need … owing to the danger … during … coming period of time… It is not too much to hope that … interested friends will make great efforts… Delicate and particular … expressions of fidelity and affection … help … in remarkable circumstances pressures of contemporary life compel … no further explanation.*'

Corkran sniffed.

'Very odd. Now I come to consider it, very odd indeed. Your correspondent has made such a mouthful of it for one thing, whatever he's getting at. If he wanted to approach you in this melodramatic roundabout way why not put it into straight English? *Redolet lucerna,* so to speak, yet with all that mass of platitude available you could put the same message far more simply.' He held up the printed folder. 'For example he could have made the message read; "Miss Cambric and others are in great need of help at this time. There is some danger. There are remarkable circumstances caused by the pressures of contemporary life. No further explanation is possible." He could even have added "Yours faithfully, Anon", I see, if he had worked at it with real application.'

'Perhaps,' suggested Mr Campion mildly, 'he's a poor damned foreigner without your command of the language. Or perhaps he just wanted to make himself interesting.'

'He could be some bright lad who was profoundly bored with Lottie's brand of Victoriana and was whiling away an odd evening with a joke instead of listening to literary chat. Do you take it seriously?'

The thin man paused before answering.

'I like Lottie,' he admitted defensively. 'She could have been a Marie Tempest or an Edith Evans if she'd given her mind to the theatre, which is where she really belongs. If this isn't a joke, it's a cry from the heart. That's why I came to you, rather belatedly. Has anything happened which could get her into trouble? You still collect a trifle of gossip here and there, I hope?'

Corkran refolded the brochure, holding it in one hand near his mouth and pursing his lips. He began to blow thoughtfully on the sharp edge as if the whistling rustle would bring him inspiration.

'If this is a genuine appeal,' he said at last, 'we may assume it comes from a foreigner – possibly someone from behind the Curtain. I don't know, but there's something in the choice of phrase which I can hear in the Russian rather than, say, the French idiom.'

'The Soviets use the place quite a bit, or they used to when I was a boy,' said Mr Campion reminiscently. 'It was a permitted form of escape. Dull and educational in theory but rather amusing in practice, if you treated the servants properly. Better than that barracks in Highgate in any case. Does that still go on?'

'Oh, yes. They include the Turrets in most of the conducted tours for their nationals and favoured visitors. Young writers and musicians who don't offend against official thought sometimes get a weekend there. It has even been taken seriously and used as propaganda to describe the kind of decadent imperialist lives we still lead over here. *Life* ran a story about the place a couple of years ago and they pirated all the pictures and used them with somewhat different captions.'

He held out the folder. 'That's the odd thing about them, Albert. I've never known a White Russian who wasn't by way of being a wit and never met an official Red who had more than an elementary gleam of humour.

Just as well, perhaps. If they had *that* ingredient they would be twice as dangerous as...'

He broke off abruptly as if he had lost his train of thought. Mr Campion waited politely.

'Something occurred to you?' he suggested at last. 'An exception which proves the rule?'

Corkran continued the pause for some time, one eyebrow raised and the other contracted in a frown.

'Yes,' he said finally. 'Yes, in a way. Have you ever heard of Vassily Kopeck?'

Mr Campion considered.

'Kopeck. A little round man, with very black hair, going bald – a childlike smile – draws slightly rude pictures on menus and writes simple jokes under them. Apparently naïve, but rather endearing. Is that the chap you're thinking of?'

Corkran stroked the lobe of his right ear and when he answered his tone was regretful.

'It could well be, though I've never seen the fellow. An attaché of sorts, I believe, but then they have so many. They come and go and it isn't easy to keep tabs on them all. You've met him?'

'Once – no, twice, now I come to think of it. At a reception of some kind, in tow with a man called Perdreau, who's a rare-book dealer, and – now we might be getting warm – at a dinner of the 1897 Society. Not at the Turrets, but then we Victorians do ourselves proud wherever a good chef is to be found. Yes, I remember little Kopeck. And another thing...' he paused. 'You don't look happy, Elsie. Am I treading on forbidden territory?'

'You could be. But go on.'

'He knows my christian name, because there was some light chat about social changes and the niceties of affectionate diminutives. Albert is all right, but out of date and therefore slightly comic. Bertie is completely U, on account of the late monarch. But Bert remains solidly plebeian. It struck him as being remarkably funny. He could easily be my correspondent. There's a fair shade of odds that he's been down to Lottie's place, for he was just the type. Anything known, as they say?'

His host continued to tug at his ear. Although both men knew each other well, he was not at ease. He was still cautious, giving ground reluctantly. Finally he sighed.

'This is hearsay and no more. I gathered it quite accidentally when I went back to the Department the other day to clear up a point which we thought it best to keep off the record – as this must be, you know. Kopeck has disappeared.'

'Defected?'

'That's just the point. He hasn't asked for

asylum, at least he hasn't approached our people on the subject. That is certain. No, as far as I know he's just vanished – a very difficult thing for a man in his position to do. They're looking for him. Rather urgently, I gathered.'

'Have they made the soft approach?' Campion used the technical phrase which his companion accepted without hesitation.

'Oh, yes. Very civil and kid glove. It was regrettable if one of their people had been seduced by Western decadence but would we let them know? You probably remember the form. Then something a bit stiffer at a higher level. For once we were just plain Honest Johns and I think we convinced them. I hope so, because we've nothing to conceal and we're not looking for trouble at the moment.

'They must have tried the Americans on the same tack?'

'And got the same answers, one assumes, or the repercussions would have stopped. I understand that is not the case. The search continues. I'd say he's either dead or in Switzerland, which is much the same thing. The odd aspect of the matter is that they haven't used the Press to stir up trouble and gain some kind of dubious diplomatic point. Newspapers have certain advantages if the story is sufficiently sensational. They can whip up three or four million amateur police-men and would-be reporters all anxious to find a needle in a haystack – it's been done dozens of times when a man goes into hiding and it is usually fatal for the poor brute. Yet there's been complete silence. That is one reason why I don't find the affair at all savoury. Do you *have* to interest yourself in it?'

Not for the first time Campion had the feeling of being back in his tutor's rooms at Cambridge. Corkran had the air of a don who disapproved the line of thought expressed by a student in an inferior essay. Campion knew the manner of old and was prepared to stand his ground.

'You said "one reason". Are there others?'

'In point of fact there are.' Corkran frowned. 'I don't know how informed you are about recent trends in the U.S.S.R. There is an unpleasant new line with undesirables and non-conformists. They commit suicide, or so their deaths are described.'

'It sounds Japanese rather than Slavonic.'

'As you say. Yet this is the explanation given to cover quite a quantity of eliminations which one assumes have a political motive. In Warsaw, where it appears to have started, twenty students studying assorted subjects, including three from the old École de Chopin, and three lecturers, a physicist, a chemist and a professor of languages. From there this form of purge has spread out to other centres of learning, Moscow, Leningrad and points south, but the attack seems to be more on master than pupil, though, of course, our intelligence is incomplete. The latest item comes from East Berlin and that is what I find disturbing. A man called Kropotkin, with whom we were lightly in touch, killed himself for no apparent reason, except that he was associated – in friendship, not technology – with several of the previous victims.'

Mr Campion digested the information thoughtfully.

'The suggestion, I suppose, is that they shared some common line of thought or information which it has been considered wise to suppress. The Politburo and the K.G.B. must feel very strongly on the subject.'

'That would appear to be the logical inference.'

'Is there any link between all this and our friend Kopeck?'

'Not that I know of, except that both men were of the same world, scholastically speaking. Intellectuals are not popular at the moment. Kopeck is a physicist of some repute – radiation is his subject – and he is half Polish. He was born in Prague, in fact, though his father was from Kiev. If he had an idea that trouble was heading his way he might possibly decide to defect – it would be understandable yet he has refrained from that step. Given that our premise is accurate, he has put himself in a totally untenable position. His passport is withdrawn and he is a wanted man. We are interested in finding him for the sake of good relations, in which case we should probably hand him over, since he has had ample opportunity to defect if he had any intention of doing so. We don't want any more scandals on our plate. His own people over here are putting out a very intensive search for him which we can hardly hinder, even if we don't actively help. Every man's hand is against him.'

'And when they catch him?'

'When they catch him,' said Corkran dispassionately, 'they will eliminate him by any method that happens to be in vogue at the time. Suicide seems to be the current fashion.' He turned directly to Campion. 'Let me give you a piece of advice, as between one ex-colleague and another. Warn Charlotte Cambric, if you think there is any real connection between her and Kopeck. Tell her not to meddle with matters which are certainly nothing to do with her – scare her a little, if you think she will respond to that sort of treatment, which I would doubt. But keep her and Inglewood out of the business. If you interfere you can only make matters worse for her and run yourself into a packet of trouble. Knight errantry is as out of date as a passing knowledge of the classics and quite ridiculous in a man of your age. I hope I make myself clear?'

'As a crystal set,' said Mr Campion. 'Unfortunately, I can't accept your warning entirely. I already have an emissary at the Turrets. He seems to be enjoying himself.'

4

The Men who Came to Dinner

The Friends of Literature of Zürich, who composed the weekend guests at the Turrets, were not an inspiring group.

Six men in austere suits and two women in coats and skirts, each a conscious essay in mediocrity, had arrived in hired cars at four o'clock in the afternoon. Despite Perdita's blandishments and the professional skill of her welcome, which was handsomely garnished by two maids in caps and aprons supervised by the new Burbage himself, they refused tea and retired directly to their rooms, scarcely speaking a word and showing a remarkable lack of interest in their surroundings. Perdita beckoned Rupert from the upper hall and they retreated together into the privacy of the butler's pantry.

'A terrible gaggle of drones,' she said. 'Not a smile in a cartload. And the clothes look as if they've been made in the workshop of a home for retired undertakers. They were booked through one of our most reliable agencies but I can't even fathom what language they normally speak. This is going to be a lost weekend; I'd put the tips at five bob a head, probably less.'

She perched herself on the green baize table and swung her legs, pulling her long taffeta skirt which was buttoned from head to foot, well above her knees. Rupert, stiffly shirted under his swallow tails, leaned against the door and regarded her with approval.

'With those faces there'll be no fun and games, that's for certain,' he said. 'Do their names tell you anything? The Swiss themselves don't go in for touring as a rule. Any clue there?'

She shook her head. 'Madame Schmidt, Mr Nascott – he's English, the thick one who looks like a sanitary inspector – Herr Weingarten, Mr Gunter, Miss Richards ... just a meaningless mixed bag. Lottie and Felix are going to have their work cut out to bring this lot to life.'

'Felix?'

'Felix Perdreau,' she explained. 'He is our entertainment man for the evening. A regular stand-by when we think the party isn't important enough to get a real celebrity. He deals in rare books, really knows about our period and plays the piano rather well. Lottie and he combine to do a bit of horse trading sometimes and I wouldn't trust his autographed first editions all the way. Not a nice chap – at least I don't care for him – but he's very useful. He has the cottage on the estate which Uncle Edwin built for Brinsley.

'Considering how very little the man wrote, Perdreau has a wonderful quantity of his original manuscripts. He found three versions of *The Lively Oracle* in a box in the attic – or so he says.'

'I've never heard of Brinsley,' said Rupert. 'Should I read him up so as to be in the picture?'

She shook her head. 'It's not important. He was a minor poet whom Edwin befriended, hoping to produce immortal verse by putting the poor little beast into an expensive hothouse. He hardly wrote a line after he was installed but there were two or three ripe scandals about him and his girl friends – mostly maids from the Turrets – and in the end one of them disappeared very suspiciously. Fortunately Brinsley died before the row came to a head and Great Uncle Edwin did his best to make sure that he was forgotten. He didn't altogether succeed and now Perdreau is reviving his memory, incorporating him into the mystique of the Turrets and doing very nicely out of it.'

A muffled buzz from above their heads cut her short and she looked up to a box which housed a row of indicators.

'That's Lottie, from her bedroom. I'll bet on what she wants – champagne instead of sherry before dinner. You'd better arrange for half a dozen to be put in the wine cooler. She always does it when things look as if they might be sticky.'

But even the golden elixir, delicately served in hollow-stemmed glasses, failed to produce a spark. The guests stood, solemn and silent, like travellers waiting for a train which is expectedly late. The two women, now in unremarkable black dresses, wandered about the Great Drawing-Room gazing idly at the bland idylls of Henry Ryland, Ralph Peacock's portrait of Lucian as a boy and mural legends by A. T. Nowell, displaying the animation a tired commuter offers to advertising hoardings.

Lottie, staunchly supported by Felix Perdreau, battled against implacable odds. His appearance was theatrical by nature and intent, for his black hair and beard were flecked with white streaks, emphasizing his deliberately Byronic air. He wore a brown velvet coat which could have been a Victorian smoking jacket, whose rich texture went well with a sallow Latin complexion. But the most striking characteristic was his voice, deep, modulated and musical, an instrument which he used with conscious skill, establishing an immediate intimacy between himself and his audience.

He was talking now to the man called Nascott, fishing delicately for background information to establish a common interest.

'We have many curiosities as well as treasures in the library here, if this appeals to you. For example, Radishchev's *Journey from St Petersburg to Moscow* – a relation of Stern's *Sentimental Journey*. The 1798 edition, of course, which was suppressed. Fascinating if one happens to read that tongue.'

'And do you?' The visitor spoke without interest.

'I have a smattering but not enough to enjoy reading in the original text. The translation would appear to be indifferent, but then the time was bad for such work. Even Derzhavin in the earlier versions suffers, one realizes ... but perhaps this is not your period?'

His companion glanced pointedly from the Second Empire clock above the fireplace to his own wrist.

'They told me dinner was at eight. It is now five minutes past. I don't like champagne and I am getting hungry.' He spun on his heel and addressed himself directly to his hostess, who was holding court to three stolid figures, none of whom appeared to understand a word of the vivacious monologue she was offering.

'Miss Cambric, do we have much longer

to wait?'

She turned towards him, amusement chasing surprise across her face, delaying her answer until she included the group in her audience.

'Be patient, my dear man. Uncle Edwin always said that a good sauce was like a good sonnet – it needed genius in preparation and wit to appreciate the result. I refuse to hurry the chef or he'll go back to the Carrefour where I found him, so you must sharpen your wits. Perdita, refresh Mr Nascott's glass in that pious hope.'

Rupert's entry with his well-rehearsed announcement came a fraction too late to save the situation. Sheepish grins from everyone within earshot showed that the shaft had gone home.

Dinner got off to a bad start. The room with its heavily carved minstrels' gallery was dominated by an Italian marble mantelpiece, above which hung the last portrait of Sir Edwin, painted by Sargent in 1902, showing him proud and successful, confident of his own importance in a world which was much to his liking. It was lit from above, so that the two eight-point antlers which flanked it, their owners brooding glassily over the table, became less absurd in the comparative gloom. Four-branch candlesticks on the table provided the only other lighting, emphasizing the opulence of silver, glass and napery. But despite the excellence of *sole bonne femme,* grouse, sorbet and savoury the occasion was chilly with social disaster.

None of the guests did more than sip at the three wines which were served and Rupert, watching curiously for some snatch of revealing conversation, gathered nothing more entertaining than that the price of macintoshes was higher in Oxford Street than in some of the Manchester stores.

The company spoke, when the occasion demanded, in English with an assortment of accents ranging from middle European to south London, talking stiltedly as to strangers trapped by accident in the same waiting-room. Lottie, at the head of the long table, had placed Nascott on her left but he answered her chaff in monosyllables, concentrating on his food, making no attempt to smile at her anecdotes. He was a heavy man, balding, with a round face remarkable only for very black eyes set too close to a snub nose. Perdreau, at the far end, poured out all his considerable charm before the studied indifference of the two women and before the port appeared he was sulking openly. He filled his glass, keeping the decanter by his side, drank at a gulp and refilled it.

A clock began striking the hour of nine, to be echoed by others in the house. Nascott checked with his own watch and a long silence settled over the table. For all the guests he had become the centre of interest and he waited until the last chime had died. It was clearly a signal which had been pre-arranged.

'Right.'

Pushing plates and cutlery and glasses away from him, he cleared a space and produced a black notebook which he opened, folding it flat and placing a pen beside it.

'Miss Cambric, your outside staff will be leaving now, if they haven't already gone. There's no point any longer in this charade. Tell your young actor to switch on the lights in here.'

He turned to Rupert. 'Stand by the table when you've finished. You are not to leave the room.'

Lottie sat very still and the frozen moment hung in the air. Her face was impassive but anger brought bright splashes of colour to her cheeks. Her dignity was as immaculate as the timing of the pause before she spoke.

'Burbage, you may do as my guest suggests, or I'm afraid his lack of manners may become even more obvious. I don't know whose lackey you are, Mr Nascott, but one cannot admire your employer's taste.'

The man with the notebook sighed noisily.

'Don't make things difficult for us, madam. We've taken over this house for the time being and you may as well face the fact. You are being paid very well for your trouble, so you've no cause for complaint. Just answer my questions like a sensible woman and we can all go home before midnight. I'm not using any threats at present but you must see that you're in no position to object. Have you got that?'

Perdreau stood up. He was a trifle unsteady and his sallow skin had paled to an unhealthy yellow.

'This is intolerable,' he muttered. 'If you'll excuse me, Lottie, I'll–'

He got no further. The women on either side of him pulled him ignominiously back into his chair and as if by an order the men rose from the table and placed themselves about the room, covering the windows and the two double doors.

Nascott picked up his pen.

'Now,' he said. 'Perhaps we can get on.' He cleared his throat. 'Miss Cambric, about a month ago, the weekend of the 29th of July in fact, you had a guest here called Kopeck – a Mr Vassily Kopeck. He wasn't a stranger – he'd been here several times before. As you know very well he did not return to his London address. Various approaches have been made to you since then, requests for information about him, and you've not been at all helpful, to put it mildly. I might say you've been a bit rude about it, but you're the best judge of that. So now I'm afraid I'm going to have to go over the ground again.'

Lottie pushed back her chair.

'Poor Mr Kopeck,' she said. 'How embarrassing for him to have such gauche watchdogs. I have no idea where he went after leaving here, as I've said on several occasions. He came, he stayed a couple of nights and left of his own volition as far as I know on the Monday morning. I'm accustomed to rising rather late and I don't question my staff about the hours my guests keep. I have not seen or heard of him since, but I'm sure he is quite capable of looking after himself. Is that all? Because I really have nothing else to add, even if I was able to.'

Nascott returned her stare with equal steadiness, his dark eyes cold and dispassionate as a butcher assessing the weight of a carcass. It was a long duel which he ended by glancing round to his supporters.

'You are helping no one, Miss Cambric, especially yourself. An organized search of the house may make a bit of a mess, but you give me no choice.'

He drew a bunch of keys from his pocket and placed them in front of him.

'These are yours. If you want to play it the hard way, go ahead and say so. It won't make two penn'oth of gin's difference. Mr Kopeck is going to be found because no power on earth can prevent it. By all means complain to the police, but you'll get nothing but a few apologies. Complain to the embassies, who are your best clients, and I can promise you will be blacklisted and so lose most of your income. Kopeck is a wanted man, Miss Cambric, and from your point of view a very dangerous one. I don't suppose you consider yourself a silly woman. Make up your mind to behave sensibly.'

He turned to Rupert, who had moved slowly forward and was now standing directly behind Lottie's chair.

'Keep your distance, young man. If we have to hit you, you won't be able to act for a year.'

Perdreau at the far end of the table suddenly raised his head and snorted.

'Hired assassins, eh? Do you know what I think about you Nascott? You're a renegade policeman, probably sacked from the Force for abusing your position. Now you've turned to running a bunch of hoodlums for the highest bidder. Very charming, very typical.'

The accusation was so unexpected and yet so likely that it stung like the calculated slap which demands a duel.

The heavy man scowled, opened his mouth to retort and changed his mind. Perdreau pressed his advantage.

'In any case,' he said. 'Your bloodhounds won't find Kopeck here. I saw him go.'

'Did you, now?' Nascott picked up his notebook, flicked back several pages and

58

began to read. 'You call yourself Felix Perdreau. Originally Francis James Partridge – changed by deed poll twenty years ago. Aged forty-five. Dealer in rare books, manuscripts and so on. My information adds "including pornography and suspected forgeries". Would you like me to go on? I'd say you were a lousy witness. Just what are you asking me to believe?'

Perdreau shrugged his shoulders. He was unabashed, and Rupert had the impression that he was pleased to be back as the centre of attention.

'Like a lot of your information,' he said. 'It is imperfect and inaccurate. I reclaimed my grandfather's name, but not his title, in 1948. Both were mine by right of birth, for my family are the Counts of Cahors. As for dealing in pornography, half the literature in the world could be so described if your mind is sufficiently tainted. You may be an expert on forgeries and falsifying books – it would not surprise me – but my reputation is above minor slanders. Do you want to hear about Kopeck, or shall I go on talking above your head?'

'Make your statement. You say you saw him go. When and where?'

Perdreau poured himself a glass and sipped it before answering. 'At about one o'clock on the Monday morning, whatever the date was. I had dined here along with Mr Kopeck and

59

several others guests, mostly, I think, ladies from Boston, but I left before midnight. My cottage stands at the head of the slope which runs down to the by-pass and at the foot of it there is a lay-by where vehicles can wait. That night there were a couple of big lorries drawn in and a small private car. Kopeck went down the slope carrying a suitcase, got into the car and was driven towards London. That indicates nothing, because the secondary road into Inglewood joins the main stream half a mile up where there is a roundabout. He could have gone in any direction. I could not be mistaken because the scene is continually lit by headlights at that hour. I hope that satisfies you.'

For the first time Nascott turned to Perdita, who was sitting alone, her hands folded in her lap, staring directly in front of her. If she was frightened she did not show it, for her face was expressionless.

'Do you agree with that, Miss Browning?'

She did not turn her head.

'I have no idea when or where he went. He said he might decide to go late in the evening and that he had arranged everything. His bed was not used, so I presume he did as he intended. He left nothing in his room.'

Lottie stood up and nodded to Perdita: the conventional signal for the ladies to leave the gentlemen at the end of dinner.

'I shall take coffee in the Music Room. It

is probably ruined by now but you may join us later if you have sufficient temerity.'

The inquisitor ignored the snub but placed a restraining hand on the arm of her chair.

'Just a minute, madam. I'm not satisfied by any of these stories and that means we shall search the house. It may take some time, so make yourselves comfortable. Miss Richards and Mrs Gunter will go with you. If I remove any papers they'll be sent back if they're not needed.' He turned to Rupert and Perdreau. 'You will stay here with one of my colleagues and God help you if you try any funny business. Don't kid yourselves – you're not in their class.'

He spread out the bunch of keys on the table, flicking at them individually with his index finger.

'Safe, store-rooms, master for the bedrooms, filing cabinets ... they're all here, Miss Cambric, except one.'

Lottie turned to him, her arched eyebrows showing surprise which slowly changed to contempt, a cold survey which he received without flinching.

'I have a few trinkets in a box in my dressing room. Until now it did not occur to me to keep them locked.'

He continued to play with the keys on the table.

'I think you know what I mean. If you don't, then I'll spell it out for you. The missing item opens the panel door into the Tomb in the garden. The lock is hidden behind one of the stone bosses and my information is that it has been used quite recently. Where is it?'

The question made no visible impact on his hostess. She straightened her back, pushed her chair firmly from the table and turned to Perdita.

'I've not seen it for many years. Have you, my dear? No? Then you must do your own burgling, Mr Nascott. I feel sure you are equipped for the task.'

She nodded formally to the company, caught Rupert's eye and gestured to the door. He opened it without interference and Miss Cambric with her escorts made an exit in the grand manner.

It was after midnight when the search ended. Before then Rupert and Perdreau had been allowed to join the ladies in the Music Room, a high-ceilinged chamber impressive with oak panelling, a mural frieze by Sir James Linton, a harp, a grand piano and a gramophone with a conical trumpet of polished brass. The two guardians sat in silence by the door on the comfortless chairs which Lottie had assigned to them.

Conversation, which started stiltedly, began to flow after Perdreau's second brandy. He talked easily and well, ignoring half his audience, discussing nineteenth-century Russian literature, a subject on which he was vastly informed, interspersing it with sudden snatches of French in which he commented or conjectured on the sullen figures at the far end of the room. One of the women certainly understood all that he said, for an occasional burst of malice at her expense brought the colour to her cheeks.

'*Bon Marché d'Ammersmith, peut-être? C'n'est pas le vrai style qu'on trouve dans l'Edgware Road. Et la coiffure – ça me rappelle Lille en plein hiver. J'ai vu la même histoire à Clermont Ferrand, il y a douze ans.*'

He was nervous, excited, more than a little drunk, but he survived the vigil without faltering and Rupert at least was grateful to him. He contributed his own occasional shaft of banter at the expense of the wardens, for the role of Burbage no longer had any point, but conversation finally dwindled to a monologue which Perdreau sustained with some gallantry.

Lottie sat hidden in a high wing chair with her back to the door, so deliberately withdrawn that after the first reaction was over no one attempted to invade her privacy. Rupert, sliding a glance at her from time to time, could not decide what emotions were hidden behind the mask.

Without the warning of approaching footsteps for which they had all been listening the door opened and Nascott appeared, dusty, tired and clearly frustrated. He jerked his head towards the corridor.

'You two can get out. The cars are waiting. As for you, Miss Cambric, I can tell you that I'm still not satisfied and I'm taking some papers and address books with me. Nothing of value, so don't try raising a howl – you'll get them all back.'

The keys, which he tossed towards Perdita, fell noisily to the floor.

'That's the lot then. If there's a mess to be cleared up it's your own damn silly fault.'

He turned to go and as an afterthought plunged a hand into a pocket and threw a large iron key with a labelled tag towards the bunch beside the girl.

'That one belongs to the Tomb, in case you don't know. It was hanging on a nail in the wood cellar, so nothing's been broken.'

Lottie spoke without turning her head.

'And what did you find there, after all your trouble?'

He did not answer her but slammed the door behind him and for a long time no one moved. Finally Lottie stood up and straightened the folds of her long mauve skirts.

'Then there was nothing to find,' she said. 'An uncouth creature. He deserved an unrewarding evening.'

5

The Client

The Intercity Inquiries Bureau had its only office in Lime Court, one of the several alleys off Fleet Street where the houses of blackened brick huddle together like gentlefolk in reduced circumstances eking out their means by discreet commerce. The Bureau occupied the whole of the top floor of number six, a group of attics approached by wooden stairs which for the first three floors were wide and gentle and for the final flight steeply breathtaking, designed for Georgian servants.

The managing director of the firm sat at a cluttered table so enclosed with filing cabinets that his method of approach to the swivel chair posed an immediate problem to the questing eye. He was not at ease because his caller's name was familiar to him as a man who had friends in high places and who was therefore unlikely to be bringing business or good news. He assessed the value of the suit, the shirt, the tie and the accent with professional skill and found no comfort.

'Mr Campion?' he said. 'Take a pew, will you. What can I do for you?'

The visitor continued to stand, appraising him equally blandly from behind his horn-rimmed spectacles.

'Ex-Sergeant Harry Nascott, late of C Division?'

'That's me. I don't make a secret of it.'

'No? It would be understandable if you did, or so they tell me. Yet it seems you get plenty of work.'

The managing director tilted his chair backwards. He was in shirt sleeves and his jowl was beginning to look blue in the unkind strip lighting of the overcrowded room. He scented trouble and bristled to meet it.

'I don't take your meaning. If you want my services they're for hire, same like for anybody else. I don't suppose you've come here to pass the time of day. What's it all about?'

'Inglewood Turrets. You were there last weekend. Assault, intimidation, theft, obtaining entry by false pretences, malicious damage to property ... I can think of a lot more, but that will do for a start. I'd like to hear your side of the story before I decide what to do about it.' Mr Campion sat down and crossed his legs. 'I've plenty of time.'

'That's more than I have.' The ex-policeman was half-expecting this form of attack and had prepared a truculent line of defence. 'You ought to know better than that, sir. That place is only an hotel under another name. My colleagues and I paid the best part

66

of three hundred quid for accommodation which we didn't use and for one meal we hardly ate. Maybe we made a bit of a mess but for that sort of money I reckon we were entitled to. No damage at all. As for theft, I took a book or two by mistake and they were returned two days ago intact with a letter of apology. I'd say the lady won pretty handsomely on the deal.'

He pulled a wire tray of papers on to the blotting pad.

'Now, if that's the lot, you can get out. I'm a busy man, if you're not.'

Mr Campion laughed. 'You forgot to add that you never discuss a client's business with strangers. In this case you're going to break the golden rule.'

'Like hell, I am. If you'll forgive the expression, you're a bloody-minded nit who's asking for trouble. Now get out whilst the going's good. I'd hate to find you'd fallen down my stairs – they're steep enough to break your leg.'

The visitor let the outburst subside and continued the pause until he had completed a mental inventory of the room. Then he produced a slim black case from a breast pocket and tapped it thoughtfully on the palm of his hand.

'A pity to throw away a successful business for the sake of one dubious account, I would have thought. Your employers are notoriously bad at paying up and very stingy on the expense side, I understand. In the meantime, have you ever seen these before?'

He opened the case, picked out a short double-stranded rope of pearls and spread it carefully on the table.

'Not very valuable – about two hundred pounds' worth, would you say? There are some initials engraved on the clasp. P.L.B. – Perdita Louise Browning. It seems they were missing from her bedroom after you and your friends searched the Turrets on Saturday night. I happened to recover them this morning from a well-known jeweller who can identify the man who asked for them to be valued.'

Nascott picked up the necklace, glowered at it and tossed it back on the table. He was very angry, afraid of losing his temper, and for the first time a little uncertain of himself.

'If you're trying some sort of game with me – it sounds rather like blackmail, or that's how I look at it – let me tell you something. I've never seen the damn things in my life before and no one would believe that I'd risk my reputation and my licence for a trashy little number like that. I've reputable clients, I've cleared with the Special Branch that it's okay for me to work for them and I've done nothing that could be held against me.'

Mr Campion recovered the string and

replaced it in the case.

'I wouldn't bet on that,' he murmured. 'Well, now, we've established one point. You think you're working for one of the embassies.'

'That's what *you* say.'

'I doubt if you could prove it, or if they'd admit the suggestion for a moment. Let me make a guess about what happened. You were called to a room in an expensive block of mansion flats, probably in Knightsbridge, where there were a couple of shiny black C.D. cars parked outside. A foreigner, someone with a good unpronounceable name suggesting that he was from the Soviet Embassy, explained the job – to put out a net for a man called Kopeck, starting at the Turrets. He told you in detail how to set about it. He pointed out that the man was wanted on both sides of the fence because he no longer has diplomatic status and therefore no passport. To avoid a public scandal the police had not yet been asked to cooperate and his own people, he explained, couldn't very well do the job because of the language difficulty. People tend to be suspicious of inquisitive foreigners. He invited you to check with the Special Branch, and very sensibly you did. That's about the picture, I'd say.'

Nascott was not forthcoming but a certain respect appeared in his tone.

'If it is, it is none of your business.'

Mr Campion settled himself comfortably. 'You must forgive me, but I know a little about the way these people operate. You are simply the mug, the cat's paw. If there was the slightest whiff of trouble you'd be out on a limb with the branch sawn half through. No one at the Embassy would admit to knowing that you exist. The Knightsbridge flat would be occupied by a total stranger and it's very doubtful if you'd get a half-penny in fees. On top of that you would lose your ticket.'

He picked up the case and held it, his elbow on the table.

'I think you'd be wise to consider your position. How much did you discover at the Turrets?'

For some time the big man did not answer. He was not a quick thinker where major problems were concerned and his caller clearly moved in a world in which private in-quiry agents were perpetually at a disadvant-age. Finally he settled for self-protection.

'I'm a professional,' he said at last. 'That's why I have a feeling that you might try something funny which wouldn't suit my book. I know your sort. Chaps like you have two different codes – one for your pals and one for outsiders. Personally, I wouldn't trust you as far as I could spit but I have to take the risk.'

Mr Campion waved the case gently.

'The Turrets,' he said. 'And Kopeck.'

Nascott surrendered. Provided that the man in front of him did not make trouble – and on reflection he thought it unlikely – the truth was probably the best course.

'He's not there. He certainly took off from the house that night and I'd bet my pension it was by arrangement with Miss Cambric. In fact, he was picked up on the by-pass by a hired car from a garage in Inglewood and driven to Cambridge. He spent the night – what was left of it – at the University Arms under the name of Bertrand, saying he was a Channel Islander. Then he hired another car and was driven to Lincoln. Booked into the Saracen's Head, calling himself Sargent. After that we lost him. My chap thinks he was called for privately but he can't be sure. If you're so interested why don't you ask Miss Cambric? She knows.'

'Does she?'

Having gone so far Nascott clearly decided to go farther, to show himself at least as an expert. He scratched his chin.

'I'd swear to it. I know a lie when I hear one, I can smell it like ripe cheese. That woman is frightened, for all her airs and graces. Something isn't quite on the square in that god-awful mansion of hers but I'd be hard put to it to say quite what. She was a cat on hot bricks, though she put me in my place like a duchess ticking off a bootboy.

And it wasn't all on account of Kopeck –
he's well away by now. Mind you, she's got
reason to be worried.'

'Meaning?'

'Meaning that my lot could be thinking of
playing it the hard way. You know, Mr Campion, I wasn't born yesterday and my
methods may be a bit rough and ready but
come to that, you're not too particular about
your own, right? Still, I get around. If I take
on a job I make a few inquiries on the side.
One of my people has been on observation
there for a fortnight. Miss Cambric's under
heavy pressure to sell to one of the big con-
tractors, Denmark Holdings. She's got a fight
on her hands. She'd be a fool to land herself
with two lots of trouble. I was thinking...'

'Adding two and two?'

'Making six. I'm small fry – expendable, as
you say, if there's a showdown – but after me,
the big boys will move in and if she's got a
secret it'll be squeezed out of her like juice
out of an orange. If Mr Kopeck is still in this
country, the kindest thing he can do is to give
himself up, for the old lady's sake. Sooner or
later they'll break her like a matchstick. If
you're a friend of hers, tell her that from me.'

He paused, openly retrieving what he
could from a losing encounter.

'On second thoughts, she wouldn't take it
from me. But you could put her wise – give
her the straight tip. I don't know why they

want this chap but if the Special Branch don't object then there's a good reason and he's not some sweet innocent flying from injustice. You see, sir, if he was any sort of agent – a spy, I mean – then I'd have been told straight away to keep my nose out of it. As it was, they as good as wished me luck. I'm saying all this because I have an idea you'll check on it anyway.'

'You'd be right.'

'No hard feelings then?'

Mr Campion stood up. 'None at all. I'll give Miss Cambric your message and your apologies. There is just one other item...'

'Those papers? To be honest with you, I took photostats for my clients and kept a couple for myself just in case. If you want one...'

The thin man shook his head. He opened the case and placed the necklace on the table.

'It's about these pearls. They cost me a few guineas this morning in Oxford Street. The box comes from quite a different jeweller. Perhaps you'd care to give them to your wife?'

6

The Spoke in the Wheel

Miss Charlotte Cambric's private office was a surprising anachronism to find at the Turrets. Apart from the casement windows looking on to the courtyard it was uncompromisingly businesslike and contained a large modern desk, a secretary's typing table, a telephone and several filing cabinets. Even the owner, discarding her contact lenses for blue-tinted glasses, had moved forward in time by seventy years. She was wearing tailored tweeds topped by a green felt trilby of the type perennially favoured by country gentlefolk of her generation.

Mr Campion surveyed her with a mixture of approval and misgiving.

'Lottie,' he said. 'I'm afraid the time has come when you'll have to tell me about your Mr Kopeck. He is by way of being a stormy petrel, as you've already noticed. Rupert told me that you had a nasty experience here last week – a storm in a teacup if you look at it that way – but a real hurricane could follow.'

She shrugged her shoulders.

'Poor little man. I'm sure he never meant

to cause trouble. And don't stare at me like that – I really haven't the faintest idea where he is. I've much more serious problems on my hands just now. Really, I sometimes wonder if the government and the lawyers aren't in league with each other to ruin the country. It's like a protection racket designed to frustrate anyone who is trying to earn an honest living. Only mountebanks and big business tycoons seem to prosper. If I had my way...'

'Just tell me about Kopeck.'

She ignored the interruption. 'I'd make every civil servant do a real job for six months every year. That'd teach 'em. It never rains but it pours, if we must talk about unpleasant topics. Today – a Monday of all days – there is a revolting person who is saying that the entire drainage system here is dangerous and since we're not on the main sewer it will have to be modernized at my expense. Another local official wants to measure the place all over again and no doubt he'll double the rates as a result. The income tax people propose to go further into my profits, though I haven't made any for two years. The chef didn't turn up last night and Perdita had to help our second cook provide for a dozen rather difficult Belgian guests. And on top of that another letter which is practically a threat from that abominable man Denmark.'

Mr Campion stiffened.

'Denmark Holdings?'

'His name is Clifford Denmark and he's the sort of efficient horror who could understand a government form, fill it in, repair a television set, and do a stock exchange deal all at the same time. He's like...' she fluttered her hands, 'like Hornblower in *The Skin Game* and Lord Northcliffe and a London omnibus rolled into one. When one sees him one only has one idea – to get out of the way. An odious creature. He wants the Turrets.'

'For a weekend cottage?'

'Bless you, no. He owns four hotels in the West End, half of Killowen Square and most of the best part of Hampshire already. He wants this place simply because he thinks he could make money out of it, by destroying it, putting up some monstrous block or even a small town – blasting his way through the controls. We're not a national monument, you know – just private enterprise. Bulldozing and bribery – that's his formula. When he scents money he regards it as his by divine right and sets about getting it like an advancing tank. No other point of view enters his head. I've turned him down four times and now I refuse to see him or answer his letters. Not that it has much effect. If he intended to call, I have the feeling he would push through the wall if the door happened to be locked.'

She picked up a piece of paper from the in-tray on her desk.

'This is his latest. The man's an ogre and how he can know so much about my private affairs doesn't bear thinking about.'

Mr Campion read the letter slowly. It pointed out that the writer had some experience in the running of hotels and large properties and went on to analyse the likely profit and loss situation of the Turrets over the next five years. The estimate was conservative and unpleasant. The conclusion was that no amount of good housekeeping and showmanship could save Miss Cambric from bankruptcy in the foreseeable future. Denmark Holdings therefore repeated their offer for the house and grounds, which was more than generous in the circumstances, and begged to remain hers faithfully.

There was nothing exceptionable in the letter but between the lines there was a picture of small clerks leaking information, officials acting under unofficial pressure, public authorities open to private bribery, of privacy that was invaded by a Big Brother who was not even a popular demagogue. Mr Campion's spine twitched.

'Could these figures be true?'

Lottie retrieved the letter and placed it under a paper-weight.

'My dear man, they *are* true. It's not the whole story, thank God, because I generally manage to skip across the ice like little Eva. Uncle Edwin had an extraordinary collection of very early gramophone recordings which he made himself of poets reading their own works. Tennyson, Swinburne and Henley for example – even Oscar Wilde – famous people of the day talking. And, of course, all the best singers. Last year I had some of them reproduced and we sell them, wickedly expensively, but they're an absolute must for any literary snob. And not all the paintings he bought were bad. Naturally, I keep the well-known period ones on the walls for show, but he did dabble in the Impressionists and they're better than money in the bank. The dear man didn't really like them and only bought a few to oblige his friends but he had the good sense to keep them in safe storage and to give them to my father before he died. The one thing Mr Denmark doesn't know about is my hidden assets, and it must be because they're insured separately and not part of the estate. Either he knows what I pay on the Turrets down to the last farthing, or he has second sight. But unless something goes seriously wrong I can hold out for a year or two. And I intend to.'

She picked up the letter, tore it across and dropped it into the basket.

'It may not be as easy as that,' said Mr Campion. 'Denmark could have other weapons in his armoury. A scandal of the right sort, for example, could undermine the reputation of the Turrets, even in this day and age it could destroy the sort of amusing fantasy business you do now. I wouldn't put it past him to introduce dry rot or death watch beetle or a crop of poisonous snakes. It sounds to me as if you had a pretty powerful enemy there. The point is, can you afford to have two?'

Lottie considered the question, making no pretence of misunderstanding him. Finally she raised her chin and her lips which had been pursed set in a firm line.

'Perhaps not. But Uncle Edwin believed in friendship and loyalty and he got a lot out of his principles – six splendid Impressionists, for example – and I have my share of his obstinacy, if you want to call it that. My dear man, of course, I don't want enemies. But I refuse to abandon a friend even if he does have the misfortune to be a foreigner. Do please clear your mind on the subject. Little Kopeck may be in trouble with his fellow-countrymen – the Russians are always looking for someone to crush – but it's really nothing to do with me. I'm not interested in politics. Even cabinet ministers are sometimes allowed to stay here.'

'But you know where he is? You helped him to escape?'

She was more determined than before.

'No, not even for you, Albert, will I say another word. He's gone wherever he intended to go, and that's the end of it as far as I'm concerned.'

Mr Campion sighed. Outside in the crystal autumn air the late harlequin roses were making a pageant and an old man was cleaning weeds from around full-budded chrysanthemums. Pigeons eddied about the courtyard. The whole scene, he thought, was as out of date as her attitude to modern problems.

'I hope you're right. Knowing where Kopeck is could be like handling gelignite with slippery fingers. If you told me just a little more I could at least...'

She shook her head.

'If you came down here just to lecture then we'll call it a day and have a glass of sherry. It will have to be in this room because I never use the public ones when I'm not dressed for the part. If you came to see Rupert you'll have to wait. He and Perdita have gone shopping in Inglewood. The new by-pass has cut it off and restored its character as a nice little country town.'

Mr Campion knew when he was beaten. He accepted the change of subject gratefully.

'How is the new Burbage doing?'

'Excellently. A nice child, and a young man of parts, if he's speaking the truth. He says he can manage a horse and trap so I trusted him with the high dog-cart – one of our exhibition pieces which we use for publicity.'

'So I see.'

As he spoke there was a clatter of hooves and a resplendent Victorian equipage turned into the courtyard. It was a brightly painted vehicle of the type now seen only on show grounds, drawn by a high-stepping chestnut. Between the enormous wheels Rupert sat erect in an eye-catching red and yellow striped blazer, whilst Perdita wore a prim blouse with puffed sleeves, straw boater tipped over her innocent blue eyes. The picture was ridiculous, gay, and, despite its deliberate antiquity, extraordinarily modern.

Rupert helped the girl down but she did not turn to thank him. She ran into the house without a backward glance and the boy did not look in her direction. He unloaded a basket and several parcels from the trap, hesitated, and was obviously relieved when the old man who had been gardening came down the slope to take charge. Walking slowly he passed directly beneath them to the kitchen door.

'Dear me,' said Miss Cambric. 'Now that's very odd. They seemed to be getting on so well together. I do hope they haven't quarrelled. In a minute I shall be driven into saying "I don't understand young people nowadays," which I suppose is the most age-betraying remark in the world. The sherry is in the middle drawer of that filing cabinet.'

As Mr Campion poured the drink the door opened and Perdita came in just ahead of Rupert. They stood awkwardly together, hardly acknowledging the presence of a visitor.

'It's about Jannerat, the chef,' said Rupert.

'He's dead,' said Perdita. 'He's killed himself.'

In an office of Inglewood police station, a bright neo-Georgian building which was decently recessed between rival self-service stores in the High Street, two experienced professionals, Constable Hobart and Sergeant Easterbrook, were using the same words.

'Well, he killed himself, that's for certain,' said the constable.

They were engaged in the complicated business of preparing a statement of evidence for the inevitable inquest, making certain that their handling of the routine was impeccable.

'We've reason to suppose that,' said Easterbrook. 'But get it in order, right? At 10.15 in answer to a request from the occupant, Mrs Grace Wilmot of 19 Kelvedon Avenue, you effected an entry to bed-sitting-room, locked on the inside, on the first floor and there discovered the body of Alexander Ambrose

Jannerat, a sub-tenant, about thirty, male, coloured, a British subject born in Kennington. O.K. so far? Identification by Mrs W. and that red-headed boy from the Turrets who came inquiring. Dr Cawnthrope summoned 10.30, arrived 11.15 ... well, we needn't bother about him.'

'I never seen anyone go so white in all my life,' said the constable. 'The boy, I mean. I shouldn't have let him in, but I was a bit shaken myself and the woman was carrying on so. Hysterics and I don't blame her. He helped me with her and it seemed best, him knowing the deceased and she being useless.'

'It's the blood,' said the sergeant. 'Some can't take it. A cut throat makes a nasty sight.'

'You can say that again. Last mess I saw like that was when I was a lad and a doodle-bug landed right where we're sitting now. He made a job of it, I'll give him that. Three trial cuts with his own knife – it was still in his hand – and then whoosh!'

'Why, d'you suppose?'

Hobart pushed back his chair. He was a middle-aged family man, dull without being actively stupid. Inglewood was his whole horizon and its suburban comfort had robbed him of ambition.

'Gawd knows. He worked four days a week at the George here and two at the Turrets –

Saturday, Sunday. Nothing known, always seemed cheerful. Came, they say, from the Carrefour, a posh joint in the West End, where he didn't get along with the boss cook. A darkie born in London often doesn't have much in the way of background and when the Met boys go around making inquiries most of his friends just won't want to know, or that's my bet.'

'No pals down at the Oasis?' Easterbrook had a wide understanding of his district and the café was high on his Doubtful list.

'Ah, it could be. He used it sometimes, very late, and I've shifted him and one or two others like him out of the place more than once. Disturbance, but not to say breach. I'll ask around.'

'You do just that. Did Cawnthrope say anything?'

'Grunted and puffed a bit – you know his form. Clear suicide, he said. Probably late Saturday night when his landlady heard him come in. No second party present, or had been, so far as either of us could see. Furniture all straight, curtains drawn, door locked, lights on and note in deceased's handwriting on the table. What more do you want?'

The sergeant sighed. 'Search me, Charlie. But that note – it's out of the ordinary, if you follow me. Not what you'd expect, really. What was it again?'

P.C. Hobart turned back a page in his notebook.

'The exact words were: "Poor bloody fools. You know less than nothing." I don't care for the tone of it, myself. I'd say it would take a bit of explaining.'

7

The Tower of Babel

The news of the death of Alexander Ambrose Jannerat spread out like ripples on a pool. By noon a reporter from the *Inglewood Gazette* knew at least as much as Sergeant Easterbrook and relayed the information to his local master, who thought it worth forwarding to the news editor of *The Globe* in Fleet Street, which was at the centre of that powerful Press network. The item rested for an hour amongst many others on a large metal desk before an assistant decided that a story might lie behind the dead man's scribbled message. On the off-chance he ran a small paragraph, far down on the second news page. He was not optimistic, but *The Sunday Globe*, the sister paper, was short on crime that week and it could be worth a follow-up.

L.C. Corkran, from long habit a voracious patron of the world's Press, read the five lines over his morning tea, clipped them and placed the cutting in a file which contained other stories of suicide. Sooner or later a pattern would emerge, and he was not happy at the thought. He genuinely liked Charlotte Cambric but it was difficult to stop an obstinate woman from playing with fire if she set her mind on it. Now the flame was coming closer: perhaps that would be sufficient warning. Partly to salve his conscience and partly to ease the inescapable itch of curiosity he rang Mr Albert Campion's London flat and was surprised at the sharpness of his disappointment when there was no reply. Finally he dismissed the matter; his successors would no doubt observe the paragraph.

The chairman and managing director of Denmark Holdings found the story on his desk when he entered his office on the top floor of Denmark House at nine sharp on the Tuesday morning. It was outlined in blue pencil and lay amongst several others, for his reading came to him pre-selected by an efficient aide. He read it carefully, a scowl giving place slowly to a chuckle which was sufficiently audible to reach the sharp ears of Mrs Draper, his secretary, in the next room. He pressed a digit on the intercom and a man's voice answered.

'Wykes – Room Two.'

'About the man at Inglewood who killed himself. You marked the item.'

'Sir?'

'Find out why...'

He switched off, surveyed the shining array of numbered buttons, a new model incorporating closed circuit television and his latest toy. He began to play with each in turn, shaking the entire building.

In an expensive penthouse in Knightsbridge, furnished with professional anonymity, a dapper man with a bland satanic face, made modern by a dark downward turning moustache, considered the paragraph. He sat very still for some minutes and then wrote rapidly, covering two sheets with meticulously legible characters. Having ended, he became immobile once more, for he had placed his thoughts on paper with the simple purpose of clarifying them. Finally he tore the sheets across, dropped the fragments into a metal basket and dialled three figures on one of the two telephones on his desk.

'This is Moryak. There is a Press story which you will find on the second page of *The Globe* this morning, at the foot of the third column. It should be reported, but without comment. No further action.'

In his office in Lime Court, the proprietor of Intercity Inquiries also gave his mind to the paragraph. It was not news to him, for an informant had telephoned him within an hour of the discovery of the body, but he was not pleased to see the story in a national daily. In his opinion the less public interest there was in the Turrets, the easier would be his task. He had got off to a remarkably poor start, although he had fair hopes of his present line of inquiry. It involved a great deal of work but, if he played his cards properly, the account could still prove valuable.

There were two aspects to the problem and both of them were well in hand. The first was to establish precisely who his client was so that his own interests would be protected if some new difficulty should arise and the second was to fulfil his instructions.

A photostat copy of Miss Cambric's personal address book lay on his table, heavily scored and noted. A long job faced him and he was only half-way through it. He applied himself to the telephone, concentrating on names and numbers within an easy motoring distance from Lincoln, dealing through contacts in Leeds, Hull, Sheffield and Scarborough. The process had been going on for two days, without any significant result. A map spread across his table, covered with circles and crosses.

Like a gourmet who saves a particular morsel for a *bonne bouche*, he had kept an entry from everything except peripheral inquiries but these had been significant. The number indexed as C.M. with no name, Baxstable (Yorks) 021, appeared in block capitals written in Miss Cambric's own round hand, but beside it in a script which the photo copy reproduced very faintly were the pencilled words 'Cheesecake Charlie'. He had resisted the trap of calling the number and betraying himself by using what he suspected might be a code word, and he had discovered that the number was ex-directory.

He inscribed it in large figures on a sheet of paper and began to cover the surface with clumsy doodles including notes about a possible route. Goole? Market Weighton? Great Driffield? *Baxstable,* he wrote again. *Pop. 850. Market Wed. The Baxstable Arms. 4 bedrooms. Garage. T. Baxstable 004. London 221 miles.*

Finally he pressed the bell under his foot and addressed the startling blonde who put her head round the door.

'Yolande, I'm off. Maybe a couple of days – no use sending a boy to do a man's job. You can get a message to me at this number, but only if Mr Williams gives you the O.K. Ask for me under the name of Kirk – he'll get the point of that. So long, and be careful if you can't be good.'

The girl raised chipped enamel fingernails to straighten the artificial pearls at her neck.

'Look who's talking,' she said.

The village of Baxstable squatted like a

mottled toad on a ledge apparently cut by a giant at the dawn of time into high uplands. Above were moors jagged with outcrops of rock and below lay long swathes of green pasture occasionally varied by autumn stubble. The houses and the church were of brown stone, the windows small and the architecture of that dateless character which is dictated by practical considerations of defence against wind and weather, solid boxes devoid of ornament. A cobbled cattle market, flanked on one side by an enclosed square of grass, some oak benches and three stunted trees, provided the main feature and the Baxstable Arms looked down on the iron pens from a paved walk above the level of the street.

Mr Campion drove slowly past the rectangle and followed the road which wound upwards between stone walls until he reached a vantage point commanding views over the grass and moorland on three sides. The September morning was clear and sharp, the air still as midsummer. Far above him a glider moved almost imperceptibly in a pale sky, effortless, remote and silent. Below him on his right Baxstable was half hidden in a fold of moorland and to his left lay the object of his journey, a sprawling collection of wood and concrete huts, almost a township in itself, connected by asphalt paths. A white staff from which a yellow wind sock hung inertly provided a focal point and there were other masts bearing an assortment of strangely twisted aerials. Two small aircraft and a second glider stood on a concrete runway which stretched far into the distance.

From where he stood his binoculars picked out a lodge and a gate between the stone walls, beside which was a painted board bearing the legend: *'Baxstable Research. Private Ground. No admittance without written authority. Warning: Electric fences and Guard Dogs.'*

Mr Campion was not proud of himself. He had reached this remote spot by reasoning which was open to Nascott and he comforted himself with the thought that if that unworthy man had access to Miss Cambric's address book, then he was entitled to know at least as much. If Lottie was to be protected against herself he must fight on equal terms with those who were interested in her destruction.

A day's investigation conducted in an area beyond the scope of Intercity Inquiries had revealed that Baxstable Research was part of a larger organization, Asphodel Aircraft. The airfield and workshops were used for the design, testing and construction of advanced gliders, including, it was said, experiments in the area of man-powered flight. It was not a government enterprise but enjoyed a measure of semi-official blessing.

Whilst he watched, men began to drift out of one of the range of hutments into a central building, which was evidently a canteen. The glider sailed majestically back to the field like a seagull settling on calm water and a small van sped past him towards the village. One of the aircraft, an Asphodel Executive, took off, circled and headed south.

Mr Campion continued his observations until the late afternoon, when it was clear that work for the day was over. Men and women emerged, re-grouped and dispersed into outlying bungalows, where windows began to glow. Baxstable Research, it seemed, was for the most part a self-contained community, for only two passenger trucks of workers left the gates homeward bound. Now that it was no longer possible to identify faces in the twilight, he abandoned the attempt, climbing stiffly into his car and turning it back towards the village.

After the chill of the moorland air the Baxstable Arms offered warmth, light and an unsuspected prospect of comfort. The small saloon bar was well stocked and gay with polished tankards. Twigs crackled in an open fireplace. He booked a room, deposited an overnight case, washed and descended, the irritation of a largely wasted day slipping gently behind him.

There were three men, evidently farmers, at the bar and a fourth figure sat by the fire, his face hidden behind a newspaper. Having armed himself with a drink Mr Campion waited until the inevitable moment came when the paper was lowered to allow its owner to survey the company. Then he crossed the room, drawing up a chair.

'Good evening, Mr Nascott. Staying long?'

The heavy man eyed him steadily before acknowledging the greeting. Despite its stolidity his face betrayed, as ever, the thought sequence which was in process. Resentment gave place to secretiveness with the need for self-protection finally gaining the upper hand. He drew his chair closer and spoke in an undertone.

'You would be doing me a personal favour – and you owe me one now I come to think of it – if you would call me Mr Kirk. I don't happen to want everyone to know my business.'

'And how is business today?'

He did not answer immediately but waited until a series of mental cogs had turned. A flicker of amusement appeared, chased by caution.

'You ought to know the answer to that one, if you've been here any length of time. The security up the road is lousy. I could do a better job blindfolded and both hands tied.'

'Knock three times and ask for Cheesecake Charlie?'

Nascott snorted. 'A code name for the boss, nothing more. His private pals use it to get switched through direct. A bunch of half-wit boffins, that's what they are. No electric fences and two old wolfhounds who are so fat they couldn't chase pussy over the wall. I spotted you on observation with your glasses, and it gave me a laugh. You might just as well have walked in and helped yourself. I did. I was there yesterday.'

'You don't waste time,' said Mr Campion respectfully. He crossed to the bar and produced two large tumblers of whisky. 'My congratulations. In what capacity did Mr Kirk appear, or is that a professional secret? Inspector of office welfare?'

'Something of the sort. Employment of Aliens was what I asked about and nobody seemed surprised. The place is full of them, egg-heads from every country in Christendom and out of it, and nobody quite knowing what the next man is up to. Just the place for a foreigner to hide, come to think of it. They must have been screened at one time but the set-up isn't important any longer. I'd say that very few of them could understand a word of what the next man is saying unless he put it on paper in the form of a set of figures. Up in the clouds they are.' He laughed. 'That's dead right and not meant to be funny. Up in the clouds with wings and pedal cycles. Manpowered flight

94

they call it.'

Mr Campion considered his companion. Now that the shock of his own appearance was wearing off, the man was relaxing. He was openly pleased with his performance and no longer saw a potential enemy. Mr Campion took a chance.

'So the bird has flown?'

'Straight back to the cage, if you ask me. I'm expecting my own chips any minute now. Some of his chums were nosing round the place this morning but it was only to make sure he'd left nothing important behind, from what I hear. Not that there was anything to find. I checked his room myself. You told me I might be had for a mug – used as a cover – and you could be right at that – so I had to protect myself. This lot were way ahead of me, and my guess is that they have been all along. They put him in the bag days ago and that's the last we'll hear of him, poor bastard.'

'You're sure it is the right man?'

'As near as a toucher. Short, foreign – not that that's anything strange in these parts – probably Russian but said he was Czech. Called himself Mr Joseph, which doesn't mean a thing. Nobody knew what he was up to, and that's no surprise either. Identified by several witnesses although he has grown a moustache since he was last photographed.'

'And now he's vanished again?'

Nascott finished his drink and supplied another.

'I don't see why I should tell you all this and I wouldn't if it weren't all over bar the shouting. The subject went off on Tuesday afternoon, about five, they think. Never came back, never even took a toothbrush. So he was pinched, kidnapped, arrested, whatever you care to call it. And I'll tell you another little item.'

'Such as?'

'Such as I'll pay a pound to a rotten orange that he'll never be heard of again. Best thing, from your point of view – lousy from mine. It could have been a very nice little account, if it had lasted.'

He glanced suspiciously round the room, found nothing of interest, became gloomy and took a long pull at his whisky. 'A pair of concrete sea-boots, that's what he's got by now. Your Miss Cambric ought to be grateful. No more trouble for her and nothing for you to do but to trot back with the good news. I'm the loser. A client like that, you know, makes a nice change from everlasting bloody divorce cases, hanging about at all hours in hotels and cars.'

'Too bad,' said Mr Campion and replenished the glasses. 'You're staying the night, I take it?'

A sudden reserve appeared in his companion's eyes.

'No reason why I shouldn't. It's a free country, right? Spreads out the expenses, helps the exchequer. Besides...'

He broke off as the thought he was keeping in reserve crept across his revealing face. He opened his mouth and controlled an impulse.

'Besides, you can mind your own damn business,' he concluded. 'It's people like you who cause all the trouble. Batten on other men's brains and hard work and never do a hand's turn yourself. Well, here's cheers. I don't cotton to you, don't want to drink with you, but what the hell is there to do in this god-forsaken hole?'

Mr Campion commiserated with him, avoiding the pitfall of a *tu quoque*, and steered the conversation to more general topics. Nascott, it emerged, was a keen collector of stamps, specializing in rare forgeries. Between refreshments he spoke fluently if not always coherently on the subject, with all the zeal of a prophet in search of a convert.

'Best of them come from long term prisoners – stands to reason, when you come to think of it. American crooks in Sing Sing or San Quentin. Stands to reason. A good forger needs time, right? Well, he's got time – all the time in the world. So what does he do? I'll tell you what he does. He unpicks the centre of a stamp with a needle and weaves it back –

fibre by bloody fibre – upside down. May take a year just for one stamp but what does he care? Fibre by bloody fibre. Worth a fortune if he can get away with it. Picture of Lindbergh flying the Atlantic *upside down*. Worth a fortune...'

He broke off to examine the latest arrival at the bar, staring at him with what the newcomer evidently regarded as unjustified curiosity, for he crossed the room and returned the glare belligerently. On the pretext of refilling the glasses, Mr Campion intervened, persuading the man discreetly towards the general company.

'Forgive my friend,' he said. 'He's a stranger in these parts. Rather short-sighted, I'm afraid. He's waiting for a man he doesn't know very well.'

'Oh, ay?'

Nascott was still explaining the niceties of philatelic deception when he returned.

'...posts the letter to some address that doesn't exist, if you follow me. That way it gets a postmark. Very important mark – postmark – very important. It's a dead letter, see? Dead as a bloody doornail. The man doesn't exist – the address doesn't exist. Both dead. But not sad at all, that's the clever part. Returned through the Dead Letter office to the chap who sent it, with a postmark. Damned clever and ingenious like the Chinese. Here's cheers.'

The room was becoming close, for the fire had been replenished with logs which gave out a considerable heat. Nascott continued his discourse.

'I'll tell you what I'll do. I don't like you – never did, come to that – but I'll tell you what I'll do. I'll show you six of the finest forgeries in the world. Works of art, just as if they'd been painted by Michaelellangellico. Masterpieces...'

His head nodded gently forward and he slept.

Mr Campion escaped from the sweltering glow to the comparative coolness of the counter and restored himself with a supply of sandwiches. Custom in the saloon had been heavy during the forepart of the evening but now it was thinning to a few regulars occupying established positions. There was a larger and more popular bar at the back of the inn and the farrago of sound which swelled through the open doorway compensated for any lack of conversation. He explored the intimacies of the local paper, absorbed the price of sheep, the proceedings of the Women's Institute and the Young Farmers' Club. The director of Intercity Inquiries began to snore.

An hour in which time dawdled and sagged to the limits of boredom passed before a young man put his head round the inner door and Mr Campion, who had been waiting for just such an appearance, caught his eye.

'Looking for Mr Kirk?'

The boy nodded. He had a cheerful intelligent face, not improved by a mixture of engine grease and acne. The voice was sharp and quick above the flat tones of the background.

'S'right. Passed out, has he?'

'Just sleeping,' said Mr Campion. 'Can I take a message for him?'

'Silly old goat. I've got something for him. He said he was keen to get his hands on it.'

'He's not in a receptive mood, I'm afraid. Did he mention by any chance that there might be something in it for you?'

The young man grinned sheepishly.

'S'matter of fact, he did. I wouldn't have bothered myself, except it doesn't belong to me and it's still worth a bob or two if it's cleaned properly. His pal Joseph made a right muck of it and said I'd splice it for him.'

Mr Campion produced a notecase.

'Would a fiver cover it? I'd like to settle the difficulty for him, since he's indisposed at the moment. It'll be in safe hands.'

The grin widened. 'If you ask me, you're a right chump, as they say in these parts. Kirk said two quid, which is more than it's worth. Yours for five of the best and you can chase your mate in the corner for the change.'

He placed a small spool of recording tape on the counter.

'Kiss him good night for me. It was nice knowing you.'

8

Questions of Allegiance

Mr Hilary Wykes, the occupant of Room Two in the head office of Denmark Holdings, was a man who cultivated elegance to within a hair's breadth of effeminacy. It was a tribute to his instinct for success that he never crossed the borderline, since that would have weakened his standing in either of the two pools in which he swam so skilfully.

He patronized one of the best tailors in London, belonged to two of the best clubs and was one of the best racing drivers ever to refuse professional status. He was seen at the best first nights with a succession of news-worthy ladies and rumour frequently touched him, yet he avoided scandal. In Deptford, where he maintained a workshop-garage, he was the centre of an admiring circle of mechanics and hangers-on and the girl who ran the flat above was reputed, in-accurately, to be his mistress. Officially, and indeed usually, he slept in the set of rooms he called his cottage in a Mayfair mews.

Only his very large nose, a family feature, prevented him from being handsome and his dark hair, carefully greyed at the sides, had the suggestion of a curl. His barber considered him the finest client an artist could wish for.

Many people regarded him as Clifford Denmark's second in command, an impression which he encouraged when it was politic to do so, but the truth was that in that empire no such animal existed. He was a useful servant but he enjoyed less security of tenure than the doorman. One of Denmark's curious conditions of service in the upper echelon was that his staff signed certain undated letters and cheques before they were appointed, and these were held as a perpetual sword of Damocles in the event of their giving dissatisfaction.

Wykes feared, disliked and admired his employer in precisely equal proportions; but at the moment fear was the dominant emotion. He stood before the big desk and was thankful to be carrying a folder, since it gave him something to do with his hands.

'The Turrets,' said his master. 'The chef who killed himself. I said to find out why.'

Hesitation was the first mistake and Wykes was too experienced to make it. He plunged in.

'Hard to say. I've been into it pretty carefully and it looks like an accident – that is, it has no significance. Chap may have been in love, or got drunk, or was just plain bonkers anyhow. Incidentally, I'm pressing on with the rights-of-way question. I think we can force her to close the main entrance...'

Denmark struck the desk with the flat of his hand, making the nearest telephone rattle.

'Don't try to sidetrack me. There's been some trouble down there and I'd know all about it if it were one of your schemes. A whole party – twelve people – walked out on a Saturday night. You should have known that. As it is, you'll find out why within twenty-four hours, or else. And now this man, who was valuable to the Cambric woman – one of the main attractions – goes and cuts his throat, and you say it is an accident. God help you if there's someone else operating in that area and I'm not the first to know. What else?'

Wykes shifted his weight and opened his folio.

'I've arranged for Helen Diaz to make a scene there next week with a new boy friend and an old lover. *The Globe* are going to cover it through Tony Evelyn, who does their gossip. Some of the diplomatic set and their camp followers will be there, including old Van Tromp, who is as sticky as a Baptist.

It ought to be a ripe little story.'

'And who the hell is Helen Diaz when she's at home?'

'At home she's the wife of Vittorio Bellini, the film director. Abroad she's an up-and-coming star who plays flaming bitches in Anglo-French highbrow films where all the best scenes are censored. Delicious. She's out to improve her image as the world's most sensational termagant. At the moment she's winning.'

'A pin prick. Lottie Cambric will ride that into the ground and probably enjoy doing it. What else?'

'I think you know most of it.' Wykes made a pretence of referring to notes. 'Her rates are going up and she's got one or two more problems which should be reasonably costly. We're keeping the pressure up – being splendidly beastly. Another project is proving difficult, but it's well in hand. If you remember you said you didn't want to know anything about it.'

The hint of a challenge was ignored.

'Not really good enough, is it? There's a packet – a thundering great packet – of solid cash waiting to be picked up there. I want to see some action. Get out and get on with it.' Wykes moved to the door and turned as a thought occurred to him.

He returned to the desk and waited until his employer decided to look up.

'Just another item. I don't know if it's worth your time but...'

'I said get on with it. What's keeping you?'

'There's a man in the Outer Hall who is asking to speak to you personally. He says it's urgent and important and he's prepared to wait all day.'

'And this is a situation you can't cope with? Sometimes I think I'm mad to employ you. Turn Mrs Draper loose on him if you're incompetent.'

'I have. She agreed with me that you ought to see him. A very obstinate type and not a great thinker, I'd say. But my built-in radar tells me that when he says "A certain property you're interested in" he means Inglewood.'

The man at the desk pressed the intercom and his secretary's expensively faultless voice responded. 'Yes, Mr Denmark?'

'The man outside – should I see him?'

'I think so, sir. He could be someone for our I.T. file. His name is Nascott.'

The prospect from the long picture window in L.C. Corkran's living-room could well have been painted by John Piper in dramatic mood. Rain scudded over the Downs, masking them briefly in veils of water, yet through the erratic breaks in the storm clouds light filtered, pricking out patches of colour to emphasize darkness at noon. Autumn had arrived with a flurry of leaves as the trees leaned against the torrent. Corkran shivered.

'A whisky-and-soda morning, in my opinion. I'm afraid you had a difficult journey. At least you came *vento secundo*.'

Mr Campion agreed. 'It chased me all the way from East Grinstead. And if you're offering me your Glenlivet I'll take it with water.'

They drank their whisky in silence and it was some time before the visitor broached the subject which had brought him to Sussex.

'You said you had the transcription? Does it justify your trouble? You were so off-hand about it on the phone that I caught the ancient and fishlike smell of security. A pity that neither of us speaks Russian.'

His host rubbed his nose on the rim of his tumbler and a gust of rain, loud as a handful of pebbles, struck the window.

'The Department has the original tape,' he admitted. 'I had to use Morgan – long after your time, if I remember – to do the translation, so I didn't explain how it came into my hands, though I may have to. Fortunately he understands about the mechanics of these things, which is more than poor Kopeck did, it seems. Morgan says the spool was in an appalling mess, broken in several places, sometimes recorded twice, with a background of music or other words spoken in

English, as you know, and others in Russian. He seems to have intended some sort of broadcast, a personal statement, and to have been trying it out – thinking aloud.

'The trifles I heard were exasperating. My guess is that at one point the whole thing became unwound and he threw it away. Perhaps he had second thoughts or ran short of tape. Reconstruction seemed a job for an expert.'

'Morgan,' said Corkran judicially, 'is an expert and he has made a very good job of translation and restoration. Pieces had been joined up in the wrong order and he's sorted them out.' He crossed to a walnut bureau and produced sheets of typescript. 'Quite an ear for music, too. He identifies a lot of the background. I'll be expected to keep this, so read it with care. Brackets, by the way, indicate when the speaker has lapsed into Russian.'

Mr Campion read the document slowly.

'Tape opens with "Una terribil tosse" *from* La Bohème, *Act 3; probably BBC recording from transistor. Section of weather and shipping forecast also BBC.*

'Man's voice. *Good morning ... good evening* ... (how to say?) *perhaps hullo and greetings* ... (Comrades? My friends?) *My name is Vassily Kopeck ... Kopeck, Vassily? ... I am fifty-six years of age and I am citizen of the U.S.S.R.* (I was a citizen ... I used to be...) *I speak to you now because since I am troubled* (my conscience is troubled) *of a grave matter ... event ... possibility* (something of horrible possibilities) *of which I must, I must speak. I have given great thought to this thing because...* (No, I have pondered in my heart.)

'*Various musical excerpts follow here. Part of Borodin's "Song of the Flea" – Chaliapin? – which seems to be a gramophone record. Mozart's 19th in F, K. 459, Third Programme, with announcer's opening. These are extracts only. No code significance is indicated. They are probably experiments with the tape recorded at random.*

'Man's voice.

'*...to establish that I am free man I read you a headline from* The Times *newspaper of today* (to show that I am at liberty ... no to prove that I speak). *To prove that I speak four weeks after I have left* (cut myself off ... have no longer any status...) *but yet have not asked for ... not defected ... so am at entire liberty to speak without pressure.* (I am free at this time to speak. No government knows when, from where, I speak.) *Today, September 4th, the headline reads "T.U.C. reconsider verdict. Woodcock's statement." Also a letter about migration of birds signed by Lord Redcar on page 11. This will show that I am not speaking to you from an old ...* (record, disc, electronic tape) *... made before this date. If there has been some search for me then I am not discovered, so I speak for* *myself and no person can say "he is a traitor to his country and words* (a bribe for protection) *have been put in his mouth".* (Not for the soft life but because this must be said). *I shall now try to explain...*

'*N.B. There is some background noise which could be single engined aircraft taking off during the foregoing. Section of Haydn's* Clock *follows – BBC? – transistor?*

'Man's voice. *N.B. Very poor recording. Speaker some distance from microphone.*

'*If it is known it can be prevented* (understood – if it is understood). *A warning can be given. So many deaths.* (These people do not understand but they...) *People everywhere must be alarmed... Alerted...* (no remedy, no cure can call back the dead). *Eaten up like ... forest fire.* (Not the secret of life but of death ... thought ... the Thinker is deceived.) *I will explain...*

'Tape ends.'

9

Enchanted Evening

There were many reasons for the survival of the Turrets as an expensive curiosity in a sophisticated, swinging world; but the greatest was Miss Charlotte Cambric's skill as a hostess on those occasions when she gave her whole mind to the problem. No normal man ever left her table without the secret conviction that the occasion had been designed especially for him and most of them flattered themselves on having added their own notable contribution, even if the best of their witticisms eluded them on reflection. Older women discovered that they still possessed style and enough charm to compete with their daughters where intelligent men were concerned and the younger ones forgot to be bored because of the excellence of the food, the element of fancy dress and the promise of lamp-lit dalliance which was part of the beckoning magic.

Of the twenty guests in the Small Drawing-Room on Saturday evening, Mlle Helen Diaz was unquestionably the most decorative. She alone had opted for complete period costume: her gown of heliotrope silk, a masterpiece of discreet indiscretion, had come from the first act of *La Dame aux Camélias*, though there was no hint of tragedy about her *grande cocotte*. French, Greek and Chinese blood, a much publicized mixture, gave her a porcelain skin and dark hair that conveyed all the menace of Medusa. A miniature set in gold held an orchid on her left shoulder. At her side the escort of the moment, whose mass of yellow curls surrounded the face of a delinquent cherub, passed unnoticed, despite the fichu of Brussels lace at his neck and a Damascus silk dinner jacket.

Boysie Brown, the darling of the teenage world, was accustomed to immediate recognition and adulation. His eyes searched the room for devotees and already the promise of petulance quivered on his lips.

Felix Perdreau in his frogged velvet coat bent low over the star's pneumatic décolletage, kissing her finger tips. It was a gesture of unquestioning surrender which she expected, understood and approved: the first phase in a charade which never failed to excite. She produced her soul-destroying smile.

'I was batheeing tonight in a tin armchair. A beeg fire and a *femme de chambre* to pour 'ot water over me from copper pots. This is for me. When I am naiked I come alive. On my Greek island always I am naiked and I am most beautiful then.'

Perdreau's voice supplied the desired caress.

'Sappho herself would be envious. I'm glad our humble hip-bath was a success. It's a forgotten pleasure today. Old Cambric, you know, always had one. Perhaps it was because although he put wonderful marble affairs in every suite he forgot the central heating.'

'So? On my island I 'ave five *salles de bain*. Now I am 'aving six. In my bedroom a tin bath, copper pots and a beeg log fire. For my next picture also, such a bath. *And no bubbles.* Bubbles are *pour épater les bourgeoises.*'

'Perfection,' said Felix gravely, 'is beyond modesty. I shall make the Odeon my temple and worship at your shrine.'

Lottie Cambric, her eyes exploring every group in the room, touched Perdita on the shoulder and whispered without moving her lips.

'Take that blond boy away from Felix and pour butter all over him. He needs an audience, so seduce him with champagne and starry-eyed wonder. Talk pop to him.'

'I dig you, cat,' said Miss Browning. Propelling the red-headed Rupert, now firmly established in the role of Burbage with his napkin-wrapped magnum, before her she set about her task, limpid and adoring.

A young man with a sly smile, the eyes of

112

a cautious gazelle and a midnight-blue dinner jacket, had been hovering within earshot
of Helen Diaz and her new conquest, a
champagne glass held professionally by its
base in his right hand. Lottie bore down
upon him with open delight.

'Tony Evelyn, my dear boy. You look magnificent. I do respect a man of your generation who has the sense to go to a decent
tailor. Edwin always used Poole, but I
suppose he's a trifle square for today. Let me
guess – Ramsden, or Sergeant Wilson?'

His smile became almost honest.

'Right first time, darling Lottie. What can
I hope for this evening? You're the best
gossip in the business when you're in form.
Thank God you never went into the Street.'

She gestured to a maid in a cap and apron
who refilled his glass and lowered her voice
so that he had to bend to catch the words.

'Try old Van Tromp. I think he's going to
bid at the Weingarden sale at Sotheby's next
week and that could put several noses out of
joint, particularly the people from the Boston
Modern who are coming over specially for it.
He won't tell you a thing of course, so go
fishing through his wife – she's the pretty old
dear with the emeralds – and she's mad
about Bracque and Chirico. She also breeds
schipperkes.'

'I know the lady.'

'Of course you do – you know everyone.

113

One of the nice things about you is that you never drop names except in your column. I've put you next to her at dinner.' She caught his arm. 'Oh, before I go and talk Morris and Ruskin to dear old Trevithic, who is stone deaf anyhow – and all for Free Cornwall–'

'Who? I must be getting deaf myself.'

'Charles Trevithic, dear boy. He speaks fluent Cornish, or so he says, and who's to contradict him? No, not about him. The Diaz girl.'

Mr Evelyn concealed his interest by looking about as if to make sure that she was indeed in the party.

'Too many headlines already for me, I'm afraid. She's not *intime* you know, any longer. Just news.'

Lottie sighed. 'Not even news now that Lord Feste, who owns nearly all the papers your lot don't, is expanding his empire. The animated kinematograph next, I'm told, and she's part of the deal – just like an extra cottage on some estate one happens to have bought. It'll be extremely worrying for her when she finds that *The Globe*, who've been playing her up very nobly, drop her like a hot potato. Your people are terribly mean when it comes to mentioning anything that belongs to Feste. I suppose you couldn't fit her into a tiny paragraph, just for old times sake?'

114

She did not wait for his reflexes to adjust themselves but swept on to a lonely figure by the window who was pulling the curtains aside and looking down into the courtyard. Gerhardt Mond of Ciné Mondial was a tough, untidy man, running to fat, with a fringe of dark curls and the brooding air of a bust of Beethoven. He released the fold as she approached and opened his arms, holding her at a distance.

'Lottie, *Liebchen*. You are going to present me to some beautiful creature who will make the evening for me, yes? This is good and I will behave myself for once. Not the Diaz. We said all that was to be said, mostly by signs, two months ago. This is finished, like a meal in Vienna, which was perfect but one does not wish again for some years. A wonderful cook, but her repertoire is limited. What have you for me this evening?'

She laughed and raised her head so that he could kiss her formally on both cheeks.

'A new chef. This is his *début* after poor Jannerat. There are partridges, I think, and some La Tache and – oh, yes, a sweet which was meant as a surprise for you – iced zabaglione.'

He continued to hold her between his arms.

'Poor Jannerat,' he repeated. 'Poor Jannerat. A wonderful sauce chef. He was quite a young man, the papers said, and with no

115

reason at all to die. Lottie, did you know that there are parts of Europe where suicide is increasing? So it is *Zeitgeist,* they say, but I hear other explanations. Has any of this reached you?'

She shook her head, her eyes round with unconvincing innocence. 'Nothing. You're taking me out of my depth and I have to keep both feet on the ground tonight. I won't be lectured on the morbid psychology of emotional young servants from the colonies.'

'No? Then I will repeat some gossip to you instead. Two days ago I was at a party – I always go to parties, just like the politicians – where I heard your name mentioned. It was the merest chance, be assured of that, for I was not eavesdropping. My keyhole ear is much sharper when it has been alerted. No, this was an occasion of twenty or thirty voices all speaking together – as they are here now – and by chance all but one stops. You know how it is?'

'But, of course. One sometimes gathers real gems that way. I hope this was repeatable?'

Mond paused before he answered, as if he were searching his memory for some extra detail to add colour.

'It was a flat voice,' he said at last. 'Slav or Mittel-European, like mine. I shall not tell you his name because if you know what he meant, then you can guess it. He said – very slowly, almost with a sigh – "Poor Miss Cambric". It was – how to put it? – as if you had been dead for a long time.'

'Gerhardt, you told me that deliberately to try to frighten me. Admit it, now. You're far too big to bully me.'

He shrugged his shoulders.

'Perhaps I am imagining. Perhaps I am inventing. Perhaps I am not minding my own business. But all the same I have a sort of feeling that you have been behaving like a silly girl. If you want to do something mad, learn how to ski, take up ballooning or put money in my next film, but do not go swimming in pools where there are sharks or even ugly little killer fish. I hear a small rumour in one place, half a sentence in another and a whisper some place else which was not intended for my ear. So I add them up and so I tell you a little story. Maybe it's true, maybe it's not. If I don't speak, then my conscience ruins my digestion for the evening – if I do, then I am risking some dreadful rebuke such as being put next to Mrs Van Tromp for dinner. What am I to do?'

Lottie turned from him to look across the room.

'Dear Gerhardt,' she said, 'such a kind thought, even if you've got your sums all wrong. You shall have two rewards and mix the ingredients for yourself. Miss Heffer comes from Santiago via Benenden and is so beautiful that you need do nothing but admire. She is going to write a book when she thinks of something to say, but don't worry – it hasn't happened yet. She will be on your left. On your right is Lady Crump, whose jokes are quite on a par with your own. Edwin used to say that a dirty mind was a constant source of pleasure and Elena Crump is both the proof and the pudding. Come over and meet her.'

Before Rupert retired to make his official entry as the announcer of dinner, the buzz of conversation had reached that particular pitch of intensity and warmth which to an experienced ear spells success.

The meal was one of those triumphs of planning and sheer hard work passing as spontaneity which maintained Lottie's legendary reputation as a hostess. Felix Perdreau monopolized Mlle Diaz, preventing her from establishing a private court to which husbands only were admitted. He wove a silken cocoon of flattery and wit about her which she accepted like a hammock on a sunny lawn. He spoke in French except for occasional lapses into Greek when he found some particularly outrageous item of gossip or innuendo to cosset her vanity.

Boysie Brown, his defences yielding under the penetrating oil of Perdita's unashamed attack, revealed the personality his agent

118

had spent a year trying to conceal, a mixture of snobbery, intelligence and rustic cunning which bore no relation to his reputation as angel-faced child who had carried his voice innocently from a cathedral choir to a lead in pop.

With the elements of disruption happily absorbed, Lottie ruled her table unchallenged. Van Tromp, acknowledging some naval ancestry, told his best story of wartime resistance as a barge master whose craft mysteriously sank whilst carrying cement, blocking a pen of U-boats. Lady Crump offered a gloriously indiscreet tip for a Newmarket horse owned by a rival, and Tony Evelyn, under pressure, gave a vicious imitation of the Prime Minister attempting to persuade his editor to fly an unlikely kite. Señorita Heffer bloomed and blushed beside Gerhardt, admitting in immaculately articulated school-girl English that her ideas for a new contribution to literature needed nothing except germination.

It was a tradition at the Turrets that there should be music on one of the two evenings of a weekend. This was sometimes supplied from the remarkable collection of private recordings made at the turn of the century by Sir Edwin, now preserved, recorded and played by what purported to be an original gramophone of the period but was in fact an ingenious deception concealing an advanced stereophonic machine. When there was live talent available Lottie had the instincts of an impresario. Her guests expected Victorian family entertainment of a high order and she rarely disappointed them.

Felix received her signal from a distance. He crossed the music room to the baby Steinway, opened its shining walnut lid and began to play very softly, the notes forming no more than a background to the clatter of coffee cups and conversation. His touch had much the same caress as his voice and Rupert, busy with a salver of cream and sugar, thought how typical of him it was that he should possess this elegant talent. He recognized the work, a Chopin *étude* in D flat major, admiring the choice, for it is marked *'sostenuto'* and demands attention by slow building and iteration. Before the final chords faded Perdreau had the attentive respect of the entire company.

There was no applause, for the less experienced of the guests were uncertain of their ground and Lottie broke the silence.

'Felix, my dear. You should sing for us – your voice was made for ballads. Give us something that Edwin enjoyed when this room was first built – Sullivan. Or Victor Herbert. No one seems to remember him today. He stayed here once in the old days, before he went to the States and became famous. Such a handsome man, Irish, I

120

think, with a very pretty Viennese wife – a Miss Forster.'

Perdreau laughed. '"The Time and the Place and the Girl"? What about going down memory lane with Amy Woodford Finden? Or "The Road to Mandalay"?'

He strummed a few bars, paused and turned to Helen Diaz, who was staring directly at him over the glass of brandy cupped in her hands.

'If you wish it,' he said. 'A ballad then, made to my mistress' eyebrow.'

He bowed towards her over the keys, stating the melody in single chords, and improvising a variation before he began to sing.

'I dream of Jeannie with the light brown hair...
Born like a shadow...'

It was a virtuoso performance, endearing, affectionate yet deliberately unprofessional, bringing a tear to the eye of Lady Crump. Finding itself in so unexpected a setting it rolled incontinently down her cheek and retreated into the folds of her chin. She led the murmur of genuine approval which built into a round of applause.

'My dear Felix, you sing like a real man. What a change after the tuneless *castrati* of today. Do it again. Do it again and again.'

Helen Diaz, who had unpinned the orchid

on her shoulder, undulated towards him and placed the ugly flower above the keyboard.

'Yes,' she said. 'Again – more *nostalgie*. I am most 'appy when I feel I am going to weep for *histoires du temps passé*.'

He turned his head and smiled, looking suddenly twenty years younger.

'Your servant, madam.'

Very softly he began to improvise on one air after another 'The Ash Grove', 'Greensleeves', 'I know where I'm going', and 'O Mistress Mine', twisting and tricking out the melodies with *arpeggio* flourishes. After some minutes, when the conversation showed signs of returning, he broke the sequence with a warning chord and sang again:

*'Oh, the days of the Kerry Dancing
Fiddlers scraping the pipers playing
...gone, alas, like our youth too soon...'*

Even Perdita, who knew the act and the limits of Perdreau's repertoire, admitted to herself that he was on top of his form. He was a natural exhibitionist, too experienced to overplay his hand. As the last vibrations died he picked up the orchid, placed it in his buttonhole and walked to the sofa where Mlle Diaz was enthroned. There was a footstool near her feet and he rested on it, an elbow on the cushions at her side, sunning himself in her approval. She straightened the flower possessively, underlining the significance of the gift.

Perdita could sense that, despite all her wiles, she was losing ground with Boysie Brown. He had been standing beside her at the coffee table, petulance becoming visible on his pouting lips. He did not join in the applause but turned his back and put down his cup so sharply that it rattled in the saucer.

Lottie caught the warning note. She bore down upon him, confidential and appealing.

'That was splendid, wasn't it? Felix has just the right amateur touch for a Victorian evening, don't you think? I suppose it would be wrong to ask you to make it a real triumph for me? Perdita tells me you sing like what she calls a syncopated archangel – an unlikely phrase but wonderfully expressive and exciting. Could you – would you?'

Boysie surveyed the room: he had become the centre of interest, a fact which gave him infinite satisfaction. Not all the glances were approving and there was a challenge here which he had no intention of resisting. If Miss Cambric wanted a colourful guest and Tony Evelyn was looking for an anecdote he was in the mood to supply both.

'O.K.' he said, 'I'll have a bash.'

A popular idol rarely achieves success by accident and Boysie Brown, after leaving his midland cathedral, had come up the hard way. He had played and sung with sweating overworked groups touring suburban dance halls, camped in vans, gained experience in north country clubs and hit the jackpot of popularity by a mixture of perspicacity and merit. A light baritone voice and intuition where audiences were concerned brought him very near the top of the profession, for he was a genuine musician, a guitarist of real brilliance and an able pianist. This was not a moment for the type of performance which had won him myriads of adoring teenagers, but for a display which would put Felix Perdreau into the background for the rest of the evening.

He moved to the piano and began to play, making a direct invasion of the older man's territory by singing 'Sweet Genevieve' with such tenderness that opposition melted without resistance and the whole room warmed to the sentimental charm which was part of his stock in trade. 'Linden Lea' and 'The Foggy Foggy Dew', had equal success and he returned to Perdita's side in a glow of triumph. She took his arm.

'Gorgeous. You could make the top ten with those any day. I never knew you sang straight. I was terrified you might shock them with "Goggle Box a Go-Go" or "Brickerhead Blues".'

'Not on your nelly,' he said, his golden

124

curls shaking as he laughed. 'I know an audience of stuffed shirts when I see one. Besides – I just had to see that pompous bastard off.' He looked round the room and frowned. 'Where is he, by the way?'

Perdita signalled to Rupert, who had been standing impassively by the decanters. This, he had been instructed, was to be a special evening and liqueurs were not to be stinted. He produced a generous measure of cointreau. Two young women, as alike as Dutch dolls, joined Señorita Heffer as she fluttered across to pour adulation over the hero of the moment. Boysie accepted their tributes with all the youthful charm for which he was famous. He blushed, conveying that he was just a schoolboy at heart, wrote his name on an expensive lace handkerchief and gave a display of naïve charm which in its way was quite as skilled as his singing. Yet his eyes still searched the room and presently he turned to Perdita.

'I said, where is that bearded wonder? Couldn't he take it?'

Helen Diaz was making sure of her own audience by flashing her devastating Asian eyes at Van Tromp, who appeared mesmerized, and holding Gerhardt Mond by the hand. Behind her Tony Evelyn hovered, introducing an occasional shaft of venom into the brew.

'Helen darling, you've a marvellously

bitchy script writer. Do you pay him the earth?'

'I offer 'im 'eaven, but he prefers dollars – just like a journalist, yes?'

The Victorian section of the evening was clearly over and the guests were giving their attention to more practical considerations of drink and gossip. Rupert wove deferentially through the various groups, reflecting with some regret that if Lottie did not call a halt to the supply of liquor there would be no black market dealings when the party officially ended. He was clearing empty glasses on the coffee table with his back to the room when Perdita's voice, casually formal, broke in on his thoughts.

'Burbage, we should get rid of some of this debris. I'll open the door for you.'

He turned to find her looking at him with a warning expression, for Boysie was still within earshot. His gloved hands made the tray difficult to handle. She followed him into the upper hall, making certain that they were alone.

'Trouble brewing,' she whispered. 'Where the hell has Felix got to? Lottie particularly wants him as a buffer state between Angel Face and that man Mond, who's getting amorous with the Diaz already. What has happened to him? He can't just have gone off in a sulk.'

Rupert shook his head.

'He was talking to her in Greek – which is all Greek to me. Then he nipped quietly out, just after Boysie's first song. My guess would be that he went off to find her a token of some sort – some of his own roses perhaps – in exchange for her orchid. Shall I chase him up? I could get down to his cottage and back in five minutes.'

'Make it four and bring him back alive.'

But Felix Perdreau was not in his cottage. It stood silent and ridiculous in the cold light of the September moon, as unlikely and artificial as if it had been designed in Staffordshire pottery. Dorothy Perkins roses round the porch climbed sentimentally over rustic trellis. The door was locked, no light showed through the silken curtains behind the lattice windows, and beside the pocket-handkerchief lawn the garage stood empty.

A mutilated orchid trodden into the gravel path suggested that the owner had left in a hurry.

10

The Sleeveless Errand

Out of the remarkable assortment of people who had a direct interest in the movements of Felix Perdreau there were two who reported the news to Mr Campion. Both of them rang him at his London flat on Monday morning, nearly thirty-six hours after the disappearance had first been noticed.

Rupert, speaking from a call box outside the grounds of the Turrets, sounded breathless and conspiratorial.

'Couldn't get through before,' he said. 'Guests to see off and all that malarky. They make me work here, you know. I think I'll go back to simple play acting when this is all over. Well, he's gone – vanished – sunk without trace. His car is missing too, so he may have pushed off in a huff, though I don't think so. He was making all the running with the Diaz and she's quite an item for anyone's notebook. There was a fine old boil-up after he'd left, with Gerhardt Mond coming up on the rails like a two-year-old. In the end I had to carry Boysie Brown to bed after he'd passed out on a mixture of cointreau and brandy. I'll tell you all the scandal later. Lottie still refuses to admit there's anything adrift. She says Perdreau obviously went of his own free will and it's no business of ours but she looks half dead when she's off guard. What do you want me to do?'

'Go back to cleaning the silver and supervising the upper staff. I hope the weekend tips have been satisfactory?'

'Perdita says they've been better, though I thought I'd done very well. Are you likely to look in?'

'It's on the cards. There's a bit of research to be done before I leap into action.'

The second call came from L.C. Corkran, his clipped tones coming over the wire, as they always did, with incisive clarity. 'This man Perdreau appears to have been kidnapped or at least coerced. We had an observer at Lottie's place over the weekend and he reports that the garage at the cottage was broken into – the lock was damaged – which suggests that there was an element of compulsion in the proceedings. I'm involved principally, because of that unfortunate piece of tape which you sequestered. It has produced repercussions and changed the Department's attitude. A fact emerges, however.'

'Our original mysterious friend is still at large?'

'That is the inference. Had he been caught in the wilds of Yorkshire, Perdreau would be of no interest. As it is, he is obviously suspected of knowing more than is good for him. Tell me – I take it you know him reasonably well – would he break easily under pressure?'

Mr Campion gave the matter some thought.

'He's a flamboyant character – possibly rather devious in business, with a shrewd idea of self-interest. It's unlikely that he would last long; knowing what he's up against, I'd give him half an hour.'

'I was afraid you might form that opinion. A pity our people didn't get to him first. I take it you still keep an eye on Lottie Cambric?'

'Four of them in all.'

'*Parate Sperate*. If you unearth anything of consequence remember that we are now just as interested as our friends – perhaps more – in finding the original cause of the trouble.'

Inglewood is twenty-three miles from central London. Mr Campion made the journey in forty minutes, arriving as the last of the morning's visitors were piling back into their coach. Perdita and Rupert, each formally attired, were collecting sherry glasses and coffee cups in the Great Hall, a chore which they clearly found depressing.

'Better go and see Lottie right away,' said

the girl. 'This stuff isn't worth drinking and the seed cake is always stale on a Monday.'

The chatelaine of the Turrets received him in her office. The weekend had left its mark on her and she looked older than he remembered. When he came to consider the question, her age had always been a mystery but her hair no longer gave the impression of being prematurely white and now it was possible to believe that she had truly known Sir Edwin when he was host to the lions of his day. Her very arched eyebrows were still black but her eyes were heavy with apprehension.

'You've no news of Felix, I suppose?'

He shook his head. 'Not a whisper, I'm afraid. Lottie, this time you've got to come clean. Helping a lame dog is one thing, but running yourself, and Perdita come to that, into real trouble won't help anyone – not even Kopeck, now. You do see that, don't you?'

'I suppose so, Albert. I may have been very silly but I'm quite as obstinate as Edwin was in his day. Little Vassily is fighting for his life and I felt I had to help. If a man is likely to be murdered you can't just stand by and do nothing. Or can you?' She fluttered her hands. 'I'm at my wits' end, my dear.'

Mr Campion looked out over the courtyard, where pigeons were fighting and flirting, to the formal gardens beyond, dominated by the urn above the empty Tomb.

'You must tell me about Kopeck,' he said. 'Why did he come to you for help?'

Lottie hesitated for some time, putting her thoughts in order before she answered. If she had any reservations they did not appear when she spoke.

'He came here several times with official parties. A dear little man with a sense of humour, but like a serious-minded child in many ways. I got to know him quite well and I suppose you could say he sounded me out very carefully before he confided in me. He asked for help – what he called "some assistance as friend to friend".'

'He wanted to borrow money?'

'I made that mistake and risked giving great offence. In fact it was the reverse. He wanted to bank money with me and from time to time he brought quite a lot – always in notes, about five hundred pounds in all. I still hold most of it. He was very formal about this and gave me no explanation. "It is taking far too long," he said. "There is a problem to be solved. You see, I am a patriot at heart. I love my country as you love this house, so you protect the good name. I want to do the same. This is most difficult because I do not think there is a great deal of time".'

She was giving a vivid imitation of the

132

man, conjuring him into Mr Campion's mind's eye out of a memory which became clear as she spoke.

'You thought he meant to escape – to defect?'

'Of course I did – just at first. But he was very insistent that this was not his idea. I even offered to arrange for him to meet Freddie Hale of the Home Office, which would have made it simple, but he refused absolutely. "This I must do for myself," he said. "I must be in limbo to speak freely – not a polite guest of your government."'

'You've no idea what he wanted to say?'

'I simply cannot imagine, though I've racked my brains. It was something that worried him – frightened is the better word. He was building up his reserves here, apparently waiting for something to happen and getting more scared every time he appeared, poor little man.

'Then I think he had a warning, perhaps the one he was waiting for, though it seemed to come unexpectedly. He arrived unannounced one Saturday evening, saying he must get away in a great hurry. He refused to hide here, which was just as well as it turned out. I think he'd made plans and they'd fallen through or gone astray. He had some idea of moving about the country, going from hotel to hotel and never stopping for more than a night. It seemed a very uncomfortable arrangement to me and not likely to work because he is so obviously a foreigner.'

'Is that when Perdreau came into the picture?'

'Felix? In a way he was in it all along. He speaks some Russian, rather more than he pretends – but then he has a wonderful ear and can make the right sort of noise in a dozen languages. He's – well, you know him – he's *simpatico*. Yes, Felix had the idea of sending him up to Baxstable and he made the arrangements. Charles Manning, who runs it, is an old friend who's been here once or twice. Quite brilliant, when you come to consider it. To find him there would be like looking for a needle in a haystack – or so we thought.'

'Until Nascott appeared on the scene?'

She nodded. 'That frightened us because the wretched creature stole my private address book. Felix made a dash for the North as soon as we realized the danger and whisked the little man away.'

'Where?'

'Oh, my dear, that's the very thing which is disturbing. He didn't tell me. This was Vassily's idea, I believe. He thought that having done something to help him I could be in some danger and the less I knew the better. He was very worried that he might be causing trouble and he was trying to mini-mize it – to protect me. Felix said that he didn't think he was suspected and since someone had to make arrangements it would be safer for me if I really knew nothing about them.'

She leaned back in her swivel office chair, not relaxed but tired and, despite her plump figure, fragile.

'Felix is an impetuous creature. He may see himself as Sir Galahad but I don't think he has great physical courage.'

'Could he be blackmailed? This is usually the first pressure these people try.'

'I'm afraid he could. This is slander and I'll deny every word of it but I suspect he isn't always very scrupulous with his books and manuscripts, yet he is such an expert on the subject that you'd have to get up very early in the morning to catch him out. Would they use physical violence – pincers, rubber truncheons – the sort of thing one reads about as happening in a Police State?'

'They might if they thought it would work. It depends how long he could hold out. If I could get to Kopeck first and smuggle him away from wherever he is then Felix would cease to be important to them. I suppose you really – scout's honour – have no idea of the hiding place?'

Lottie shook her head slowly, making the gesture final and convincing.

'Felix has so many connections – so many odd friends and not all of them presentable.

There are very few, I imagine, whom he could rely on in this sort of difficulty.'

'Tell me about him. He has an office or a shop of some sort just off Bond Street, I believe, dealing in rare books – special commissions for libraries and private collectors – that's really all I know. What else?'

She sighed. 'That's nearly all I know, too. He sometimes goes off on long trips abroad, buying more than selling, I think. He used to have a flat in Brighton, but gave it up two years ago, when one of his best clients who lived in that area died. He's a bachelor but there are always plenty of women to flutter around. He likes admiration but he gets bored very easily and I think that the trouble is that the girls he finds entertaining mentally don't attract him in other ways and, of course, vice versa. It so often happens with that sort of man. He's quite invaluable to me and I think that I could say that if there is any real affection in his soul it is for me.'

She paused, still searching her memory. 'Oh, yes – one other thing. He watches his health very carefully. I think you could call him a hypochrondriac, if that's the word I want.'

'Any reason for it?'

'He thinks he has a weak chest. Last year he spent a fortnight in a clinic of some sort; but my impression is that it was one of those expensive health cure establishments which provide good excuse for idling about in comfortable surroundings. It was at Dovecote, of all ridiculous places.'

Mr Campion seized on the name.

'Dovecote – near Clacton. All nannies and kiddies and green lawns. Safe bathing and no common public houses, bingo halls or cinemas? What was the name of his hideout?'

'He never told me. I think he wanted to give the impression that it was very select and important, so of course it may have been quite commonplace and dull. There could even have been a young woman involved, perhaps a girl he doesn't altogether approve of.'

She smiled reminiscently. 'Yes, it could have been that. He is very discreet about his amours.'

'It is a long shot,' said Mr Campion. 'But it looks like the only one in the locker.'

The glorious year for Dovecote was 1912. At that date the last of the sea-front mansions was completed, the lawns were laid out and by-laws passed by shrewd property-owning councillors forbidding any intrusion upon the untrammelled respectability of the resort. The facilities for bridge, tennis and croquet are excellent and for visiting fathers there is a reputable golf course; but in the main it attracts the wives of the wealthy, their children, *au pair* girls working as their

137

nursemaids, and invalids. The town has grown considerably but only by reproducing itself like an amoeba, using the same unimaginative but highly successful formula. There are forty private hotels, nearly a thousand furnished houses for seasonal letting and a multitude of nursing homes, hydros and establishments where every medical attention is expensively provided.

Mr Campion arrived at the Royal Victoria, a superior Edwardian hotel (open to non-residents) in time for an exceedingly dainty tea. The fact that he supplied himself with the local trade directory did not improve his standing in the eyes of the elderly waiter, who inquired if there would be anything more and presented a bill before he had concluded his second cup. Partly in self-defence and partly because the task before him was likely to be protracted, he booked a room and continued his suspiciously commercial reading.

Five newsagents were listed in the town and he called upon four of them in turn, asking the same questions and receiving the same unsatisfactory answers. The fifth, an archaic tobacco and confectionery store selling buckets, spades and miniature shrimping nets, proved more helpful. It was nearly six when the bell inside the door announced his arrival.

'I'm Gibbons Market Research,' said

Campion, 'inquiring into the distribution of scientific journals. How is the demand with you?'

A myopic dwarf whose pebble lenses gave her the expression of an inquisitive toad put down her knitting and gave her mind to the problem.

'Scientific? Well, let me think a moment, dear. We do six *Everyman's Weekly Doctor,* and ten *New Scientist,* four – no five – *Modern Home Nursing* and thirty-two *Capt. Blazer's Science Rocket.*'

'Splendid. No recent additions, I suppose?'

'Only oddments – special orders and that.' She opened a dog-eared ledger. '*The Alembic,* one; *Neo-Physicist,* one. There's no call for them to be stocked, you see. Both of them asked for special last week and until further notice.'

'We at Gibbons,' said Mr Campion, 'like to know our readership. If they were ordered by someone who isn't a registered practitioner he should pay the full rate. I hope there was no question of a reduction?'

Her eyes moved independently, cautious and globular behind the thick lenses.

'Mr Williams wouldn't allow that, dear, so I couldn't say who reads them, I'm sure. They go to Wayland Hall, some sort of private hotel for cranks – on the front, of course. Very quiet, very elite. People like reading about their own troubles, though it only makes them worse, if you ask me. Still, I shouldn't grumble, it's a very good account, settled every month and no trouble at all.'

'Wayland Hall,' said the market-research inquirer. 'I'm glad it's a respectable address.'

The large tudoresque house had an enclosed glass veranda running almost the full length of its monstrous façade. Despite its size, modesty prevailed when identification was concerned, for it bore only a small brass name-plate beside the white lintel. The desk in the foyer was unattended and Mr Campion looked round the twilit room with its deep leather chairs in search of help.

In a far corner Felix Perdreau sat sprawled, his head back and his eyes closed. His face was ashen and only his heavy breathing showed that he was not dead but asleep.

11

Second Call

Perdreau was not easily roused. In response to Mr Campion's gentle pressure on his arm he opened his eyes and stared into the distance without comprehension or curiosity. The thin man continued his grip and finally the tired eyes began to focus.

'Campion,' he muttered. 'I know you, don't I? What odd wind brings you here?' His whisper was hoarse and he licked his lips as if he had spent the day in a high fever.

Apart from a quartet of dowagers gossiping in a far corner, the room was deserted.

'I've come from Lottie. She – er – guessed or deduced where you might be. What happened to you on Saturday night?'

Perdreau ran his hands through his hair, pressing his temples. He was not unkempt, though his oversize bow tie was loose and the collar unbuttoned.

'Saturday night? And today is Monday, they say. It seems a century ago. No sense in secrecy any longer, I suppose. If you've come from the Turrets you must know too much already. I was kidnapped like the son of the Duke of Burgundy in *L'oiseau des Brumes*, if you remember those *contes de fées*.'

'But not by an eagle, I gather?'

'Two vultures ... there may have been three, or a dozen for all I know. I was showing my paces to a pretty vixen called Helen Diaz who had a beckoning eye. I escaped for a moment to find her a token of my intentions, a book of Greek love songs very vulgarly bound in white samite and printed on imitation parchment – a tourist's trophy, but flashy enough for her boudoir. Outside my own front door I was blacked out, quite literally. A cloth over my head, a jab in my arm and the next thing I knew – but long after, a lifetime later – there was a searchlight in my face and disembodied voices asking questions.'

He broke off. 'My head feels like Cinderella's pumpkin about to produce a coach and four. Could you get me a drink?'

'A long whisky and soda?'

'Almost anything will do. My palate is dead. There is a little dispense door just behind you. Knock on it – softly for my sake – and say it's for me.'

When Mr Campion returned the sick man held out two unsteady hands, drank the liquid in one long swallow and arched his head backwards.

'I'm returning to sanity.'

'Good. Now about these questions. How much did you tell them?'

Perdreau groaned. 'God knows. Everything there was to tell, I'm afraid. They kept at me for hour after hour and my mouth was dry as the Sahara. Whatever they did to me gave me a thirst that was unendurable – blinding. A jug of iced water just out of reach was all the torture they needed. Thumb screws have nothing on that when it comes to killing resistance. You'd sell your soul for a mouthful. In the end they had to give me a few drops because my voice packed up and my tongue turned to rotting leather.'

'And they got what they wanted?'

'I'm not proud of it. I told them all about this place, the name he was using – Eugene Lambert – the telephone number – everything. My whole will power simply wilted away. I think I was drugged or doped because I kept on waking up to find myself still trying to talk – wandering – mumbling about rare editions, book sales and all the tricks of the trade. It could ruin me if they thought it worth recording.'

'Could you identify your inquisitors?'

'I doubt it. Grey men, grey faces – classless accents. There was one with a long narrow head, Slav cheek bones and a black moustache like a professional pall bearer or the portrait of Henry the Fourth. He hardly spoke at all but I felt he was in charge. It was he who decided that there was nothing more to be got out of me. He brought me coffee when it was all over – very bitter and drugged, I suppose. I slept again after that.'

'And when you woke?'

'When I woke it was quite early this morning. I was lying on a bed in a sleazy hotel in the Euston Road with the overnight case I keep in my car unpacked on a table beside my unpleasantly dirty bed. When I asked the man in charge, he said I'd been brought in by two friends and he'd only accepted me because although I was stinking drunk I wasn't making a song and dance about it. The room was paid for in advance. I was registered in my own name and he handed me a ticket for a garage just round the corner where my car was parked. There was a bathroom – just – and a breakfast which made me as sick as a dog. I ask no sympathy, only understanding.'

'You have both,' said Mr Campion. 'They seem to have done a very efficient job on you. Having recovered your car I suppose you drove here to find out what happened?'

Perdreau clasped his hands between his knees and bowed his head.

'I had to. I remembered blabbing it all out. It kept coming back to me like patches of nightmare and for some reason I lacked the moral courage to telephone. I drove straight here and damn dangerously because I kept falling asleep on the road, or very nearly. It was no use, Campion. Kopeck's gone.'

'This time they've caught him?'

'It looks like it. I came here, asked for him, and they said he left suddenly – yesterday – with no explanation. By then I was dead beat and feeling so woolly that my mind refused to function. I took a room – I've stayed here before, you know – had another bath and slept again. Then I came down feeling a trifle more human but the woman who runs the place, Mrs Furlough, was out and nobody seemed to know what had really happened. I just went to sleep again, and I'd be there now if you hadn't roused me. What a mess, what a bloody miserable useless wicked mess. I could use another drink.'

'When we've talked to Mrs Furlough. There's a cosy little office behind the reception desk where she presides, if I know this kind of establishment. Lead me to her. I'll need your support if she's going to confide in me.'

The room, like its owner, was undeniably feminine. The walls were clinically white, redeemed by three Nash water-colours; a silver bowl of roses made the big desk radiant; and green curtains patterned with golden fleurs-de-lis kept the room gay even at the depressing hour of twilight. Mrs Furlough, petite and patently efficient, had repeated the ebony of her hair in glasses angled to give an oriental slant to her eyes. Twenty-five, thought Campion, and regretfully added fifteen years as he took her hand. Perdreau made formal introductions.

'Felix, you still look utterly overhung. I think you should go to bed. I'll have chicken sandwiches and a corpse reviver – my own particular – sent up. Take my advice and do it now.'

He sat down heavily and shook his head.

'In a minute, madonna. But just now it's the man I brought here we have to ask about. I know he's gone, and if his bill isn't paid I'll see to it, but tell me again what happened. This morning I had great difficulty in understanding the meaning of words.'

She laughed, revealing superlative teeth.

'I'm not surprised. As an expert I'd say you'd been mixing vodka with several other potent spirits. Well now, little Mr Lambert – I always felt I should call him Monsieur, because you said he was more than half French – he left us on Sunday morning, just when we thought he was settling in nicely. He paid his bill, since you ask, and walked out just as the first gong was sounding for lunch. Very wrong for a man on a special diet after a breakdown, but I couldn't stop him. He didn't even order a taxi, but walked away with his silly little cardboard suitcase and a magazine under his arm. He was obviously not going to explain, so that was that.'

'For no reason at all?' inquired Mr Campion. 'No message – no telephone call?'

'There was an inquiry in the morning, but I didn't bother him, since the caller said not to. I took it myself, it being Sunday and no girl for the switchboard. A secretary, a woman from the London flats where he lived, ringing to check his address to forward him some letters. It was the man who appeared just after he'd gone who was just a mite macabre. He arrived in a big black C.D. car which was chauffeur driven and very impressive. He asked for Mr Lambert in a grim sort of V.I.P. manner and refused

146

to take no for an answer. In the end I had to show him the receipted bill which our guest had left on the desk, and the empty room. He said it was very worrying because he was needed urgently in London. He took a lot of satisfying and even when he left I don't think he quite believed me.'

'A man with a mournful face and black moustache?'

'Very with it – like a pop singer, only a proper hair cut – that's him.'

'Extraordinary. Did he miss Mr Lambert by minutes or hours?'

'Half an hour, perhaps. I know he arrived during lunch and the boy fetched me off the dining-room desk to deal with him.' She turned sparkling black eyes on Mr Campion. 'It was the second call – the one Mr Lambert took himself – which seemed to decide him to go. It must have been, because I didn't tell him about the first.'

'The second call?'

'Yes, from someone who wanted you, Felix. It was a muffled sort of voice, and a very bad line, asking if you were here and when I said "No" it said "Is a friend of his staying?" The caller described Mr Lambert, but obviously didn't know his name. Then I suggested "Lambert" and the caller said, of course, that was right and could they speak to him. I switched it through to the veranda where he was sitting. The talk only lasted thirty seconds. He just went upstairs and packed after that.'

'A man or a woman – young or old?'

Mrs Furlough shrugged her shoulders. 'Your guess is as good as mine. Either, I'd say, and any age below ninety, but it was the worst line in the world – probably cross country. London calls are better and New York sounds like the next room.'

Campion surveyed his companion from above outsize spectacles.

'Who?'

Perdreau threw up his hands and it was sometime before he answered.

'I was the only man in the world who knew he was here – until they broke me. Or so I thought.'

12

The Better Part of Valour

'The time is approaching,' said Mr Hilary Wykes of Denmark Holdings, 'when I expect to see a few results. I'm sure you'll agree?' He examined his finger nails, which were distressingly dirty, for there are oily traces from the interior of even the best engines which refuse to be removed. He disliked the man to whom he was talking, scarcely bothering to conceal the fact.

'On a retainer like yours, even allowing for the expenses of your organization, which appears to consist of a repulsive woman called Richards, an office girl, two full-time ex-narks, and a fat oaf who hangs round the gardens of the Turrets, you are doing quite comfortably. It won't last, you know. Up here we are simply interested in the end product. Do you get the message?'

The proprietor of Intercity Inquiries, to whom the question was directed, did not respond. He was unsure of his ground, treading warily, yet anxious to give an impression that he was accustomed to the type of business into which he had stumbled. He protested with professional dignity.

'You've had one Confidential from me. We arranged for them to be weekly. Two days before the next one is due. I warned you this might be a long job.'

Wykes was sitting behind an impressive desk on whose green tooled leather surface sat two telephones, the closed circuit T.V. intercom, a scale model of a 1926 3-litre Bentley and an open office file. He ran his fingers through the folios, reading sentences at random.

'Among the visitors during the weekend of the 7th October were Mr and Mrs Heindrik Tromp, Miss Helen Diaz, Señorita Heffer –

you've misspelt her name, by the way – Mr Gerhardt Mond... There appears to be some irregularity in the matter of tipping and the handling of the *tronc* system... The subject visited the Forum Club, which is for ladies only... Inquiries are proceeding into the possibility of obtaining access to the concealed telephone wires, which are situate underground...'

'Nascott, this is long-winded tripe dressed up in police court bafflegab. Sick making. There's nothing new in it – nothing I couldn't have told you myself. If I showed this nonsense to Mr Denmark he'd probably fling you out of the window. Do you really tell me this is the lot?'

'It's early days. Less than a fortnight–'

'Nonsense. The reason for using you – in your own words – was that you'd been nosing around the place for some time, had a woman on the inside on your payroll, and thought you were on to something which might be useful to us if not to your previous employers. Don't be stupid, man. You sold this story of yours to Mr Denmark and in my experience no fly has ever settled within a hundred yards of him. You'd never be able to put one over on him in your entire lifetime unless you really knew something. Now what about it?'

Nascott shifted his weight in the chromium and plastic device on which he was sitting.

His eyes flickered round the room.

'Is this in confidence, Mr Wykes – between you and me, I mean?'

'Certainly not. What are we paying you for – what do I get paid for, come to that? If you're on to something, the sooner I know about it the better. Spill it, man.'

'If you insist, sir. I did turn something up, three nights ago, but I don't care for it and I don't want any part in it until I can get a few more facts. You're not paying me enough to risk my licence and if it comes to a showdown it might be thought I'd committed a misdemeanour already. I don't like to speak clearer.'

'You're going to have to. Lucidly. Otherwise you're out.'

The visitor extracted himself from the depths of the chair with an effort. It had not been designed for a man of his bulk and he perched himself cautiously on the edge, nearly overbalancing in the process.

'If you must know,' he said, 'I found the body of a man and there's good reason to suspect murder. That's plain ugly, but it's the long and the short of it. Tapping telephones is a risk but concealing information of that sort is a criminal offence on its own. Now I've told you – and if under pressure I tell you the whole strength – all I know – it makes you a party to that offence. You could be charged, along with me. Do you want me to go on or shall we forget this little talk ever happened?'

'Go on.'

Nascott paused to allow the instruction to emphasize itself.

'Very well, then; but don't say I didn't caution you. In the grounds of the Turrets there's a mausoleum – they call it the Tomb – a sort of stone bootbox-shaped affair with an urn on top of it, like you see in church-yards, only much more sizey. I always thought they lifted the top off to put a coffin inside but this one has a small door at one end, part of the panelling. There are brick steps down and two stone shelves, one each side when you get down, almost six feet I'd say. In the early days I understood it was used for storing blocks of ice, though the old man, Sir Edwin, meant to be buried there – with room for the rest of his family, I sup-pose. Now on the Saturday evening when I first searched the place there was evidence it had been recently entered, though it was quite empty. I don't know if I told you this, sir, but I can smell fright – it's my job sometimes – a kind of an instinct. Any good policeman can do it. Miss Cambric was definitely frightened when I said I'd been there. I didn't chase her about it at the time because I thought that whatever had hap-pened there was nothing to do with my inquiries about Kopeck, whom I'd reason to believe was still alive. But there were certain signs which I took note of, being in the habit of observation.'

'Spare me the jargon. Tedious, you know. Get on with it.'

'There were some marks on the stone floor to suggest something had been dragged across it and under one of the shelves there was a new two shilling piece. I thought at the time that something illegal might have been stored there – cases of liquor that she didn't want on the books, for example. You never know what will give a woman a guilty conscience, especially if she's accustomed to being honest. After I'd traced Kopeck up North I forgot about it until the situation changed. Then I saw that anything I could get on Miss Cambric might be useful to you, so I did some more investigating. I told you, if I remember, that I had the full plans of the house and estate. It was a lot of work: I had to go to the British Museum and look at art magazines of the period. I looked them up first to see if there was any possibility of a secret room in the house where he could be hidden. There wasn't one.'

Wykes leaned forward. 'Get to the point, man.'

'After I got my chips from my other client I looked up the drawings again – I'd had photostats made of them and they're very elaborate, elevations and all. Under the first compartment of the Tomb there is a bricked space, intended by Sir Edwin for himself, I suppose. Three stone flags on the floor cover it and they lift out fairly easily if you've got the strength. One of them has a concealed ringlet. Three nights ago I went back and opened it up. There's the body of a man there – quite recent, I'd say, though it's hard to tell in a cold spot like that. Strictly speaking, I ought to have reported it to the proper authorities immediately, but I thought it best to try and find out who he was before I did anything. If we knew that, ahead of anyone else, it might strengthen our position with Miss Cambric. Do you want me to proceed?'

Wykes did not answer the question. He fingered the leather strap on the model car, unbuckled it and lifted the bonnet. He was still playing with the toy when he spoke.

'Describe the man.'

'About fifty, thick set, receding brown hair, scar on left cheek due to accident or war wound many years ago, no particular outstanding features, small snub nose, big mouth, grey suit, grey muffler, brown gloves, sneaker shoes. Cause of death hard to say, but it could have been a blow on the head. No identifying papers, and tailor's label removed from coat. A burglar or a professional sneak thief, I'd say. To tell you the truth I didn't care much for what I'd found and didn't stay overlong.'

He paused. Wykes, still apparently engrossed in the toy, did not respond.

'You see, sir, this sort of thing sounds as if it might be wonderfully useful for a bit of pressure, but I've got to think of my position. I'm an ex-officer and no excuse for not knowing the law. I'm chancing my arm as it is. It might be rather different if I could ascertain who the man was, so we could start inquiries from the other end, if you follow me. I've put out a few feelers, but as it stands the information is a bit too hot to handle and I don't quite see how it could be used without it kicking back on us. If you like we could do an anonymous letter to the police or a phone call. Wouldn't it be best to forget this little chat?'

The man behind the desk pushed back his chair and for the first time faced his visitor squarely.

'Mr Nascott,' he said. 'I don't have to tell you about the times when it is wise to keep your trap shut. This is one of them. All right: case dismissed. Keep at it in a general way but for God's sake cut out your long-winded reports – only contact me when it's worth it. And give that Tomb a wide berth. Just forget it exists.'

A sleek car more suitable for a funeral than a wedding wound through the serpentine drive past elm trees and laurel bushes to the forecourt of the Turrets and halted before the gothic porch. One of the two uniformed men in front leapt out to open the door for the passenger and pulled at the wrought-iron bell to announce their arrival. Had it not been for the modernity of the car the scene belonged to another age: the formal afternoon call of an important visitor on a great house.

Rupert, in an alpaca jacket over a waistcoat with broad horizontal stripes added his own quota of archaic dignity.

'Miss Cambric is not at home, sir. She does not receive visitors except by appointment. Perhaps I could deliver a message?'

'My name is Moryak,' said the caller. 'Have the goodness to take Miss Cambric my card and say that I am quite prepared to wait.' He produced the pasteboard from an ivory case.

'I will ascertain if Miss Cambric is available. Perhaps you would care to be seated?'

Left to himself the caller examined the Great Hall with its divided staircase, gallery and heavy panelling as curiously as any tourist. The showcases of original manuscripts by Browning, Tennyson, Dobson, Swinburne and all the late Victorian masters held his attention for some time. Sir Frederick Leighton's painting of Clytemnestra and Sir John Millais' portrait of Sir Edwin himself looked down impassively between antlered heads and trophies of colonial wars.

It was a considerable vigil. The man with the black moustache, which a previous generation would have found comic, made full use of it, for he had an inquiring mind and seldom wasted time. After twenty minutes Rupert reappeared.

'Miss Cambric will receive you, sir. If you will come this way.'

He led the visitor up the staircase to the Small Drawing-Room where Lottie was enthroned in the largest of the quilted-velvet armchairs. She did not rise to greet him but nodded to acknowledge the formal bow. Her ribbed silk coat and skirt suggested antiquity without being slavishly in period.

'Mr Moryak. I recall that we had some correspondence a few weeks ago. If you have come all this way to reopen the subject then I'm afraid you are wasting your time, and mine. I really have nothing to add to what I said in my letter.'

He did not reply immediately but pulled a chair directly in front of her and sat down uninvited. When he spoke his voice was cold and clipped as if he were carving the words in the air with a scalpel.

'Miss Cambric, I don't think you quite understand your position. To make this clear I will outline the situation, so I ask you to listen very carefully. Please not to comment until I have finished.

'You have befriended, so to put it, the man

Vassily Kopeck, who is one of our nationals, and you have done all you can to prevent us from making contact with him. This would be understandable if he was a defector, a person seeking an easy bourgeois life who did not have the wit to ask for asylum in the proper way. Foolish but understandable.

'This is not the case with Kopeck, as you must realize by now. He is an educated citizen, one who knows all about the existing channels for betraying his country – yet he has not used them. Do you never ask yourself why? No?

'Then I will tell you. This man is a criminal who is wanted by your country and mine. Unfortunate but true. We have placed this information with your authorities and they are co-operating with us.'

He picked up his card, which lay on an occasional table by Lottie's chair and wrote on it.

'If you do not believe me, I ask you to call this number on the extension I have shown. These are your own people and they will verify what I tell you.'

Miss Cambric's frozen expression did not change.

'Oh, but they have already spoken to me. They had the courtesy to make an appointment and I told them what I'm telling you. I have not the faintest idea in the world where Mr Kopeck is and nor have any of my staff.

A friend of mine has been seriously molested by hired thugs acting presumably on your instructions. I have asked the authorities to ensure that this kind of uncivilized behaviour is not repeated and they have promised me protection against it. Really Mr–' she picked up the card – 'Mr Moryak, I find this conversation a pure waste of time.'

'I regret. Your friend may have had an unpleasant experience but it would be simple to complain to the police should he wish to, yes? I personally know nothing of it.'

'Then you may go.' She stood up to emphasize the dismissal.

Moryak did not move. It was a deliberate gesture intended to offend. In his experience a woman in a bad temper was at a disadvantage.

'I have not finished with the matter yet, madam. Ring that bell if you wish. Your red-headed lackey – a hired actor, I believe – can assist my men in what they have to do. They already have my instructions.'

Lottie turned on him, bright patches of colour in her cheeks.

'Mr Moryak, you are not in your own country. I have friends who can make your stay here impossible. If you persist, I really will create such a fuss that you'll find yourself deported.'

'I think not. Control yourself and listen to me. I have an informant who says that a body is concealed in the little stone building which stands in your grounds. It could be that of the man we are looking for. I have to satisfy myself on this point, and you will not prevent me. If you attempt to do so I shall lay my information before your own police and they will naturally investigate it – indeed, I shall wait until they arrive. You have a choice but the alternative could be most unhappy for your reputation.'

He had expected the attack to break her defences. The colour left her cheeks and her circumflex eyebrows rose but she held her ground. A long pause showed that she was collecting her thoughts.

'The last people to go into the Tomb,' she said, 'were professional bullies who were almost certainly in your employ. I am becoming used to hooliganism and even violence wherever your hirelings appear. What they did there I have no idea.'

'I ask to see this Tomb. If you have nothing to hide and a crime has in fact been committed then you will welcome an investigation. You are a good citizen, yes?'

Miss Cambric did not reply. An embroidered bell-pull hung beside the fireplace and she tugged on it, producing a distant jangle in the depths of the house. When Rupert appeared she was sitting at an inlaid rosewood escritoire with her back to the visitor. She spoke without looking up.

'Burbage, this man and his bodyguards wish to see inside the Tomb. Will you open it and go in with them, please. After that they will be leaving.'

She did not move when they had gone but sat staring in front of her, tapping her fingers on the unopened leather blotter on the desk. A flurry of pigeons announced that the courtyard had been crossed and the ticking of the clock became insistent. Presently she unlocked a drawer, pulling it out and placing it on the velvet surface. Behind lay a ridiculous little secret compartment, a box on the end of a thin wooden lath, containing a single envelope. She returned the drawer to its socket and for some time the missive lay untouched. Finally she opened the unsealed cover and read the contents, a letter in incisive characters, boldy inscribed.

'To those of my heirs whom it may concern...'

A knock at the door made her turn sharply and Rupert appeared. He was considerably shaken but still playing his part.

'Mr Moryak is back, madam. He wishes to speak to you.'

The man pushed past him and looked round the room, as if to make sure that Lottie was still alone. He was impassive but his colour had vanished and a blue vein beat visibly in his temple. He hesitated for a fraction of a second as if uncertain where to place himself and turned to Rupert.

'Close the door. Stay where you are.'

'Well?' said Miss Cambric. 'You must tell me all about it. Have you found Mr Kopeck?'

Moryak sat down, coiling himself into the chair as if he were a steel spring which if released might propel him through the ceiling. His anger charged the room with the apprehension which precedes a thunderclap.

'My informant was right,' he said at last. 'There is a body in the Tomb.' The restraint in his voice made it icily impersonal.

Lottie sighed. 'I was rather afraid of that.'

'You knew of this fact?'

'I have suspected that such a discovery might be made sooner or later. After all, what better place could there be for a body than a tomb?'

'My business is to secure the arrest of a criminal. This – this discovery, as you call it, is nothing to do with me. Nothing at all. It is, one assumes, a matter for your own police.'

'Perhaps,' said Miss Cambric. 'Perhaps. Burbage, you are the more trustworthy witness, so you had better tell me what has occurred. Foreigners when they come up against the unexpected are apt to lose their command of English.'

Rupert cleared his throat. He was determined to stay in character and he spoke slowly as if he were giving evidence in court.

'Very good, madam. I went with this gentleman and his two chauffeurs to the Tomb as you instructed me. I took the key, but the lock no longer works properly – in fact, it's been smashed. Under the flagstones inside there is a sort of bricked vault, the actual place for a coffin, I suppose. At first, there didn't seem to be anything to see – the bottom is covered with loose pebbles or granite chips. Then they started rummaging around in them and I'm afraid that there is a body.'

'But not Mr Kopeck?'

'Oh, no, madam. Not that I've ever seen the gentleman. This is a skeleton – a mummy perhaps. It seems to have been there a very long time.'

The pause became an uneasy silence.

'What would you wish me to do, madam?'

'Nothing at the moment. Mr Moryak, as you say, this is none of your business, but since your intrusion has produced this discovery, I think you should know the true story in case your twisted mind imagines a different explanation.'

He was still angry but a new expression crossed his face, a mixture of curiosity and admiration.

'You are remarkably calm. Perhaps you knew of this – this circumstance – long ago?'

Miss Cambric turned upon him, her eyebrows conveying unmistakably that he was an interfering boor who just – but only just – merited an explanation.

'I have known something about it for many

years, ever since I inherited the Turrets, in fact. Sir Edwin left a letter for me and I have been re-reading it.' She picked up the folio on the desk. 'It concerns a wretched man, a very second-rate poet called Cecil Brinsley, whom my uncle befriended and installed in the cottage where Mr Perdreau now lives. He was ill repaid for his kindness. There were many scandals about the man, one in particular concerning a servant girl who disappeared. Fortunately Brinsley died before the trouble really came to a head and my uncle, I believe, compensated the girl's parents very handsomely. He did however leave this letter which he wrote in 1900. I shall read you a section of it.

'There is no doubt in my mind that this fellow Brinsley has concealed the body of Lucy Kent, a maidservant in my employ, somewhere in my grounds. Whether he killed her or if she made away with herself I cannot guess, but I am confident that she died during the summer of 1895 in the cottage which I mistakenly bestowed upon him. Should the body at any time be discovered after my own death then it should be given Christian burial in her full name which is Lucy Anne Kent, daughter of Jonathan and Mary Anne Kent of Inglewood, born 1878. I do not consider, however, that a further search would serve any good purpose since both parents are respectable and I have done what I can financially to ease

their distress. They have seven other children.

'Well, Mr Moryak, I hope you are satisfied.'

It was some time before he reacted. When he spoke his tone was conventional, giving the platitudes no wrapping of sincerity, as if he were using the stream of abuse as a safety valve.

'Shocking imperialist decadence. Our aristocrats at their worst were not so depraved – so cynical. This is tyranny, capitalist wickedness ... murder ... it should be exposed.'

'I'm afraid,' said Miss Cambric, 'that it will have to be.' She replaced the letter in its envelope and returned it to the drawer. 'Such a pity. Newspapers – sensational stories – more sale for the Brinsley poems – many more tourists and probably the wrong type, coming to the Turrets for a year at least. Mr Moryak, if you could really use your brain you would know that it would have been much kinder to have left that poor girl in peace. Rupert, will you show him out?'

13

The Proper Charley

Mrs Hetty Sims, a part-time parlourmaid at the Turrets, had taken off her apron, wrapped her head in a scarf and scuttled up the back drive to a call box just as soon as she was able to escape without being noticed. There was a policeman outside the Tomb, Sergeant Easterbrook with his Inspector were still in the house and an official van waited in the courtyard to collect a burden for the mortuary.

Her voice came clearly over the line to Nascott in his Fleet Street office, sly as a whisper, cautious as a hunting cat.

'It's an old scandal – seventy years old, they say – but I thought you ought to know. Any use? ... Harry, are you still with me? I say, is it any use to you?'

'Maybe. Was that all they found?'

'My God, isn't it enough? What more do you want? Harry, what's eating you? You talk as if you've been asleep all afternoon.'

'Let me get this straight. This chap Moryak turned up himself, did he? They searched the place and that was all they

166

found – just a skeleton?'

'I chatted up one of the policemen. That's all there was to it. He's a local and he says it's an old story. The thing you ought to be worrying about is who tipped them off?'

'I know that one.'

'Then it *was* you. I thought you'd been sacked by that lot. You don't sound pleased.'

'Just a bet with myself which I lost. I don't like clients dropping off the hook before I've finished with them. There's another bloody snake in the grass somewhere, so keep your eyes open.'

'Harry, what *did* you expect them to find?'

'Forget it.'

Nascott replaced the receiver. He sat still for some minutes, swearing under his breath like a surly dog, anxiety and bewilderment chasing each other across his face. He had made a miscalculation and the consequences might be serious. He had failed in his attempt to regain a useful account and placed a second in jeopardy. It followed that something must be done, and speedily, to strengthen his own position before the news from the Turrets reached Denmark Holdings. It was half-past seven in the evening, which meant that the story would make the morning papers if they thought it worth using. He had the night before him to arm himself against disaster.

Presently he stood up, brushed ash from

his waistcoat and began a systematic search through the nearest of his filing cabinets.

The information was elusive and he began to swear again. Finally he closed his eyes, forced his memory back into a subconscious pigeon hole and produced what he was looking for. He had not been a policeman for twenty years without learning a trick or two.

In Fleet Street he took a taxi to Deptford.

Green Road is probably the most inappropriately named thoroughfare in all London. Nascott paid the cab off by the bridge where Deptford creek moves sluggishly into Greenwich Reach and turned by way of Stowage into Wraggs Fields, a grim area of blackened brick relieved occasionally by tenements, eating houses, small workshops, grocers and newsagents, a slum village sandwiched between warehouses with an entity of its own supporting three prosperous bars. The China Clipper and The Six Bells, garish with honky-tonk pianos and piped recordings, failed to produce what he sought but in the Marlowe Arms the décor and even the air seemed unchanged for a century. It was a long tunnel with a bar on one side lined with varnished wood, so narrow that it was difficult to pass, opening out into a low room under a central skylight. A horsehair bench ran round three sides and the mahogany tables were fixed to the floor. In the farthest corner a man was sitting alone, a pair of steel-rimmed glasses set so deeply into the ridge of his broken nose that they seemed to grow there. At twenty he might well have been handsome despite the injury but at seventy he presented a wreck, a huge head above a chest which had kept its size by virtue of a massive rib-cage.

As Nascott approached him he looked up from the book which from its India paper and dark binding might have been, but was not, a Bible. The voice which had once been deep was now rheumy and abrasive.

'I hope I'm seeing ghosts,' he said. 'I thought you was dead.'

'A drop of gin, Mr Marcus. You still drink gin?'

'Sergeant Bloody Doublecross Nascott. Make it a large one. I'll need it if you're staying long. You don't look too good to me, but then you never did.'

He raised his head to scan the visitor from head to foot, revealing a neck like a tortoise above a collar which no longer fitted.

'Yes, you're a worried man, Sergeant. I read you same as I read this book. It does my eyes a power of good.'

Nascott produced two large measures of spirit and sat weightily before the old man. He was in no mood for banter. The conversation was best kept to business.

'Charley, I'll be honest with you for once. I need a bit of info, and it's for cash if you've

169

got the right goods.' He opened a notecase and placed three folded pound notes on the table under his own glass. 'Now don't get me wrong. You know I'm working for myself now – so no one's going to get into trouble, and that's straight up.'

The old man emptied his tumbler and planted it significantly against the newcomer's offering.

'Get up and get me the other half. My memory doesn't work so well when I've a thirst on me.'

Nascott returned to the table, but kept the drinks firmly gripped in front of him.

'It's no trouble to anyone,' he repeated, 'if you know the answer you're doing yourself a favour and that's all there is to it. I want the name – nothing more, I give you my oath – of a small-time breaking-and-entry man, working country houses, maybe someone who comes from these parts. Fiftyish, fat, brown hair going bald and with a scar – a deep one – on his left cheek. Do I ring any bells?'

'Not a tinkle. If he lived here he wouldn't graft here and he couldn't fence here. Are you sure you've got the right racket? I might put a name to that scar if you pressed me but the party in mind doesn't work that sort of lark and never has. What's it worth to you?'

It was some time before Nascott replied. The notes had vanished and he glowered across the table, his expression changing to speculation followed by resignation. Finally he opened his wallet again and pulled out a small transparent envelope containing a stamp, which he held between fingers and thumb before his opponent's face.

'Maldive Islands, 1906, overprinted in Ceylon. Not worth a packet but hard to come by.'

The cupidity of the collector was aroused and a freckled hand lifted. Nascott withdrew the bait.

'Let me get my lens on it.'

'When you've coughed, Charley boy. Not a moment before.'

'You're a hard man, Sergeant. I've never known an offer from you that wasn't a *gezumph*. I wouldn't put it past you to print it yourself.' A wheedling tone crept in. 'Let me see that surcharge.'

'The name, Charley. The name.'

Surprisingly the old man removed his spectacles to polish them with a scrap of wash-leather from a metal case, a process which made his eyes water. The task completed, he took stock of the customers at the nearest table, cocking an ear towards their conversation. He leaned forward and spoke in a whisper.

'You could be meaning Barney Buller. He was in a crash twenty years back and went through the windscreen. A tin plate in his skull, too, so I've heard. Was that mentioned?'

'Could be. What was his line?'

'Fast cars – get-away cars – used to be. That was before his crash. He drove for one or two of the boys but the smash-up fixed him for that. He did a couple of years for it, which was bad luck, because the stuff was still on the back seat and the rest of the mob got clear. A jeweller's in the City, I seem to recall.'

'And now?'

The broad shoulders jerked. 'He hangs around. Flogs cars that ought to be scrapped. Fixes two write-offs together and makes one that looks O.K. You might find him in the Seven Stars in Slype Street.'

'There's a racing chap who uses that one, or his mechanics do. Name of Mister Hilary Wykes. Is he with that crowd?'

'Not to say *with*. He hangs around. The Wykes lot are on the level, which is more than Barney Buller ever was. He hangs around in the Seven Stars and so do they. If some of 'em do a bit of business in spare parts with him on the side I shouldn't wonder, but it wouldn't be anything much.'

'Is that the lot?'

'There could be a little something to come, but not before I see that Colonial. I'm treating you fair, Sergeant. You do right by me.'

The little envelope changed hands and the old man held the contents suspiciously to the light of the white-globed lamp which hung from the centre of the room, appraising the watermark through a jeweller's lens which, having raised his spectacles miraculously to his forehead, he had screwed into his right eye.

'Looks like a right 'un. You don't inspire faith, but...'

'Barney Buller, remember?'

'Ah, as to that, it could be a matter of guessing, putting two and two together. He's not been too strong in the head since his smash but that's no great change. I did see him a time or two last year with Lew Goodman, who had a nasty fire in his fur warehouse, and once with Mrs Arkwright – the old lady, not the daughter-in-law – just before they were burnt out. You've got a very foul mind, Sergeant, like a cesspool only not so sanitary. You might make something out of it.'

Nascott parted from his old acquaintance on terms of near-cordial abuse. He had solved a problem and felt that the situation was well in hand. He left the Marlowe Arms at a jaunty pace, making his way by a series of cuts into the better lighting of the main street which bisects the Borough of Deptford in a long arc.

He was pleased with himself and intent on a personal reward in the form of a drink in less sordid surroundings. It was after ten, too late to reach the West End even if he could find transport.

The man who was following had no difficulty in keeping him within sight, for he paused often, trying to locate a suitable hostelry. The shadower had been given precise instructions, which promised to be tricky, but Nascott was making the whole thing simple.

Ahead lay the neon lit portico of Nick's Gala Casino, once East's Electric Cinema Palace, a pool of brilliance which emphasized the drabness of the pavements on either side. A shop front jutting irregularly into the street provided cover and the man, who had drawn almost level with Nascott, stepped aside, leaning drunkenly in the shade.

He carried a gun with a long silencer under a folded newspaper and he fired at the precise moment when two quarrelling revellers were ejected from the casino. It could not have been easier.

14

Press Day

There are always some members of Parliament who, for a regular retainer, which is sometimes surprisingly low, are prepared to advise big businesses on matters of government and sometimes to ask questions on their behalf. They are not popular with their colleagues, who regard them with the same distaste which doctors feel towards those of their profession who specialize in the imagined ailments of wealthy women. Public Relations men on the other hand are happy to know that they are available, for a question in the House can be a useful way of drawing indirect attention to an important client or an advertising campaign.

Mr Leslie Entwhistle, the member for Cobblestone East, dabbled lightly in this practice, especially on occasions when the Government could be embarrassed by a suggestion of bias against fellow travellers; and it is possible that, had he known the facts, he would have acted on them without the yearly emolument which Denmark Holdings paid for his wise counsel.

He confirmed his devotion to this extra-mural employment by telephone on the morning following the shooting of the Director of Intercity Inquiries.

'It's for this afternoon, my friend, and as innocent as a babe unborn. Aye, to the Home Secretary. It's what we call an oral, so he'll be there to face it. But the wee supplementary to follow has the sting you're seeking. He knows what it's all about and he's a cautious man, but he'll not be able to dodge it.'

'Have you talked to the Agence Varga?'

175

'I have that. They're not a reliable body of men but they know well enough where their interests lie. They made the initial approach so I felt it my duty to tell them all I knew. I wouldn't put great faith in the gentry.'

He was understating the case. The Agence Varga is the least reputable of international news vendors, specializing in scandal and rumour, and having, it has been said, access to every disreputable back-door on the political scene. The official Soviet agency, Tass, like Reuter of the free world, does not acknowledge its existence, and the Press, by contract, exclude any mention of the source; but many inspired whispers and infected straws in the political wind drift from continent to continent on its tainted breath.

Wykes purred. If he had to touch pitch he preferred a long pair of tongs and they had not been easy to come by of late.

'Good. Put up a stylish show, won't you? Best interests of both countries – suspicious incompetence by our people – sinister protection of private interests – all that. I want headlines.'

'You'll get them. No bother at all.'

Having dealt with one news story, Hilary Wykes turned his attention to another. The popular papers, and *The Globe* in particular, had made a front-page display of the story of Harry Nascott, for it was happily in line with the editorial policy of the moment, a righteous crusade against the underworld and its protection rackets.

'DEPTFORD SHOOTING,' it announced:

Private Eye Attacked. An inquiry agent whose office is in London's Fleet Street was shot last night by an unknown gunman outside Nick's Gala Casino, in Thameside Deptford. Harry Nascott, 45, an ex-police officer now running a private inquiry bureau was found lying on the pavement outside the club at 10.30 p.m. and is now in the Deptford Memorial hospital suffering from gunshot wounds. An official said early this morning: 'He is still unconscious and must be considered as dangerously ill. He has made no statement.'

This is the third case of shooting to occur in the open street within the past four weeks. Nick's Gala Casino is owned and operated by the Cellini Brothers and it was here that Billy 'Flick-knife' Franks, now serving a two-year sentence for protection racketeering, was arrested. Mr Emile Klementz, manager of the club, stated that Nascott was not a member and had not visited the premises during the evening. 'We have a very exclusive clientele,' he said. 'Election is controlled by an independent committee.'

Mrs Helen Richards, a member of Mr Nascott's staff, said that the work of the bureau was confidential and that there was no indication as to the inquiry her director was making at the time of the attack. 'He was certainly working, since he lives in Kilburn and we know of no social contacts in that neighbourhood.' (See page 10, The War Continues'.)

Wykes consumed every variant of the story but it remained basically the same: a cause for serious anxiety. He spent some time talking to the mechanics in charge of his workshop and to the girl in the flat above it, but found no enlightenment. Nascott had not contacted them and no one could be found who had seen him in the area. Nick's Gala Casino was in their opinion a clip joint for mugs and if anyone got clobbered through paying a nosy visit it was their own bloody silly fault and only to be expected.

By a happy chance the master of Denmark Holdings was in New York and this, for the moment at least, relieved the necessity of drawing attention to the story. Hilary Wykes, a superstitious man, touched his model Bentley for luck and abandoned his office for Lime Court, Fleet Street.

His appearance added to the confusion which was bringing the work of Intercity Inquiries to a standstill and it was some minutes before he had the undivided attention of a handsome chestnut-haired woman, who appeared to be the only member of the staff with the ability to understand more than half a sentence.

She eyed him with speculative approval, nodding towards a minute cubby hole containing a stool, a chair, a typing table and tea-making equipment, which made space uncomfortably limited.

'We'll be cosier in here. Mr Harry's spoke of you. You're the Denmark Holdings Account? Can I help you?'

Wykes balanced himself elegantly on the edge of the desk.

'You know about it?'

'I should do. I work on it.'

'Good. Then you can tell me what Nascott was doing in Deptford last night.'

She shook her head. 'Nobody here knows that one. Mr Harry keeps very good files on everyone but himself. We've had journalists asking the same thing all morning and there's a couple of C.I.D. men in his private office looking through his papers. But they won't find anything and that's for certain. When it came to what he did himself he was like an oyster. Deptford's a long way from the Turrets. It may have been quite a different inquiry – divorce perhaps. We do a lot of that.'

Wykes was too experienced to show a reaction. He considered the woman in front of him and was inclined to like what he saw. Beneath the amiable matronly veneer there was a sophistication and a hardness which appealed to him.

'Tell me about yourself,' he said. 'Where

do you fit into the picture?'

She opened the door by a fraction to make sure that they were unobserved, closed it again, and sat down on the typing stool, indicating that he would be more comfortable in the other chair.

'My name is Sims – Mrs Hetty Sims. I've worked for Harry for five years – ever since I married and left the Force. Now I'm a widow I'm still carrying on with the job. I'm supposed to be a part-time servant at the Turrets. I dress up in Victorian aprons and caps, do the beds and room service and wait at table. Miss Cambric likes older women, because the younger ones are inclined to giggle and wear the wrong hair-dos.'

'All that long-winded stuff he sends me in fact comes from you? You're his only contact there?'

The idea amused her, bringing a confiding feline smile. 'Harry always writes as if he was giving evidence in court. Me, I don't put anything on paper. If it's urgent, I telephone. Today is a bit different. I nipped up when I read the news to find out what was happening. As for being the only contact, that's not true. We're giving the Turrets absolutely top priority and there's others besides me. You get value for money, never you worry.'

He sat for some time as if considering the information and finding it important.

'You're interested in delicious money – a

little folding paper – something on the side, perhaps?'

'Perhaps.'

Her smile was still there, revealing nothing but cautious encouragement.

'If he lives, your Mr Nascott will be away some time. I was thinking of a private arrangement between you and me. Wildly confidential. Do you have any ties?'

'Can't afford them in my job.'

'Good.' Again he hesitated, assessing her character with a frankness she clearly found pleasurable.

'For money, then. Quite a nice little present that no one need ever know about. My idea might not be particularly comfortable and it could take a week or two. Am I being interesting?'

'The way things are in this office I could listen to you all night.'

Very slowly Wykes allowed his mouth to widen into a smile which had a curious resemblance to the lips of the woman on the opposite side of the desk. They understood each other very well.

'My dear girl,' he said. 'My very dear Mrs Sims. I think you and I could do business together. I'd like to take you out for a drink but perhaps it wouldn't be wise. You see, I've got something in mind which requires a strictly commercial outlook. You could be just what I'm looking for.'

It took them half an hour to settle the transaction.

Mr Campion, too, had spent part of the morning reading the Press. The story of the pathetic occupant of the Tomb had not made the headlines which had greeted the shooting of Nascott but the two heavier dailies thought it worth a mention and *The Times* had achieved an erudite little scoop, connecting the discovery with the romanticized scandals surrounding the memory of the poet Brinsley, a piece of sound professional reporting in which the influence of Felix Perdreau was apparent.

A copy of the latest issue of *The Alembic*, the learned monthly journal which Vassily Kopeck had taken along with him even in the rush of his escape from Dovecote, lay on Campion's desk. He had read it from cover to cover.

Like many of its kind, it consisted of a series of articles on subjects incomprehensible to the layman, in this case the intricacies of biochemistry. The editorial matter formed the central section, the outer folios being given over to advertisements for technical equipment, recent commercial chemical products, and notices of staff vacancies designed to increase the brain drain, if not from Britain to America, at least from firm to firm.

Amongst the minor miscellany was an

item which had caught his eye. It occupied only three lines.

Farthing Enterprises, Ltd
Suitable contact is sought to handle
completed product. C.O.D. Box 764

Mr Campion considered the entry for some time, finally resorting to his encyclopedia. 'A Kopeck,' it said. 'Originally a silver coin, but copper since 1701. It represents one hundredth part of a rouble and is the smallest unit of Russian currency.'

A kopeck – a farthing. The possibility of a link was too tantalizing to be ignored.

The publishers of *The Alembic* own a large group of such technical journals and the editors are only occasional visitors to their office. The advertisement manager is the essential mainspring of the paper, a hard working permanent member of the staff. Mr Campion located him by telephone with comparative ease. He recalled the space booking and regretted that the privacy of a box number had to be respected under house rules. No; he, personally, knew nothing of Farthing Enterprises, Ltd. They were a new name in his experience, which was a matter of fifteen years. He was sorry, old boy, to be unhelpful but a letter would of course be forwarded immediately it arrived. He'd see to it himself.

The Register of Companies, in its negative way, made a more enlightening contribution, for an exhaustive search showed that the firm of Farthing Enterprises, Ltd. did not exist.

Over a solitary lunch at his club Mr Campion contemplated his next move. Finally he retired to the writing-room and addressed an envelope in block capitals to Box 764.

'A suitable contact,' he wrote, 'will be at Liverpool Street railway station main line bookstall at 6 p.m. on Friday, October 27th, carrying a copy of *The Alembic* under his left arm. Immediate cash will be available for satisfactory delivery of completed product.'

By the late afternoon it was apparent to Hilary Wykes and to all readers of evening newspapers that Mr Entwhistle had fulfilled his promise. His parliamentary question had been simple enough on the surface but, once asked and answered, it opened the floodgates on a story which the Press had been keeping on ice for some time. No longer held in check by polite Whitehall requests and D notices, they launched out into a sensation which, with any luck, would keep the public happy for weeks.

'Can the Minister' (asked Mr Entwhistle with the innocent air of an habitually delinquent child) 'state the procedure in the case of an alien immigrant who has had his passport withdrawn and remains in hiding in this country?'

The Home Secretary, true to his reputation, had given nothing away. 'Every effort,' he said, 'is made to prevent illegal immigration and if a specific instance is brought to my notice inquiries can, of course, be made.'

Now came the sting. 'Has the Home Secretary been informed of the case of Vassily Kopeck, an ex-attaché of the Soviet Embassy, who has been apparently residing in this country for the past three months without a passport?'

'The case,' said the Minister, 'has been brought to my attention. I can assure the Hon. Member that appropriate steps are being taken to discover Mr Kopeck's whereabouts.'

Entwhistle persisted.

'Has there been any approach made by this man to ask for asylum?'

Frankness had never been a characteristic of the Home Secretary. 'As the individual in question,' he said, 'has not yet been traced, the question does not arise.'

The exchange had been brief but it was enough.

'Vanished Diplomat,' said the headlines, adding, 'Nationwide search for missing Soviet attaché.'

A blurred photograph of Kopeck taken at a dinner of the 1897 Society appeared in every paper and on every television screen, coupled with such scraps of biographical information as could be officially garnered or privately invented.

By the time the first of the morning papers was put to bed in Fleet Street the Agence Varga had supplied as much detail as any hungry news editor could wish and a great deal more than most of them thought wise to use from so dubious a source. Were there criminal charges to be brought against the fugitive once he was caught? No information, said Tass. No comment, said the Embassy's Press officer.

Again the Agence Varga was willing to fill the gap. Vassily Kopeck (they understood from usually well-informed sources) was wanted for embezzlement of funds and there was a second charge connected with sexual abberations among students and intellectuals which was so serious as to suggest that he was dangerously insane. He was known to be a friend of Miss Charlotte Cambric of Inglewood Turrets, England's leading private museum of Victorian treasures, a popular hostess with the diplomatic set, and it was thought that he had disappeared in the course of a weekend party held under her roof. As a story, it was agreed in the taverns of Fleet Street, it had practically everything a journalist could desire – scandal in high life, crime, international intrigue and sex.

Unanimously, they did justice to the banquet.

15

The Client

Lunch at the Turrets, except during weekends, was an informal meal served in a small room next to Miss Cambric's office, connected with the kitchens by a lift-shaft from which the food appeared announced by a speaking-tube whistle. Lottie in tweeds and blue-tinted glasses presided and her guests made no pretence of belonging to another century. It was not an occasion which called for her theatrical gifts as a hostess.

L.C. Corkran, precise but a trifle peevish, sat on her left, whilst Mr Campion occupied the third chair.

'This place is in a state of siege,' she announced. 'The Upper Sixth from St Brazils' – fifteen of the ugliest girls I've ever set eyes on – had the greatest difficulty in getting through the police barrier this morning, and the tradesmen are complaining that their vans are searched every time they arrive with a couple of mutton chops.

'My telephone, which is supposed to be a dark secret and is ex-directory in any case, hasn't stopped ringing for two days and four American visitors in a Rolls-Royce – which you'd think was above suspicion – turned out to be journalists. How long will it go on?'

Corkran brought an eyebrow down in a frown.

'My dear girl, that's what I've come all this way to discover. Do you realize that you and Albert have dragged a respectable civil servant out of retirement simply because the Department feels I'm the only person capable of bringing you to your senses? You've made yourself the centre of exactly the sort of diplomatic and Press storm which I spent my best years trying to prevent and you sit there eating potted shrimps as if you were discussing the impact of a curate's flirtation with a girl guide.'

Lottie was not altogether contrite. She had recovered a great deal of her *panache* and in her modern clothes she looked precisely what she was: an efficient business woman in charge of a concern which was encountering difficulties. Support, if it was obtainable, would be useful, but she was not prepared to make large concessions to obtain it.

'You haven't answered my question, Elsie. I said, how long?'

'Until Kopeck is found. If you feel some responsibility – some urge to ensure his safety – then it would be best if we reached him before his own nationals get their hands on him. Do you know where he is? The last time you were officially asked that question you offered us some terminological inexactitudes.'

'Only because the whole thing was outrageous. If you'd found him he'd have been handed over like an ox to a butcher. Your Mr Whatever-his-name-was practically admitted as much.'

'The situation has changed since then.' Corkran was speaking slowly, almost as if making a prepared statement. 'Kopeck apparently has something to say – probably something rather shocking – which he wants the world to hear and he hopes to make it quite clear to his own countrymen and to us that he is not acting under pressure from any political side. He may have his curious moral point of view but I'm bound to admit he's behaving in an extremely odd and embarrassing way. He's been living in a dangerous limbo now for a considerable time – a matter of months. In the end he will have to accept either asylum or death. He must know that.

'At this point when every agent, every journalist and practically every morbid sensation hunter in Britain is looking for him he has a potential audience which will never be greater. He must know that, too, if he is still alive. Yet we have no word from him. *Have you?*'

He shot the question at her with unexpected sharpness, but she remained unruffled.

'Certainly not. If I had I might have considered telling you, even if only to save him from his atrocious associates. I don't enjoy the kind of publicity I'm receiving at the moment and I may as well confess that it's having a very bad effect on my better bookings. I really do not have the faintest idea in the world where he is. That's the truth, Elsie, my dear man. You look so stern that I wish I could fib to make you happy.'

Mr Campion intervened.

'Forgive me,' he said, 'but someone knew he was at Dovecote – someone who rang him up in the nick of time to warn him of danger. It certainly wasn't friend Perdreau and I don't believe it was you. Does an idea occur to you?'

For the first time Lottie was disconcerted. She took a sip of Chablis and looked from one guest to the other over her tinted lenses.

'I'm afraid that was Perdita,' she confessed. 'You can't blame the child, Albert. She arrived at the idea of his hiding place by the same process of deduction which you used. The only difference, of course, was that she knew of Felix's little *affaire* down on the coast. She's clever and takes after Edwin when it comes to getting her own way. I

190

spoke to her rather sharply about it, because I thought she might be endangering herself, but she was quite impenitent.'

The two men spoke together.

'You don't think...?'

'She doesn't know...?'

Lottie shook her head.

'She doesn't, thank God. That is the one thing of which I really am completely certain. She's an outwardly demure minx and there are times when she's capable of lying magnificently, but this wasn't one of them. It was about the last conversation we had.'

A whistle followed by a rumble and thump announced that the second course of the meal had arrived by the service lift. Lottie produced three *tournedos* from the mobile cupboard before she settled to enjoy the effect of the inference she had made.

'The *last* conversation?' said Corkran. 'Where is this niece of yours now?'

'I dismissed her, of course. My dear man, having behaved as she did, she became a liability – to herself as well as to the Turrets. As soon as the whole story became public property the last thing I wanted about the place was a young girl who might want to put herself in a position where she felt she ought to protect me. Good gracious, no. She's left my employment and she certainly won't be back until this melodramatic business is all over. I'm afraid these beans are frozen but at least the potatoes are fresh. They're the new kind, which take up far too much space in the garden, but keep their flavour. Albert, you look worried.'

'I am,' he admitted. 'I hope you packed her off to some nice safe place – a convent with high walls and a Mother Superior who happens to be a Judo Black Belt, for example?'

Miss Cambric gestured towards a decanter. 'Elsie, would you taste it? Les Enfants Douces – long after Edwin's time, but it was his favourite wine. No, Albert, certainly not a convent – most unsuitable for a girl of her emancipated spirit. In fact we both accepted that it would be far better if I had no communication with her. She had enough money for the moment and a great deal of common sense. We both agreed that she should go to earth in whatever way she chose and speak to no one at all. So I have no forwarding address and she may be in Scarborough, or Leamington Spa or as far away as the Isle of Wight, for all I know. You need not worry about her. Wigs are so cheap these days – they change one's whole personality – that I'm quite sure she won't be traced.'

She turned to Corkran. 'Much safer, really, don't you think? After all, your own surveillance here is not absolutely successful, is it? Last week a very nice young man who's been masquerading as a gardener was knocked over the head when he was wandering about the place late at night. He wasn't seriously hurt but he didn't recover his senses until dawn. I suppose you knew that?'

Corkran was embarrassed. 'I did, in fact. Lottie, you're treating this whole business far too lightly. The people we are trying to deal with have very few morals as we understand the word. That boy was attacked because he was trying to protect you, though what good the assault did I fail to see. Last week a man was shot in the street – a silly fellow called Nascott who made himself a nuisance here once, I understand – a minor pawn in the game. I suspect he was trying to serve two masters and one of them objected. The opposition really is quite ruthless.'

He paused to make sure that the words were making the desired impression.

'I was going to say that I do not wish to frighten you, but that is the precise reverse of my intention. Our colleagues beyond the veil, which is made of steel rather than iron, may feel that Kopeck dead is worth more than Kopeck alive. In cases like this they sometimes allow the idea to be known. A reward in the form of negotiable currency could attract various unsavoury inter-national characters and some of them are highly skilled. The point I'm trying to make is that you are the focus of all this interest –

the most likely link between them and a fortune. This is no *brutum fulmen*, but a hard fact. Short of depositing you in the Bank of England I don't see what to do about you.'

Miss Cambric considered the suggestion, taking a sip of burgundy in the process.

'I cannot see,' she said, 'that I am in any personal danger at all. Surely nothing is to be gained by physical violence where I am concerned? My dear man, the very fact of your visit is a protection. If I had anything to tell, I am far more likely to say it to you than to some anonymous blackguard bribed by that satanic-looking reptile Moryak. I've made a statement to the Press – had to do that for the sake of peace and quiet – and that's as far as I'm going. The truth is that if I'm useless to you then I'm equally useless to them. Won't they see that?'

'Very probably. Moryak has a logical mind. Now that he's had a personal brush with you he will realize that you're unlikely to react to direct pressure. But pressure can be applied in more ways than one. If Kopeck is still alive – and the continued activity suggests that he is – then he will try smoking him out.'

'How?'

Corkran hesitated, putting his thoughts in order, dividing what should be omitted and what should be presented to his hostess. The mantle of a senior lecturer sat well on his shoulders.

'We know very little about Kopeck,' he said at last. 'His subject as a physicist is solar radiation, deep X-rays and so on, a field of which I'm profoundly ignorant. He was given diplomatic status to enable him to move around freely – to pick the brains of our people, in fact – and to act as what might be called an industrial spy under the banner of scientific liaison. Albert met him briefly and liked him. You met him several times and also found him attractive.

'The only additional information – and this is a matter of inference – is that he appears to have a conscience. If the pressure on you, Lottie, became intolerable, he might feel it right to surrender himself and to his own people rather than to us. I'm afraid you'll have to accept all the protection we can arrange for some time yet. You wouldn't consider closing the Turrets for a month or two? It would make...'

He was interrupted by a knock at the door. Mrs Hetty Sims in cap and apron, every inch a Victorian parlourmaid, came in bearing a wax sealed envelope on a salver.

'For you, ma'am.' She bobbed, her face as expressionless as a doll, and withdrew.

The hostess read the letter twice before handing it to Campion, who had recognized the decorative modern script from a distance.

'*Dear Miss Charlotte,*' it ran,

I am sorry to leave your employment but I wish to retire from domestic service and shall be away before this letter reaches you. Will you please regard any wages due to me as cash in lieu of notice? I have greatly enjoyed working for you but I feel I can be of no further use.
  Yours faithfully,
  R. Burbage

P.S. Hetty (Mrs Sims) is an informant working for Nascott. She telephones his office daily. She will not open this, though she would if it were not sealed. The Indian cleaner and washer-up called, I think, Attaboy, who is only casually employed, is also a suspicious character. He reads Chairman Mao and Trollope in his spare time. A fat man named Williams, who is the chap who knocked me over by the Tomb on my first day, hangs around Inglewood, generally in the Red Lion, is up to no good since he is a friend of Mrs Sims. The new under-gardener, Simon Willing, hopes you do not know he was banged over the head one night last week but I think you do. He is one of ours. So is Carpenter who has been replacing Oatsby your chauffeur while he's away sick.
  Please give my regards to Mr Campion. A very kind and clever gentleman I have always thought.

P.P.S. Before he left for outer space our friend made Perdita a present. It hangs on the wall of her bedroom. Perfectly genuine I think and nothing concealed in it. Mr C. might find it of interest.

'A wise child,' said Mr Campion. 'If a trifle impetuous. Lottie, do you think I could book a room at the Turrets for a week or two? In the meantime, of course, it would be interesting to see the gift.'

Their hostess was still absorbing the letter and its implications. Her eyes had widened and her arched eyebrows had risen to wrinkle her forehead.

'But I know what it is,' she said. 'I noticed it weeks ago. How silly of me not to connect it with him. Such an unlikely piece of decoration to hang between a Picasso plate and a pop montage, but then I let her furnish the room as she pleases because it's in what used to be servants' quarters.

'It's a rather splendid icon.'

16

Dangerous Corner

Out of the bataclan and hysteria which the Press whipped up so gratefully around Vassily Kopeck, only two facts emerged. The first was that no one had any clear idea of his mission as a diplomat or a scientist.

His fellow physicists in Britain had taken him on trust because he was clearly more knowledgeable on their subject than most visiting firemen but his personal contribution to research was a mystery. He had listened attentively, asking astute questions and even drawn attention to relevant work which was being done behind the Iron Curtain. The information he provided was not secret to the initiated but there had been times when he was undoubtedly a valuable catalyst.

The eminent inarticulate men with whom he had been in contact found it difficult to explain their work even to science correspondents and the majority of the brotherhood were loath to associate themselves or their laboratories with anything which suggested sensationalism.

The Press, moreover, were late in the field.

There had been other inquiries into Kopeck's associates before the news of his disappearance broke and the second inquisition produced unanimous, if uncoordinated, retirement into professional shells.

The other concrete fact was that he was popular. Off duty he had been amusing, a man who appreciated food and wine, a guest who was always prepared to sing for his supper.

He had made contacts resulting in affection, if not deep friendship, in Birmingham, Edinburgh, Bristol, Reading and Cambridge and no man spoke ill of him.

The Director of Amalgamated Electrical Research unbent to describe him in *The Globe* as 'one of the most charming and intelligent companions a man could wish for. He is a dedicated worker and to suspect him of trivial misdemeanours is nonsense. He is utterly uninterested in politics. My wife and I entertained him frequently and found him an admirable and witty guest. He liked to draw on tablecloths, which is an expensive habit, but the results were always worth keeping.'

On the strength of these reactions the Press decided that he was an industrial spy, possibly torn by opposing loyalties and that the key to the mystery lay in discovering where the second magnet was hidden. Both of the heavier English Sunday newspapers turned teams of experts on to the subject, a decision which resulted in almost identical front pages for their weekly review sections. Both editors were profoundly relieved when, in good time for the following issue, the ex-President of an emergent African state, who had been presumed dead at the hands of his colleagues, appeared in Moscow fully prepared to tell the world of his adventures.

In the meantime, Kopeck had been seen drinking in the bar of the George V in Paris, travelling by Aer Lingus to Dublin, studying a Coptic manuscript in the British Museum, flying a kite on Clapham Common and washing dishes in the kitchen of a private nursing home for alcoholics near Tunbridge Wells. In Edgbaston an elderly Cypriot waiter was detained for several hours before he could prove his identity and at Dover a door-to-door canvasser dealing in tracts announcing the end of the world was equally inconvenienced.

The Globe alone received twelve letters purporting to come from the missing man, supplying a variety of reasons for his behaviour, ranging from the romantic 'I am the son of Princess Anastasia and therefore the true heir to the Russian throne' to the practical 'I have placed an atom bomb in a London cloakroom and it will explode unless I receive a million pounds by next Tuesday.'

Despite the welter of newsprint no genuine

trace emerged. Kopeck had vanished as effectively as a cat who turns a corner in a London fog.

Inglewood Turrets, the only tangible point of interest in the mystery, came into the glare of deceptive limelight. It was, *The Globe* (among others) hinted, a centre of political intrigue, a place where the diplomatic set, under the cover of culture, disported themselves with film stars, wealthy divorcées and the disreputable froth of café society. Astute legal advisers in Fleet Street vetted every inch of copy to ensure that no actionable libel was uttered, but the inference was plain to every reader.

Lottie's bookings dwindled to the point of disaster and cancellations flooded in, for there is no company in the world more sensitive to the breath of scandal than the privileged group which travels with C.D. number plates.

On the Friday when the story was a week old, Mr Campion arrived at Liverpool Street station at a quarter to six in the evening. He had chosen the time carefully so that Messrs Farthing Enterprises, if they wished, could contact him with the minimum of publicity. The bookstall faces the main departure platform for Eastern England and the Continent, and at that hour it was at its busiest, an untidy concrete rectangle over which thousands of city ants scuttled towards their weekend escape routes to the country. Disembodied voices distorted through echo-chambers boomed instructions and no man or group, with one exception, paid attention to an ephemeral neighbour.

With his copy of *The Alembic* displayed beneath his arm the thin man examined racks of gramophone records, tables laden with re-maindered books and watched small mountains of papers and magazines melt, only to re-form with reinforcements. He buried his head from time to time in a paper so that an easy approach could be made from behind but he remained isolated and apparently unnoticed.

Half an hour passed. He began to wander afield and turned to browse among the paperbacks, where space was confined and the crowd was thickest, but he remained alone. Finally he escaped from the crush, holding *The Alembic* to his chest, as if it had been a label.

'This is for you, man.'

The soft Jamaican voice belonged to a very young porter. In his hand he held a slip of folded paper, torn from a timetable.

Mr Campion delayed the messenger.

'Who gave you this?'

'A ge'man, sah. Ah dunno him, but he said to give it you.'

'Tall or short? Young or old?'

'A young ge'man, sah. Gone to catch his train. Ah didn't see him too good. He jes' gimme this paper, point to your backside, gimme half a dollar and go ... O.K.?'

'O.K.' said Mr Campion.

The message was printed with a ball-point pen in block capitals.

'No go-betweens. Face to face or not at all.'

It was late on the following evening, a Saturday, before Mr Campion found it possible to return to the Turrets. The new Burbage, a role now stolidly played by Carpenter, a man from the Department who had originally appeared as a chauffeur, was waiting to intercept him at the porch when he arrived.

Miss Charlotte's wardrobe had not been entirely successful in fitting such powerful shoulders and their owner was uncomfortable. A green smudge across his stiff shirt front and a made-up tie which was well off centre made his appearance unconvincing.

Between the outer door and the main hall there was a porch furnished in gothic discomfort.

He put down the suitcase to delay the newcomer.

'A word in your ear before you go in. The guests are upstairs in the Music Room – only five of them. American schoolmarms, I think – with Miss Charlotte and Mr Perdreau.'

'Trouble?'

'You could call it that. I don't think they noticed anything, but the old lady doesn't miss much. In any case she's bound to find out because of the damage.'

'What happened?'

'Someone fired a shot through the window of the Small Drawing-Room just now. By the luck of the nine blind ones there was no one there, because they'd gone in to dinner right on the dot. It smashed a diamond pane, went right through the curtain and landed in one of the pictures. No real harm, but quite a mess because of the broken glass. I've cleared most of it up.'

'Did we catch the visitor?'

'Didn't get near him. The duty men on the gate heard the shot and so did Simon Willing, who was having a beer in the kitchen, but it's a dark night and they were too late. The chap must have fired from the shrubbery by the Tomb and at that distance he couldn't have been aiming at anyone in particular. Just trying to make trouble.'

'Very close to succeeding. What about the lay-by on the bypass? Is that covered?'

'Night and day, ever since the big fuss started. A walkie-talkie man in a car who's in touch with the main gate and another in the grounds. We ought to have dogs on a job like this, but the old lady won't hear of it on account of the guests.' He ran a finger round the inside of his collar and noticing the stain on his shirt rubbed at it ineffectively with a handkerchief. 'I couldn't do much myself because I'm supposed to be on duty waiting at table. We don't think he went that way. Nipped into one of the gardens of the houses over the ridge and dodged back into town most likely. Not that it matters much – that side of it, I mean–'

He broke off, embarrassed by his un-accustomed clothes and what he clearly regarded as a personal failure.

'If there was no alarm then the chap had a wasted evening,' suggested Mr Campion by way of comfort.

'I don't see it that way. We missed a trick. I look quite enough of a Charley in this rig without outside help.'

'Remember the tips. Your predecessor told me they were very good if you kept your wits about you.'

The new Burbage picked up the suitcase and replaced it as a thought occurred to him.

'Two shillings, for six large bags, so far. But there was a little something I thought I ought to pass on. Our chaps in the lay-by mentioned it, so it will drift up to you in the end. They take the numbers of every car that parks there and they're all checked for owners. Two of them were interesting, they say. Does that mean anything to you?'

205

'Almost too much,' said Mr Campion. 'I hope they're not following up their researches.'

Within the Turrets the suggestion that nothing had changed in eighty years, or was ever likely to, remained unshaken. In the upper hall, a dark panelled gallery which ran the length of both wings of the house the scent of a cigar lingered like the ghost of the original owner and from the Music Room a voice which had once been the glory of the operatic world drifted in limpid, dateless enchantment. Geraldine Farrar was singing *'Connais-tu le pays?'*

Mr Campion paused to listen before retreating towards the Small Drawing-Room. It was locked. He tapped twice without any response and had turned away before Lottie's voice halted him.

She had opened the door only a few inches and her tone was determinedly conversational.

'Such a lovely soprano. I heard her once in *Bohéme* at the Metropolitan and when I met her I expected to find a blonde – somehow her voice suggests that colouring – but she hadn't been wearing a wig. A beautiful woman. I couldn't resist adding her to Edwin's collection, though she was a year or two after his time. Come in, if you want to, Albert. There's nothing to see, or there won't be in two minutes' time.'

Mrs Faversham, known as Babette, the petite housekeeper who acted as ladies' maid over the weekends, was perched on a pair of steps by the window, making adjustments to fresh curtains. The damaged draperies lay folded on the floor and a picture with a jagged hole in the top left-hand corner leaned against a chair, facing the wall.

'It was one of Yeend King's sunsets and no great loss, in my opinion. I've put a Farquaharson sheep-in-snow scene in its place – a larger painting than poor Mr King's, to cover up the damage to the wall.' She nodded towards the Music Room. 'I shall give them all a good night drink in here just to prove that nothing has happened – that is, if I can get hold of Burbage. He's a nice boy, but not nearly so good as his predecessor.'

Mr Campion closed the door, relocked it and sat down.

'I'll deputize as second footman,' he said. 'Lottie, you ought to take Elsie's advice and shut up shop for a bit. Tonight's little episode could be literally a warning shot across the bows. If the room had been full of people – even if no one was hurt–'

She shook her head. 'Edwin never tolerated outside interference and I certainly don't intend to make changes now. If you ask me this is the work of that abominable man Denmark, making capital out of the other business. If you could find some way of scotching

207

him you'd really be helping. I'm right, aren't I?'

Her black eyes, bright as if they had been emphasized by a full theatrical make-up, flicked a challenge which he could not deny.

'You could well be. The difficulty is that his own fortifications appear to be rather stronger than ours, and the only key I have has been broken in the lock. It may take time to mend. You have a full house next weekend?'

Mrs Faversham had finished her curtain hanging; the picture and the ruined drapery had vanished with the step ladder.

Lottie surveyed the room with satisfaction.

'Perfect, I think. Edwin had dozens of sunsets and enough sheep in the snow to keep Bradford in wool for a year. No one could remark a difference. Yes, Albert, a full house next weekend. Twelve, or thereabouts. I cheated – just a little – by inviting Molly and Jack Croesus, who are as poor as church mice and have been ruined by their name. I asked her once why she didn't change it but she said her maiden name was Gold and that had been nearly as bad. They're sculptors and never pay any bills anyhow, but very good entertainers – always on my free list. I hope you'll be here?'

'I will,' he promised, 'wearing my bullet-proof vest from Mafeking and armed with a gatling gun.'

In Deptford Memorial Hospital, ex-sergeant Nascott lay half awake, breathing stertorously. A frightened man, he was concentrating on saving his own skin, reporting himself to be weaker than he was in truth and seeing no visitors. He had learned by telephone of the dismissal of Mrs Sims and the disappearance of an Indian employee at the Turrets who had not been on his payroll for long. Only Williams remained, a very dubious link, for he had been the subject of an unfriendly warning from two strangers who were plainly members of the Special Branch.

Through waking and dreaming, bouts of temperature and fits of shivering, pain and unconsciousness followed by terror, Nascott clung to one fact. If he managed to survive he had enough on Hilary Wykes to hold the account at least until the Turrets surrendered. After that, with any luck, there might be a sum in settlement. Not blackmail but a gentleman's agreement for silence and services rendered.

So far as was possible he had followed the accounts of the search for Kopeck but long hours and countless drinks in the company of pressmen had taught him a cynicism which increased as each batch of papers reached his bedside. The missing man was now hidden in a mysterious sanatorium near Davos according to *The Globe,* whilst others had glimpsed him on an all-night coach to Newcastle and sleeping amongst the tragic flotsam that finds shelter in the crypt of St Martin-in-the-Fields.

'Dead,' muttered Nascott in his dreams, and worried the night sister who had just come on duty. 'Dead ... dead ... dead. Long odds he's dead. But if he isn't...'

The woman straightened his pillows and lifted his hand to release the evening news-papers on which it rested. She folded it care-fully and placed it in a wastebin, whence it was removed the following morning by the cleaning maid. A minor story on a minor page remained unread. 'In Moscow,' it said, 'the poet Oleg Tchernawitz, who gave evidence in the recent literary-subversion trial, has committed suicide.'

The mumble from the bed was only just audible. 'If I could get there first ... worth a packet...'

The private ward on the top floor gave on to a corridor at the far end of which was a cubby hole used by the houseman as an office and a refuge. Mr Campion found the occupant, a plump, bearded young doctor too tired for superficial politeness, apparently immersed in all of the thousand problems which bedevil such appointments. He assessed the visitor with a calculating eye, for he had been warned to be helpful.

'A sick man,' he said, 'still in a state of shock, or pretending to be. He's scared stupid and it's not surprising. *Must* you see him?'

'It could be important.'

'You're not some sort of policeman?'

'Not even a journalist.'

'Good. He's said all he knows, or all he's prepared to say, which seems to be very little. When you've been as close as that to curtains, it's inclined to make you cautious. Personally, I'd tell the lot of them to take a running jump.' He yawned and pushed his glasses to his forehead. 'Any special reason why you should see him?'

'Several.' Mr Campion was diffident. 'Or I wouldn't have been allowed to reach these heights. Would it hurt if I talked to him?'

The young man shrugged his shoulders. He was nearing the end of his term of office but not above enjoying the authority which a patient in the news had brought. To emphasize his position he delayed his answer.

'I don't think so. He has plenty of lucid intervals when he reads the papers and calls his office. In the ordinary way we wouldn't allow this sort of thing – he's still under sedation – but he made an issue of it and it helps to restore his confidence. A head wound like that – it cut a groove in his skull, you know – is a slow business. If you live in a dream world you may not like your private nightmares. You can frighten yourself sense-less without extra aid. No, a respectable outsider might help to put his feet back on the ground.'

He stood up. 'He's in number seven. If he's asleep and you've time to spare, just wait for him. His consciousness comes and goes like a baby's.'

'I'll do my best,' the visitor promised. 'I wish him well.'

He stood for some time at the foot of the bed looking down on the bandaged figure who lay back, his eyes half-closed, offering no acknowledgement. Nascott had lost weight and his newly shaved jowl was pale blue beneath parchment cheeks. Presently he began to speak in a contemplative mumble.

'Silly bitch. Bloody ... silly ... double-cross-ing ... bitch. Find a replacement – plenty where she came from. Must keep going.'

He continued the monologue for several minutes, his thoughts racing and dawdling alternately, the words scarcely audible.

'Crafty, you know, dead crafty ... have to pick the right man ... have to know where to look. Sitting on a gold mine...'

The voice trailed into silence, the breath-ing became a series of heavy snores ending in a reverberation which shook the dreamer into wakefulness. He opened his eyes, took in his visitor and grunted.

'You,' he said making the word abusive.

'The something-for nothing merchant. I thought you might be calling. Brought any grapes?'

'Not even lilies,' said Mr Campion. 'You've been talking to yourself. Very obliging of you but you should try to control the habit – it could be dangerous. You mentioned gold mines, amongst other things. They can be tricky, too, if your claim isn't staked.'

Suspicion, apprehension, dislike and grudging respect moved in succession across Nascott's revealing face, leaving a simple scowl.

'You can go to hell. Get out before I ring for the sister.'

His visitor sat down. 'I came to bring a word of warning and to collect a little information. Whether you like it or not, I've had my share of the bargain. Let me give you yours.'

'You're a right bastard. You can't help me. Nobody can.'

'That gold mine of yours. My guess is that you have a theory – some little thought that occurred to you whilst you've been recovering – and you're wondering how to find the best market. Take my advice and forget all about it.'

The Director of Intercity Inquiries closed his eyes and rested his head on the pillows. He was not quite asleep but his face for once was expressionless.

'Do me a favour,' he said at last. 'Get lost.'

'I aim to please,' persisted Mr Campion. 'It was just a warning – between old enemies.' He did not move. Beyond the window of the small white room the hooting of tugs, the rattle of cranes and the querulous natter of gulls re-stated the immediate presence of the river.

Almost imperceptibly Nascott turned his head. He was awake again. 'I could make a packet,' he said. 'A real packet. And neither you nor any other interfering know-all can stop me.'

'Indeed? I would have thought your market – even if you happen to be right – was very limited. There's Mr Moryak, of course, but you sold him a pup last time you had any dealings there and my information is that he's not a forgiving type. You've had a taste of the mood he's in. I'd keep out of his way, if I were you. Then there's a man called Hilary Wykes whom no doubt you know very well. He, or his employer, want that particular pot kept on the boil. I'd say you'd lose a good account if it was known that you had betrayed their interests. What's left?'

'The Press.'

The visitor sighed. 'I suppose I couldn't appeal to your better nature? There are excellent reasons why Kopeck shouldn't be found just yet.'

'Tell me one.'

Mr Campion leaned closer, eyeing the man on the bed directly over his spectacles. 'The first is that if you breathe a word to anyone within a mile of Fleet Street – or even if I think you're thinking of it – I'll make it my business to see that you lose your licence. An ex-police officer is expected to know the rules about concealing information on a major crime. You know exactly what I'm talking about. There's a second reason which I would have thought you might have spotted.'

'I don't get it.'

'You're losing your grip. The best market – the only safe one – for any ideas you have is right under your nose.'

Nascott considered the statement for some time before he grasped its meaning.

'You?' he said at last.

'Who else?'

'And suppose I'm wrong? I could be, you know. I wouldn't normally admit it to a smooth talking con-man like you, though I've an instinct for that sort of thing – that's why I'm the best in the business. I could be wrong, but I'll give you a pound to a rotten orange I'm not. I get inspirations at times because I take trouble with my background information.'

He was talking rapidly now as if the erratic dynamo which kept him from extinction had suddenly taken hold.

'What's in it for me? I run a business, Mr

Campion, not a patriotic do-gooders' society. My hunch is for sale and the terms are strictly cash. Cash down before delivery of goods, right?'

The thin man at the bedside leaned forward.

'What I'm buying,' he said, 'is not your guess but a fortnight's silence. Silence from me – silence from you. After that you can go ahead. If Kopeck is still alive one side or the other will have found him by then. If Moryak gets there first, you'll lose. If it goes the other way, and if your hunch is right, you can claim to have been the man who solved the mystery and your story won't be officially denied. I can guarantee that. It should be worth quite a lot in the Sunday market.'

'I hold my tongue for two weeks and don't even tell you what I'm thinking?'

'It's as simple as that. Try not to talk in your sleep.'

For the first time the vestige of a smile crossed Nascott's face. 'You know, you're a very strange piece of goods. Old-fashioned – out of the ordinary. It crossed my mind that you were going to try an old trick of mine on me. I call it the trading-stamp lark. I swap a stamp, something with a known value, for a bit of special information. Better than pound notes, sometimes, unless the chap happens to be a collector. No troublesome explanation about how he got the money – he simply sold an item he happened to find in an old album in the attic. Just for a moment I thought you were going to try to work it on me. I remember what I told you the night you stitched me up. Funny, that – remembering what you say when you're over the eight.'

Mr Campion opened his notecase and placed a small envelope on the bed.

'Just to seal the bargain,' he said. 'A three anna, chocolate-and-carmine New Delhi 1931, printed in reverse colours. You collect forgeries, I believe.'

'You're on.'

An unsteady hand moved towards the trophy, hesitated and dropped on to the sheet before it could reach its objective. Abruptly the current had weakened and the patient was asleep again.

In the courtyard outside the hospital there were several taxis awaiting custom from retreating visitors. Mr Campion took the first and gave directions. He was followed, he noticed with interest, all the way to his club.

17

Showdown

Felix Perdreau, moving about the workroom on the first floor of his cottage, was, as ever, a theatrical figure more elegant than reality by the merest fraction. He was dressed in a tattered gold brocade dressing-gown with a high collar and long full skirts, his cuffs folded back to leave his forearms bare. With his white-flecked beard and falling forelock he suggested an alchemist from a gothic novel rather than an astute restorer of rare editions. Books lined the walls and overflowed in drunken columns on to the floor. A pot of glue which had recently been heated was still steaming in a saucepan, a hand-press and a bench littered with tools, chemicals and inks added to an atmosphere of erudite hocus-pocus.

At the moment he was engaged in the rewarding business of blending two imperfect copies of *Tamburlaine,* produced at slightly different dates, to make one complete example of the 1590 edition. The task demanded patience and an exhaustive knowledge of the methods of sixteenth-century printers and binders, but he was an unhurried craftsman who took pride in his work especially when it was essential that his skill should go unrecognized.

Today he was obtaining a peculiar satisfaction, for he needed the peace which the task provided. Here the various problems were all capable of solution. Touches of verisimilitude – a nobleman's bookplate from a library that had once been famous, the crabbed signature of a bygone owner on the flyleaf, traces of sealing-wax, a child's scribble half erased – brought with them a tranquillity which was missing from the outer world.

He was so absorbed that he did not hear the crunch of footsteps approaching the cottage. A knock on the outer door made his heart jump uncomfortably and his face became sallow.

Mr Campion noted his distress and apologized mildly for being the cause.

'I wanted to catch you before dinner,' he said. 'Lottie's guests are going to be a mixed bag, I believe, and the Music Room will be no place for anything but a chat about the pre-Raphaelites. You don't look altogether happy?'

Perdreau ran a hand through his hair, making a white strand like the crest on a wave of black curls.

'Just a complicated task which marches

slowly, in the manner of the Duke of Bilbao's army. I was enjoying myself, to tell you the truth. Another world – an escape – sometimes has therapeutic qualities. Getting and spending we lay waste our powers. A drink, perhaps, before we consider today's peck of trouble?'

The ground floor of the cottage consisted of a surprisingly large L-shaped room contrived by removing partitions from what had once been three small compartments. A baby grand stood by the far window, bookshelves heavy with fine bindings covered most of the walls and a Kirman rug glowed before a dying fire.

Mr Campion accepted a long whisky from an array of bottles and decanters in a mahogany corner-cupboard, sipping it slowly until the silence became embarrassing. The host sat, hands between knees, some distance away from the music stool, his glass untouched.

'Diplomatic mission?' he said at last. 'Or just a neighbourly visit, a breathing spell before a surfeit of Victoriana?'

The visitor sighed. 'You could say I was the man who called about the body. It would be an unhappily accurate description.'

Perdreau did not raise his head and his white forelock drooped dejectedly over his brows. His hands were still clasped.

'You're too acute altogether. I've always

suspected that this sort of showdown with you might come sooner or later. It's been a nightmare time, Campion. Wicked dreams abuse the curtained sleep. But, why now – now, when there seems to be a chance that the whole damned business could be brushed under the carpet? Someone else has taken a hand in it, as you must know very well. God knows why, but at least the shadow has lifted.'

'Because of the someone else. I don't want to fight on two fronts if it can be avoided.'

'And can it?'

'If I can draw one or two more high cards I may have a hand worth playing. I must know the truth about the man in the Tomb.'

Perdreau stood up, emptied his glass and refilled it, keeping his back to the visitor.

'How much do you know already?'

'A good deal, I'm afraid.' Campion's voice was so diffident that he could well have been discussing a minor social gaffe. 'I know that a man was killed, probably in the Turrets, some time in early September. He was a small-time crook called Barney Buller. I have this from our one-time guest, Nascott, by the way, though I doubt if he knows that he told me. The stranger was an insignificant and unpleasant character who had been specializing in his later years as an incendiarist. His employer was almost certainly someone in Denmark Holdings, a gentleman called

Hilary Wykes, who is the cat's-paw and hatchet-man of that institution.

'The fire-raiser's body must have been hidden in the Tomb very soon after his death. At some point Nascott found it there and since he's a man without conscience he tried to sell the information in two different places, an idea which was damaging to his interests and pretty nearly fatal to his existence. Wykes was evidently the first to get the news and it must have been a considerable shock, since it was entirely possible that the link between him and Buller could have been traced. I have no doubt that he or his friends whisked it away the moment they knew what had happened. It's probably at the bottom of the Thames by now wrapped in lead piping. Incidentally, *was* there anything on the body – a notecase, a letter – any identification at all?'

Perdreau returned to the piano stool. He struck a deliberate discord, paused and, as if to apologize for a show of bad manners, played three chords with his left hand, sustaining the final notes until the reverberations had ended. His head remained bent over the keyboard.

'Not a thing.' Dejection was making his voice flat. 'If you exclude an empty envelope addressed to a man who turned out to be a plumber in Stoke Newington. I went over to that repellent wasteland to find out, but there appears to be no connection. I suppose I'd better tell you the whole story.'

'It may not be important, but it might strengthen my hand.'

'Not important?' Perdreau snorted with weary indignation. 'It's important to me. I've not had two hours real sleep since it happened. That infernal night is bitten into my brain like acid on a copper plate. It was so simple, so unexpected...'

'So accidental?'

The man in the dressing-gown raised his head at last.

'You guessed that? It was the merest chance, Campion, I give you my word. A discreditable episode but you may as well hear it without the varnish of self-apology. That night – it was a Sunday – the guests were unusually wearisome and sat up far too long for my taste. I withdrew by way of the cellar because – the fact must be faced – I was short of a bottle of whisky and my intention was to help myself illicitly. I crept down the staircase of the Oubliette, as old Edwin called it, as silently as any other petty thief. When I got there I found that I wasn't alone. There was a marauder moving about the place with a torch and it took me some time to discover what he was up to. When I did it was almost too late. He had made a kindling pile, several in fact, and the matches were actually in his hand. He was bending down, very close, with his back towards me. I hit him with the first thing that came to hand – a cold chisel for opening wine crates, I think.'

'On the head?'

'No. Just on the shoulder. It wasn't even much of a blow. I was aiming at his wrist to stop him striking a match. He pitched over, hit the floor as if he'd been poleaxed and never moved again. It was as simple as that.'

'If it's any comfort to you, he had a remarkable skull with a tin plate in it. He could have died at any moment merely by banging his head on a doorpost. What happened next?'

'Next?' Perdreau brushed back his forelock. 'Next I sat there for an hour – two, maybe – wondering what the hell to do. I'm a man who likes the sybaritic life, Campion, and it occurred to me very strongly that a scandal, to put it at the lowest, would involve me and the Turrets in a lot of trouble. The Kopeck business was already brewing. Looking back, perhaps I was light-headed. I'd had one or two more than my share in the course of the evening, trying to beat dull care. I was sozzled but not stinking when I arrived, but I sobered up pretty smartly when I saw what I'd done. I carried him up to the Tomb on a wheelbarrow and put him under the flag-stones. It seemed a providential way out. Does that make me a murderer?'

Mr Campion was deliberate. 'Not in my

224

book. Unwise, perhaps, but not homicidal.' He stood up. 'Lottie knows about all this?'

'Very little escapes her, I'm afraid. She's never raised the question, except with her eyebrows, but I think she saw me cross the courtyard, for it was an uncomfortably bright night after the storm. She was certainly frightened when Nascott made his search a week later.'

'He spotted that, which is why he went back for a more careful look around.'

'And now?'

'Now,' said Mr Campion judicially, 'you have twenty minutes to change, restore your confidence and to nip over in time to support Lottie at dinner.'

The company for the weekend at the Turrets was divided into two opposing groups of equal numbers, the entertainers and the entertained. The balance was not happy: too much yeast can ruin the best of brews.

A sense of unease hung over the party, for the house was still considered newsworthy by the popular Press and the story of the shot through the window, though staunchly denied by Miss Cambric, had reached the papers in a highly coloured version with suspicious speed. Two cancellations had resulted and the gaps had been filled at the last moment by hardier souls who were expected to be decorative, if financially unrewarding. Two security men in plain clothes had vetted each arrival as they entered the drive, adding their own turn of the screw.

An elderly professor of English literature from an American university with his wife, a bespectacled mouse, two schoolmistresses from the Hague, the Bishop of Bwanaland, black and benign in episcopal purple, two acolytes whose rolling eyes suggested uncomprehending dismay and an earnest young woman trailing a bored husband many years her senior, made up the hard core of the guests who had paid for their entertainment. In her determination to keep tradition unbroken Miss Cambric had overdone the lighter side. Jack and Molly Croesus led for the new brigade in an assortment of bright garments which were too advanced to be recognized as fashionable except by the initiated. About them circulated the latest and least repressed of modern novelists, a couple of drama students of indeterminate sex and a picture dealer whose fortune was as new and outrageous as the imitation tattooing which covered most of his mistress's shoulders.

Lottie whispered to Campion as he crossed the threshold of the Small Drawing-Room.

'A terrible mixture, I'm afraid. It's my own fault for making sure of a full house. Too many teetotallers and too many total imbibers. This is a challenge, my dear man, so see if you can persuade my professor's wife to smile. Tell her she could be the wittiest woman since Millamant if she lost a few inhibitions and put six inches on her bosom. And don't let the Croesus pair sing after dinner, whatever happens. The Bishop might understand some of the words, even if the rest of the party don't. If anyone mentions Mr Kopeck, the subject is completely taboo. I've told Felix to put the word around.'

She moved deftly between her guests towards two solemn young women who stood apart sipping sherry as if its qualities were strictly medicinal.

'How lucky we are to have you here to-night, because you're both experts, I believe, on speech training. In your country they always speak such perfect English that I feel ashamed. I once bought toothpaste in Rotterdam from a girl with an enchanting accent – better than the best one hears in Edinburgh. Over here if one made the same request in Dutch one would be lucky to be offered saddlesoap. I want to hear your opinion of some voices from the past – singers and speakers. Edwin always said that Dickens, whom he met as a young man, was the greatest loss to the stage. He heard him read parts of *Oliver Twist* in 1858 for charity and said he had a magnificent presence. Unfortunately it couldn't be recorded because the machine wasn't invented at the time. Still, we have Patti, De Reszke, David Bispham, Gervaise Elwes and so many more. Even Algy Swinburne, now that he's due for revival. Edwin thought him funny and made him recite "My Sister Swallow". He was rather unkind in some ways.'

Mr Campion toiled dutifully at his assignment and found the material better than he had suspected. The lady blossomed under flattery, revealing that her husband's eminence as a scholar owed a debt to her shrewdness in the background.

Before the new Burbage announced dinner only the Bishop's supporting clergy had failed to yield to Lottie's skill as catalyst and the younger of the drama students had sidled towards her hostess murmuring, 'Could I sit next to the Prof? He's sort of dreamy and he can wiggle his ears independently. That's quite a factor in my life.'

The stage of coffee and liqueurs in the Music Room promised certain difficulties since Molly and Jack Croesus had arrived armed with guitars, clearly expecting to be asked to perform. Miss Cambric solved the problem by simple dictatorship.

'Madame Adelina Patti will sing the Bell Song from *Lakmé*, the rendering she gave in this room in 1901. After that Felix is going to show us some of our other treasures. He's made his own choice from Edwin's library of the voices of his friends. I'm afraid some of them are a little scratchy, despite the work that has been done on them. They're all what the cognoscenti call 'Pre-Dog".'

She turned to the Professor. 'Isn't that a splendid phrase? It means before they invented the trademark of the wirehaired terrier listening to the gramophone. His name was Nipper – doesn't he look it? – and he was painted by an artist called Francis Barraud whom I seem to remember lived in Bushey, quite near dear Hubert von Herkomer and his sister.'

Perdreau's performance with Mme Patti was one of the highlights of the repertoire at the Turrets. The original recording of the aria *'Dov'è l'Indiana bruna?'* had been doctored and as far as was possible the orchestral background, led by an indifferent flautist had been muted. With careful timing aided by expert re-recording, he was able to create the impression that the company was listening to a living but invisible singer accompanied by the pianist sitting in front of them.

Mr Campion, who had heard the performance once before, was respectfully impressed, for Perdreau wove a spell which was not to be denied, implying by every glance and apparently spontaneous pause that he was alternately following and leading a ghost who was within a hand's touch. The illusion was emotional and unreasonably disturbing.

The magic held long after the song had ended.

He accepted the tribute of silence for precisely the right interval and stood up.

'Now,' he said. 'I thought we might have a complete change. Mr Oscar Wilde is going to read a passage from *Salomé* for us. He wrote the play in French for Sarah Bernhardt, who never acted in it, but he spoke some of the lines here for Sir Edwin Cambric seventy-six years ago.'

The voice which emerged from the shining brass horn of the gramophone sounded effete to modern ears. The playwright, proud of his impeccable accent, spoke in the lilting *bel canto* tones affected by older actors of the Comédie Française, an exercise in elocution rather than meaning.

'Iokanaan! Je suis amoureuse de ton corps... Ton corps est blanc comme les neiges qui couchent sur les montagnes de Judée... Laisse moi toucher ton corps...'

Curiosity held the audience and the extract was too short to outstay its welcome. Lottie turned to the Professor, who was sitting next to her on the chaise-longue.

'One of our newer revivals – only just back from restoration. My uncle never really liked Wilde, though he came here twice, the second time with some rather undesirable companions, I'm told. He once said, "Cambric is like an elephant – only credible when seen in sobriety," and Edwin never quite forgave him. Still, he admired him and he did buy several of his manuscripts, which are still in the hall. He even sent him a gold fountain pen when he went into exile in Paris, to encourage him to write again. The poor man sold it the next morning to his hotelier. Felix, who have you got for us now?'

Perdreau laughed. 'Something thoroughly respectable, but a rarity all the same. Lord Tennyson, the late Poet Laureate in person.' Restoration here had been less successful but out of a fog of whirring scatches the boom of a patriarch with a strong Lincolnshire accent echoed back over the years.

'Half a league, half a league,
Half a league onward...
...Charge for the guns...'

A detonation very close to the house shook the room and the curtains billowed on a gust of cold air. The first impact was more insulting than terrifying and for a moment no one moved. It was followed by a crack so ominous that the whole fabric seemed on the point of splitting. A second and a third came rapidly, chased by the unmistakable crash of falling timber. Again the curtains twitched on an unseen impact, screeched as they ripped apart and a window fell inwards in a shower of broken glass, stonework and twigs. Dust eddied over the furniture. A sheet of music sailed ridiculously into the draught amongst yellow leaves and scurried into a corner.

The tattooed girl squealed, clinging extravagantly to her protector, who was retreating towards the door. The younger of the drama students and the two Dutch ladies, impelled by curiosity, had almost reached the windows when a final crash of branches brought a second fall of rubble and ruin clattering on to the parquet floor. They hesitated, thought better of the venture and ran from the room.

Campion caught Miss Cambric's arm. She was standing alone, swaying as if she was too absorbed to balance, her black eyes taking in every detail of the devastation.

'One of Edwin's elms,' she whispered. 'He said they would stand for a century.'

She steadied herself, accepting his support, and looked round. Only the Americans with Jack and Molly Croesus remained. They had retreated to the other end of the room, each man holding his wife close. In the corridor a woman was laughing, high and mindless, and from the staircase came excited voices, the thump of running feet.

'*Charge for the guns*' repeated Alfred Lord Tennyson. '*Charge for the guns ... charge for the guns ... charge for the guns...*'

Very gently Mr Campion escorted his hostess to a chair and silenced the orator at the turn of a switch.

'Thank the Lord for that,' said the Professor. He went over to the gaping window frame and leaned into the darkness. 'It's a tree – the biggest goddamned tree I ever clapped eyes on – smashed right into the wall. It's made one helluva mess.' He turned back, striking brick dust from his palms. 'They always say elms can be traitors – they go when you least expect them to. Often on a still night like this.'

Miss Cambric stood up, shaken but determined. For once she could not pretend that the shock was trivial: she fought back.

'Fiddlesticks, my dear man. I know an explosion when I hear one – I've heard too many since Count von Zeppelin first started attacking us in 1915. If you'll forgive me, Albert, I'll go and see to my guests – some of the girls may be a little upset, and I can't blame them. Perhaps you'd be kind enough to go down and investigate the damage. Jack, there is still some brandy intact on the sidetable. I think a glass would be steadying to the nerves. Try to persuade the others to join you.'

She swept out, indomitable as the *Revenge*. Mr Campion would have followed her, but the young man took him by the sleeve.

'Not for us,' he said. 'Molly and I don't

find it healthy here. Say goodbye to the old girl for us, will you? We're away.'

Mr Campion found Felix Perdreau with several of the guests standing outside the main porch, staring at a spectacular tragedy. The eastern corner of the house was flanked by a group of elms, the largest of which lay sprawled across the forecourt. In its fall the upper branches had smashed against the house, breaking several windows and shattering the stucco so that the bricks behind gaped through the jigsaw cracks.

A car dramatized the scene with headlights. At the base of the fallen trunk torches flickered and the figures moved behind the broken tracery of the branches where a few late autumn leaves still fluttered.

Grim looks greeted the thin man as he approached the group and the new Burbage, his shirtfront ruined beyond recovery, gestured towards the stump which still stood like a broken tooth solidly in the ground.

'A gelignite job, they think. Simple time fuse, probably an alarm clock. It could have been planted any time in the last twelve hours. It looks as if it had been pushed into a hollow facing away from the house to make sure the damn thing fell slap on the corner.' He was very angry.

'Simple?'

'Anyone with a bit of commando training

could have fixed it. It wouldn't need a bloody safe blower – just some bastard who could get his hands on the stuff.'

'No doubt he was provided with it gratis, along with a small fee for expenses,' murmured Mr Campion. 'How do you think he got through the cordon?'

The man emptied his lungs in one furious breath.

'Cordon? Two men and a boy and me wasting my time arsing about dressed as a waiter. This place is wide open to any villain who cares to slide down a ditch – it always will be until we can get guard dogs in. It's the old lady's own fault. She's in dead trouble and she won't face it.'

Reluctantly, Mr Campion was inclined to agree. He stood for some time looking at the shattered stump where the impact point of the explosion needed no demonstration. Two cars arrived almost simultaneously on the forecourt, one heavy with local police, and from behind the house came the sound of engines being started. He was still watching idly when Perdreau appeared at his elbow.

'I think you should come back indoors. Lottie has had a visitor.'

Miss Cambric was sitting at her escritoire in the Small Drawing-Room when he entered. Her head was turned away and she did not raise it, but gestured towards the man who was standing before the fireplace, a melancholy figure with a bald head and a pinched face which suggested an albino crow.

'This is Doctor Moxton,' she said. 'Doctor, would you be so kind as to tell Mr Campion your errand?'

The little man sniffed. 'I've very little time to spare,' he said. 'I don't want to go over the ground twice, but if you wish it – if you wish it.

'The position is this. I am the Medical Officer of Health for this district and I try to avoid working twenty-five hours a day but sometimes it can't be helped – it can't be helped.

'The position is that we have a suspected case of smallpox and this is a matter of some urgency – very great urgency. The suspect is a Mrs Sims – a Mrs Henrietta Sims – who until recently was employed here, I understand. I must have a list of all her contacts for the last three weeks. In particular an Indian cook, also an ex-employee here, who apparently can't be traced. It's all very unfortunate because everyone seems to be in a state of confusion owing to a fallen tree. Elms should never be allowed near houses. They are thoroughly dangerous at all times. I hope you can help me. This is a very serious emergency – very serious indeed. I must insist that some responsible person answers all my questions.'

Lottie turned her head. Her eyes were wide, enormous in a setting which was pale as paper, her voice no longer resilient.

'Do what you can, Albert, please. The middle drawer of my desk in the office has all he needs in a silly little red notebook of Venetian leather. Mrs Faversham will help you, if you can find her.'

'Of course,' he said and held out his hand. 'Go to bed. I'll see to everything.'

She clasped it tightly, pulling herself to her feet and waiting until she was certain of her balance.

'This time, I'm beaten, my dear man. You were right – Elsie was right. I'll close the Turrets tomorrow. Poor Edwin – he'd never forgive me.'

18

The Racing Driver

Anger is not the best of stimulants when careful planning is needed. Mr Campion, who was unaccustomed to the emotion and surprised by its intensity, took various steps to reduce himself to a state where logical thinking could be resumed.

Having disposed of the melancholy doctor

he wandered out of the house and climbed to the head of the slope leading to the Tomb. Behind him the traffic on the by-pass streamed in an unbroken gully of light and far ahead occasional windows pinpointed the wealthier outposts of Inglewood. It was cold and windless with a thin sickle of a moon and anything but silent. From suburban gardens a quarter of a mile away rockets sailed into the night, cascading in carnival stars. He was reminded that this was the eve of the 5th November, the season dedicated by the English to the memory of a favourite patriot.

He returned to the Turrets by way of the kitchens, entering Lottie's private office with a mild feeling of guilt. Here he made a series of telephone calls and waited long into the small hours before the answers to his queries arrived.

Hilary Wykes among others was occupying his attention and having discovered where that gentleman was spending the weekend he gave some thought to the problem of determining the most unfortunate hour at which to call.

At a quarter to nine on the following morning, a Sunday, Mr Campion wandered into Fitzherbert Mews in Mayfair and located the flat for which he was looking without difficulty.

A long grey tourer, elegant as an Italian

ballroom slipper, its open seats and dash-board covered by a tailored tonneau canvas, stood before a vermilion front door which evidently led directly to rooms over what had once been the coach house for a mansion in Fitzherbert Square.

There was a wrought-iron balcony of Spanish inspiration outside the window above and from it hung wire baskets trailing variegated ivy. The chromium bell was engraved with a single name. The caller rang with a persistence which indicated that he intended if necessary to devote all day to obtaining attention. After five minutes the window opened and a voice called:

'What do you want?'

'You,' said Mr Campion. 'Shall we talk here or inside?'

Wyke's head was too well barbered ever to become disreputable, even after what had evidently been a difficult night. It appeared over the balcony very slightly dishevelled above a black-and-white silk dressing gown.

'At this Godless hour? You're round the bend. Who the hell are you in any case?'

Mr Campion gave his name, adding mildly, 'My subjects include arson, attempted murder and malicious damage to property. If you can't hear from where you are I can raise my voice. I thought of discussing a smallpox case among other items.'

A click from behind the door announced

239

that the lock had been released by a switch. A climb brought him into a room which was predictable to the smallest detail. Motoring prints and the autographed portraits of the masters and mistresses of the racing world crowded the walls, a browning laurel wreath hung round a steering wheel mounted above the fireplace, and bucket seats, doubtless from illustrious vehicles, provided the smaller chairs. Models of vintage cars crowded the mantelpiece.

The owner glowered at his visitor, his arms akimbo and his feet apart.

'Your name seems familiar. Not glamorous, but faintly bell-ringing. Do I know you? Only a bloody-minded oaf would knock a man up at the crack of dawn. Yet you look almost human. What exactly were you mouthing about down there?'

Mr Campion considered the room and its tenant from above his glasses with disapproval, finally tossing his hat on to an armchair which might have been designed for a racing Goliath.

'I came to tell you,' he said, 'that as from this very moment you will call off your attacks on Charlotte Cambric, force your tame doctor to admit that Mrs Hetty Sims has nothing more serious than chickenpox, which he almost certainly arranged for her, and tell your employer that it would be wise to forget that Inglewood Turrets exists. I hope I make myself clear?'

Wykes took his time before he answered, and it occurred to Campion that he was considering physical assault, rejecting the idea in favour of a protestation of ignorance, and finally deciding to discover the strength of his opponent by a delaying action. He stood his ground, thrusting both hands into the pockets of his gown.

'I'm thirty-five years old,' he said at last. 'Devastating but true. In my time there have been three tries at blackmailing me, and two shots at killing me by sabotaging cars I was going to drive. I've dodged my way out of a race mob and I've crash-landed a plane which was on fire. But this is the first time I've come across a real gibbering idiot on my own doorstep on a Sunday morning. Almost a newsworthy item. Would you like some coffee before you go? My head feels full of sump oil and your ravings are coming to me from a great distance.'

The visitor took off his overcoat, chose one of the leather monsters and sat down, stretching out his feet to an occasional table which appeared to have been made from a pile of tyres.

'Probably a sound idea. But before you set about preparing your remedy I have a thought to offer. It is a great mistake to underestimate your adversary – you want to know your own strength and his. Now in my case, I don't feel like taking on Denmark Holdings, but Hilary St John Perrault Wykes, aged thirty-nine, according to my information, is about my weight. That's why I've done quite a little research on you. I have a dossier, as they say, which could make you unemployable in any reputable concern. Now go and make your instant potion.'

A smile which had nothing of amusement in it flickered for a moment and vanished.

'Good Lord, I believe you really are a blackmailer. Incredible. Hang on for a moment whilst I brew up. After that, I shall ring the police.'

He opened a door into a recess which was hardly more than a cupboard and re-appeared in less than a minute with a tray resembling a disc wheel from which Campion accepted a steaming cup. His host crossed the room to a desk and opened a drawer, snapping on a switch.

'Tape recorder. Saves a lot of time when it comes to giving evidence. Factual, you know. I'll give you a chance by adding that Clifford Denmark takes a very poor view of people who try tricks with his senior executives.'

The coffee was better than the visitor had hoped; he sipped appreciatively before taking a diary from his pocket and placing it on the rubber-girt table.

'Splendid,' he said pushing his glasses

forward. 'Now we'll start at a date near the middle of August when you began to buy drinks in a pub called the Seven Stars in Deptford for a man by the name of Barney Buller, a known crook with several convictions and a reputed fire raiser. I have three witnesses here including the landlord who took the trouble to warn you of the kind of man you were chatting to.'

He broke off. 'By the way, I hope your microphone is conveniently close? I shouldn't like the machine to miss anything. On Sunday, 10th September this man Buller, who'd gone down to the Turrets intending to set fire to it at your instigation, met with an accident whilst he was at work and you were left in the dark about what happened. His widow, incidentally, found about two hundred pounds in a box and proceeded to blue it in a sensational style until she got frightened. No doubt the item appears as "various disbursements" in your petty cash account, but I have recovered some of the notes and you made the mistake of giving new ones in series. I doubt if your boss would forgive you for that – it was pure idleness, lack of attention to detail.

'We move now to Mr Harry Nascott, a recent recruit to Denmark Holdings but quite a public figure in his own way. He admits discovering the body and telling you about it without realizing the full significance of what he was saying. As a result the wretched corpse was removed by a couple of strong-arm men on your instructions on the night of October 17th. Shall I go on?'

Wykes had been sitting on the edge of his desk, his silken legs crossed, his hands gripping the edge. He leant over, switched off the tape and stood up.

'I've been remembering about you. I knew I'd heard your name somewhere or other. You're a friend of old Guffy Randall, who's a member of my club, and I've heard him yakking about your talents. Tedious. Both of you seem to be as up to date as a model T Ford – you in particular. You don't even try.'

A silver box stood amongst a collection of outsize cups and trophies. He took a cigarette and lit it from a flame which sprang from a miniature petrol pump.

'You're not with it, old man. You come trotting along here trying to scare the pants off me – presumably for money – with a tale that comes straight from Cloud-cuckooland. I meet hundreds of hangers-on in my business and sometimes I even buy them drinks, so your friend Buller may be among them. You say Nascott says he saw his body at the Turrets, though why he should come up with a tale like that beats me – and now it's vanished very conveniently. He's hardly a reliable witness, is he? Or don't you listen to news bulletins?'

Mr Campion was discomfited. A shock was coming and he braced himself, turning a page in the diary without looking up.

'Nascott is dead. Dreary, but true. He jumped out of a hospital window this morning and smashed himself to pulp. Too bad, eh? Bang goes your idiot story. No body – no witness – no blackmail. Perhaps you'd like to get the hell out of here when you've finished your coffee? At this time in the morning you have all the charm of a blow-out ten miles from John o' Groats.'

Wykes was standing very still, looking down on the thin figure in the armchair, waiting to pounce on some trace of reaction, a hesitation or the blink of an eyelid which could show how far he could press the advantage. For some time neither man moved.

Finally Campion flicked over another page. 'Oh, dear,' he said and sighed. 'Poor, silly, venal Sergeant Nascott. I was afraid that might happen. As you say, too bad. The wretched chap trod on some toes which are even more delicate than yours. A cruel gesture, made, I suppose, *pour encourager les autres*. He committed suicide?'

'That's what they inferred. No suggestion of an unfriendly push. It comes to the same thing as far as you are concerned. Your stooge is in no position to double-cross anyone any longer. Finished your coffee?'

'Not quite. If you like to switch your

machine on again I'll give you the gist of the statements made by two of your mechanics, Smeaton and Parmilee, about their activities down at the Turrets. By the way, you picked a rotten rendezvous that night. The lay-by just below the house is under observation and the number of every car which stops there is recorded. That includes your splendid Wykes-Lancia special now parked outside this flat and your spares-cum-maintenance van which dropped in to the lay-by at half-past one in the morning after your chaps had knocked out a guard and picked up the body. It appears that you don't care to do your own dirty work, but you keep an eye on it just the same. Shall I put the tape on for you?'

Wykes did not move. He was losing the advantage he had bought with his news but he was not broken. He hit back confidently.

'If you told me Bill Smeaton made any sort of statement, even to God Almighty, I wouldn't believe you. Not faintly credible. You're making this up as you go along.'

'On the contrary, his statement is quite clear. It runs like this: "I don't know what you're talking about. I was never there. I do not remember where I was that night and for all I care you can take a running jump up the nearest available exhaust pipe." It took several hours to extract this story and he does not propose to change it. A rugged type, your Mr Smeaton.'

He turned another page.

'On the other hand, Mr Syd Parmilee of 19 Slype Lane, Deptford – one of the best pit-mechanics in the business, I believe – is not made of such stern stuff. I spoke to two of my friends at five o'clock this morning and they were very reassuring about the prospect of persuading him to confide in them. They said it might take another four hours and would I ring them back?'

He glanced at his watch. 'It's just on nine. May I use your phone?'

Wykes had picked up a long bottle opener in the form of a spanner. He struck it sharply against the palm of his other hand, his face twitching. 'If you touch it, I'll smash your wrist for you. I don't see what your game is, Campion, but I'm not going to wear any more of it. *Niente.* You come bulldozing your way in here with a pack of empty threats and cockeyed accusations which sound to me like the tuning up for a blackmailing racket. I don't pretend to understand half of what you're raving about but I'll give you one straight warning and I mean every single damn word of it. Now listen – listen good and hard.

'You're really here on a wild goose chase concerning Lottie Cambric, so far as I can understand the gibberish you're talking. Right? Well, her principal interest at the moment appears to be in this man Kopeck, who's wanted by the police in his own country – an escaped criminal and a spy of some sort, according to the papers. God knows why, but she's trying to protect him. Still motherly, at her age. It's none of my business, but I happen to know where he is. If I have another peep out of you, I'll do the telephoning – straight to the Soviet Embassy. Think that one out.'

Mr Campion did not reply directly. He stood up, crossed to the balcony and looked slowly up and down the mews from behind the white net curtain. A car which had not been there when he arrived was parked at one end and at the other, under an archway, a man was leaning in a doorway reading a paper.

'In that Lancia of yours you could leave an E-type 4.2 Jaguar standing?'

The question was so unexpected that the scene was robbed of impetus. The reflexes of the professional forced a professional answer.

'In traffic it would depend on the driver. On the flat, with no holds barred, I could give him ten in a hundred. What the hell are you getting at?'

'Ten in a hundred,' repeated Mr Campion. 'Good. That's just what you're going to do. Get dressed.'

Simple astonishment cleared every other

emotion from Wykes's face. 'When I've kicked you out I'm going straight back to bed.'

Campion left the window and turned to lean over the back of a chair. He spoke slowly, as if to an apprentice who was deliberately unwilling to learn.

'Sit down whilst I put you right in the picture. Pay attention because time seems to be getting short. If you can deduce where Kopeck is, then others can do the same. Nascott is unlikely to have told you his ideas, but he must have given you a lot of background material about the characters connected with the Turrets, so you made your guess – it's unlikely to be more – from that. I have the same hunch myself.

'I intend to lift Kopeck out of his hiding place this very morning, because he's no longer safe there. To do that I need a fast car and a skilled driver who's prepared to take risks. You fit the bill.

'I need you because the boys outside have been following me around for some time now and they're pretty expert at the job. My own car isn't in their class for speed.'

'And why should I lift a finger for you?'

'Use your mind. Syd Parmilee is being taken into little pieces by experts and by now he will have coughed up all he knows, including your original connection with the late Barney Buller. So far I've only arranged this in order to twist your arm about the Turrets, but if I have any trouble the whole story goes out of my hands – the entire boiling – Denmark's private doctor who is pretending he can't tell chickenpox from smallpox and is making such a fuss that he's frightening more honest men – Smeaton's experience with gelignite in the army – your string of spies and informants planted round the Turrets – everything. If it does nothing else, the stink I'll raise will finish you with Denmark Holdings and I'll see to it that the Public Prosecutor gives the conspiracy his very special attention.

'The alternative is a sharp piece of driving with a passenger who is your only hope. If anything happens to me nothing can prevent the whole thing coming out.

'That's the choice and I want the answer in ten seconds flat.'

Hilary Wykes straightened his shoulders in a slow flexing stretch which was almost casual. As if to confound his opponent's story he went on to the balcony and examined the yard beneath, an unhurried survey.

'You could be right,' he said at last. The attack had vanished from his voice, leaving it bland and emotionless. 'The Jag has no business here and it's a new continental number with quite a turn of speed. First time I've seen one. Relax, old man. You've won the toss.' He returned to the silver trophies and lit another cigarette. 'I'll be five minutes. I never drive without a shower and a shave.'

19

The Brotherhood

Before the Lancia reached Piccadilly Circus, now sordid as a hangover in the Sunday sunshine, it was apparent that Wykes could handle a car with that complete authority which is as comforting to the passenger as the performance of a prima ballerina seen from an orchestra stall.

He drove with zest, foreseeing every opportunity and taking each of them with the majesty of a shark moving through a shoal of John Dorys. Fifty yards behind, the Jaguar followed, nip and tuck, equally purposeful.

'The man is good,' said Wykes dispassionately, one eye on the mirror. 'A stylist. We can't lose him in traffic. Where are we heading?'

'In principle, the Newmarket Road. If you have your private system of back doubles, now is the time to exhibit it.'

In his own element Wykes became a more credible and less affected personality. He addressed the car in affectionate murmurs as if it were a high-mettled horse capable of feeling a touch of the whip.

'That's my girl – and no nonsense from that Bentley – exquisite – just a squeeze past Dad and Mum and the kids...'

To Campion he said. 'I doubt if we'll shake them off by these cuts – they know them as well as I do. My thinking would be to go north for twenty miles or so – St Albans or Hertford – and then cross country to Thaxted or Saffron Walden. Would that fit the bill?'

'They're still with us. Try a burst of speed at the first chance and stop in a side road once we're out of sight.'

A detour through anonymous suburban streets brought them to Epping but the Jaguar remained, keeping its distance as if attached by a string. In open country they repeated the strategem, turning through a maze of lanes around Much Hadham, twisting, going full circle, finally emerging into Bishops Stortford, where the shadow was awaiting them.

'It occurs to me,' said Wykes. 'That they know precisely where we're heading. You can't expect me to beat the book on that one.'

'You could be right. I'm afraid we've made it obvious that we are going somewhere and don't want company.'

'Cat and mouse. I'm rather enjoying it. You wouldn't care for me to run them off the road? I know most of the unfriendly tricks. It is a question of letting them get ahead, cutting in, and hoping the man behind will lose his nerve. We'd have to choose a likely stretch with no witnesses. Probably they'd be a write off. Devastating – possibly final. It might cost you five hundred in repairs to us.'

Mr Campion appeared to consider the proposition.

'I think we'll stay legal apart from the speed limit. My guess is that they don't really know more than our general direction. We could beat them on a sudden turn off.'

'In Saffron Walden?'

'Below there. Newport and due east.'

Wykes moved the dial past ninety, a smile reflecting his exhilaration.

'I was right then. We're making for Stoke by Gurney?'

'No secret any longer.'

'I guessed it from Nascott's dossier on Felix Perdreau. As a matter of interest, why weren't the bloodhounds ahead of us weeks ago? Come to that, if you've known all along where he is, why didn't you do something about it? Was that so smart?'

'Several reasons. One of them is that he was as safe there as anywhere. The bloodhounds, as you say, have had every chance to get there first – yet they didn't. *Ergo*, they haven't looked there, or having looked haven't found. England's dotted with possible hideouts. This may not be the right one.'

The car was singing along the straight stretch between Quendon and Newport, weaving between traffic that seemed motionless, the pursuers temporarily out of sight and the countryside a blur flanking the sealskin ribbon of the tarmac.

'Amusing but useless in my opinion,' said Wykes, passing a pair of determined motorcyclists as if they were clockwork toys. 'Once they spot that we're turning east the game is up so far as foxing them is concerned. Time wasting. I'm only the chauffeur, of course, but if I were following me I'd put two and two together by now. Your best bet is to beat them to it and hope you've got enough time in hand.'

'Could we make it by twelve? There's about twenty-five miles of side roads, all narrow, ahead of us.'

Wykes glanced at the dashboard.

'Just about. I don't take chances in lanes even for you. D'you know the way?'

'We turn off at Clare for Stoke by Gurney – then we pray that Gurney Old Church is signposted. It's been derelict for thirty years, so we may have trouble.'

'I thought it was a monastery – Greek or Russian Orthodox or something of that sort? Perdreau bought a library from them, according to Nascott.'

They were slipping easily through a

countryside of elms, ploughed acres and tall hedges still flecked with the tarnish of late autumn, apparently alone save for Sunday-morning drivers making leisurely expeditions to favoured hostelries.

'The Order of St Athanasius.'

'It means nothing to me.'

'A Russian sect – no connection with the creed of the same name. Refugees from religious persecution behind the Curtain. They're a brotherhood, an Order of Poverty, I believe. Strict vows and, once you've taken them, a pretty uncomfortable life devoted to good works.'

Wykes skirted a miniature family car with such dexterity that the occupants were scarcely aware of his presence until he was long past them.

'Hardly my style. How do they manage to live?'

'Private subscriptions. Sale of valuable possessions salvaged from the old country – books and icons, for example. Less than twenty men all told. They're living in a tumble-down mansion once designed for a wealthy lunatic and restoring Gurney Old Church, which, according to my map, is five miles from anywhere. You turn right here and it should be in sight.'

The lane ran uphill between hedges steeply banked on both sides, the surface no better than a cart track. At the top of the ridge an open five-barred gate and a stile gave on to a wooded slope, beside a succession of fields overlooking a vale which was green and sodden.

Three elderly cars, respectable as matrons in mourning, and a collection of bicycles waited by the low wall of a churchyard where the tombstones were buried in dead cowparsley and brambles. A line of cypress marked the path to a small Norman church enmeshed in scaffolding so precarious that the whole fabric seemed on the point of subsiding into the undergrowth. Wykes slowed the car to a crawl.

'Do we park here?'

'I think we should be cautious. Try farther along among the trees.'

The track led round the stone building to a clearing opposite the vestry where the ground had been churned into ruts. Planks, tiles, bricks, ladders and discarded scaffolding lay in confusion amongst bruised blackberry bushes. The remains of a cement mixing hardened in the morning sun. From within the church came men's voices, deep and sonorous in the old-gold glory of a Russian chant. The driver turned the car full circle and switched off.

'What now?'

'We look around. Mass seems to be ending, so we can cast an eye over the congregation as it leaves. Since you don't know the man we're after, you might amble back, keeping out of sight, and watch for any late arrivals. The Jag had a telephone aerial, so there may be reinforcements. I'll be among the cypress trees.'

Left to himself, Mr Campion removed the ignition key and began a cautious tour of the chaos of scaffold and rubble. The vestry door was slightly ajar but he did not venture inside. Instead he wandered towards a trestle table on which were plasterer's tools and a pile of putty half-wrapped in newspaper.

Squatting beside the flapping newsprint was a moulded model, so comic and so innocent that it mingled almost unnoticeably with its background, a shape which was just large enough to be contained by a man's two hands.

A putty bullfrog looked up at Mr Campion with mildly curious eyes, set wide above a lop-sided grin, a caricature more than a portrait. The thin man returned the smile for a moment and bent nearer to touch the creature. The model had almost hardened and he lifted it, carrying it carefully back to the car, where he placed it on the canvas that was stretched above the rear seat.

From the church the wheeze of a harmonium drifted like the scent of smouldering leaves, the ghost of an organ voluntary. The graveyard was still deserted and he picked his way behind the building through brambles and twitch towards the cypress avenue. Wykes appeared from the surrounding trees and caught up with him.

'Two cars stopped just up the road. They sound like our friends, but I didn't care to investigate. What happens now?'

'We wait,' said Mr Campion.

The door under the half-timbered porch opened with a creak and an old woman emerged, leaning on the arm of a companion, succeeded at a respectful interval by a man in a blue suit, grizzled and poker-faced, a peaked cap under his arm. An ancient Daimler trundled them away. Two middle-aged women in no-nonsense tweeds followed, striding out confidently, taking the footpath towards the valley, and a couple with a small girl clasping a prayer book paused on the pathway.

The final group was led by a vast bearded figure in a black robe, his height emphasized by the tall black headdress and sweeping veil of the Greek Church Archimandrite. To his left and right walked two other priests, bland and expressionless in their pillbox hats and cassocks. Except for a difference in height, all three were unnervingly alike, the resemblance accentuated by black beards of the same square cut. The waiting couple bowed to them and they sailed on down the path. Eight more identical figures followed and a ninth, having retreated to make sure that the building was empty, closed the oaken door and joined them.

Wykes suppressed a giggle before it could become audible.

'Like peas in a pod.' He whispered. 'Fascinating. Don't tell me you can spot one of these rooks from the next.'

'I can't. Others are dealing with the problem.'

At the field end of the path, where a lichgate marked the entrance, the Brethren of St Athanasius were halted and a voice called sharply.

'One at a time. The rest of you stand still.'

Facing the group were three men, two with hands thrust significantly into outer pockets which were pushed forward: grim, thick-set figures in drab suits, deliberately anonymous, unmistakably menacing. The third stood apart, two paces behind. It was Moryak.

Of all the company in the unlikely setting he appeared the most incongruous: only the flecks of mud on his shoes proved that he was not an illusion, something transferred by a miracle from the centre of a foreign capital.

One of the grey men gestured to the Archimandrite. 'You first.'

The command produced no movement. A cock pheasant in the wood cackled hysterically, hurtled into the air and was gone, emphasizing the remoteness of the countryside. The couple with the child drew closer, curious and as yet unalarmed.

Strong arms gripped the priest, jerking him forward face to face with Moryak.

'Not him. But each of them in turn. They will all remain until I say.'

The examination was conducted in complete silence and without any further show of force. Moryak scrutinized each quizzical but submissive face in turn, once removing the black cylindrical hat from the head of a shorter member of the sect and walking round him as if he had been a wax dummy displaying a garment for sale.

Two men emerged from the churchyard and joined the inquisitors, waiting until Moryak had completed his inspection.

'Well?'

'Nothing there. The other door is locked. They all came out by the front.'

Campion and Wykes had been standing between the cypress trees in full view of the search. Moryak strode towards them, a henchman on either side. His voice had the quality of bitter aloes.

'You are curious allies,' he said. 'It makes me wonder why you are sharing secrets. Even so, you have not been quick enough. You are unlikely to answer me so I will give you an instruction. You will remain here for an hour under guard and after that if you are wise you will abandon your intervention and go back to wherever you came from.'

He turned abruptly.

'Jan, you will see that they speak to no one. Max will herd these creatures back to their barracks, using the car with the man and his wife and child. They may go when you have finished with it. The rest of us will move ahead to the house, except for my chauffeur, who will stay here and keep in touch from my own car. Do you all understand?'

Mr Campion found himself looking into the frightened eyes of two bewildered parents.

'What are they talking about? Are they policemen?'

'In a way. I should do as they say.'

The procession moved off in single file, the lesser brethren balancing grotesquely on ladies' bicycles, which accommodated the skirts of their cassocks. The Archimandrite, sitting aloof and dignified in a car nearing vintage status, was the last of the monks to leave, followed at a snail's pace by the family and their escort. As they moved up the track and were lost behind the curve of woodland, Mr Campion sighed.

'I feel old,' he said. 'Perhaps we might sit down.'

Wykes looked about him.

'There's a bench in the porch. Picturesque, but draughty. Personally, I'd like to smoke and stretch my legs. I suppose that's asking too much?'

The guard addressed as Jan had an unreal mid-Atlantic accent, suggesting that he had learned his English from American tutors. He stood before them, the gun no longer in his pocket but pointing openly at Campion.

'Perhaps,' said the thin man diffidently, 'we can compromise. We walk to that heap of planks and smoke without the suspicion of sacrilege.'

The minutes tiptoed by in air which was now still as a vacuum. Presently a jay chattered in the wood and was answered by the threats and calls of smaller birds. A church clock in the valley struck the hour of one and was emulated long after from a distance only just within earshot. Mr Campion stubbed out a cigarette and yawned.

'This time,' said Wykes, 'have one of mine.'

He placed a hand in his inner breast pocket, withdrew it and fired in a single movement which was so rapid that the shot was echoing down the wood almost before the man facing them dropped his gun and reeled forward clasping his right arm. He pitched on to the grass, blood spurting between his fingers.

Campion retrieved the weapon, considered flinging it into the undergrowth but changed his mind, and slipped it into his pocket.

'Very uncivilized toys,' he said. 'I wondered if and when you were going to use yours. It's been spoiling the line of your jacket all the morning. Do you often carry it with you?'

Wykes grinned. 'You said the party might be tricky. I hate bruising my knuckles – it's bad for my driving. Hideously painful too. If you must know, I've never fired one in anger before, but I'm considered the quickest draw in Shepherd Market.'

The man on the ground whimpered, staggered to his feet and collapsed on to the heap of planks. He was breathing heavily, swaying his body from side to side, his hat pushed absurdly to the back of his head.

'What do we do with him?'

'Nothing,' said Mr Campion. 'You've winged him but it's not fatal. His friend up the road will suspect that something is wrong, unless he's deaf. I think we should be on our way.'

He walked over to the Lancia and climbed into the luxury of the bucket seat. The figurine had vanished. As Wykes opened his own door Campion turned to him, offering the key.

'That was very good shooting.'

The driver shrugged his shoulders.

'I'm like you – I take precautions. A belt with my braces. You could hardly go telling tales on a friend who's got you out of a tight corner.' He moved the car forward. 'Fasten your own belt. I'm going to step on it.'

'Not yet. Take it easy until we're around the corner.'

'And risk being potted at?'

The question answered itself. As they turned from the churchyard on to the main track a man came running. Wykes accelerated, driving directly at him before making a split second swerve which forced him to leap sideways, lose his balance and sprawl.

'Dead slow as we pass our friend the Jaguar,' said Mr Campion. 'I may not be quite such a good marksman as you.'

They drew level at a crawl and he leaned from his seat, pulling the squat little weapon he had acquired from his pocket. He fired twice, placing each shot accurately in the wall of the front tyre.

'That should free us from unwanted followers. Twenty miles an hour is fast enough in narrow lanes in my exhausted state.'

Wykes looked at his watch.

'If we push along,' he remarked, 'we could still make the Bull at Long Melford in time for lunch. Delicious. I've done all you asked – and more. I have an urge for a very large dry martini which won't be kept waiting. You don't have to join me, if you're feeling waspish.'

He made a racing turn at the gate and plunged into the gully leading to the metalled road.

'You're still under orders.' Mr Campion's

voice was authoritative. 'And you'll stop before you reach the corner. I don't mean slow – stop and switch off. *Now.*'

Wykes braked so abruptly that the car slid forward a dozen feet, the tyres swearing against the affront. He was frowning like a petulant child and angry with himself for being forced into an amateur's performance.

'For God's sake, why?' he demanded. 'If you've made a muck of things, it's hardly my fault. Don't take it out on me. I want some lunch, if you don't.'

'Because,' said Mr Campion, 'I rather think we have a passenger in the back seat. So far he's had a most uncomfortable trip.'

20

The Unconverted

The object crouched behind the bucket seats, once exposed, moved in a series of jerks, each evidently calling for an effort.

At first it suggested a dusty black sack containing a bolster which had been wedged into an inadequate space. It unfolded slowly to reveal a pair of none-too-clean hands, followed by the dome of a forehead set above a bearded face in which white teeth gleamed in a seraphic smile.

'Mr Kopeck, I believe? Or have you become Brother Vassily?'

The little man made an attempt to stand, tottered for a moment and subsided into the rear seat. He was blinking in the bright sun, breathing in quick shallow gasps.

'How to say thank you? This is a great mystery to me. Perhaps I will find words when there is life again in my feet.' He stretched a leg tentatively and winced at the pain.

'No. I am not a true religious. My mother would have told me to thank God for it. Had I not been playing truant I would have missed you. I was watching from the scaffolding on the Church so I received your signal and saw my peril from a distance. My little frog has brought me good fortune.'

He turned to the handful of putty on the seat beside him and caressed it with a grubby finger.

'A good-luck piece? *Porte-bonheur?* Mascot – that is the word?'

Wykes interrupted.

'I don't find it wildly healthy here. Too much cover in the hedges for my simple taste. When can I say good-bye?'

The Lancia whispered into life and began to glide down the slope.

'Long Melford and food,' said Mr Campion. 'At a guess we have an hour in hand before the hunt is up.'

The appearance of a bearded monk in a hostelry crowded with Sunday lunch visitors made very little impact. A Rural Dean dealing delicately with a glass of Benedictine in company with a gaitered Archdeacon nodded as to a fellow of the cloth and raised his eyebrows by a fraction at the mud which spattered the cassock, but for the rest of the assembly the presence of the most publicized fugitive in Christendom passed unnoticed.

Kopeck surveyed the room, savouring the atmosphere of cooking and comfort. He gave a sigh of pure happiness.

'My good friend Bertie – that is to use your *aristo* name if it is permitted – this is like an answer to prayer. It ought to convert me, after so many hours spent on my knees. I should think of these things, like a pagan finding philosophy in middle age, but my inside does not permit. For nearly six weeks I have lived on cabbage water, turnips, potatoes, bread and the fragments of most unpleasant stewed mutton. My mother was devout and I have a brother who defected to the Church and so was lost to my world. But poverty, the poverty of the peasants of Gorky and Dostoyevsky, is not to my taste. Yet I had sanctuary, so may God forgive me if I complain.'

He crossed himself.

'You find me blasphemous? The opiate of the people is offensive to me in theory but strangely attractive in practice. It is an easy habit to acquire.'

'A T-steak,' suggested Mr Campion. 'And burgundy to wash it down?'

'I am in your hands.' A smile followed unexpectedly by a blush flickered and vanished. 'I am like a baby. I have no money, no independence and very little information. With the brethren life is hard. No newspapers, no radio, a common pause which is empty for worldly needs, no contact with life.'

'Not even a copy of *The Alembic?*'

'I am Kopeck without a kopeck – a joke from my childhood has come true.'

Wykes leaned forward. He was half-way through his third martini and his eyes were bright.

'Fascinating. Out of touch – total purdah – for all this time?'

Kopeck wagged his head. 'I remained curious. Many things – terrible soap and cheese which tasted of the same nature – came to us wrapped in newspaper and when my beard had grown a little I was permitted as far as the church on a bicycle. Grigor, the Archimandrite, who was born in Kiev, like my father, was protective to me but he lives like a man on a tower, looking at the clouds and the distance, but never towards the ground. I am sad for him – I am what you would call a dead loss. He hoped to save my soul, which he believed in, by bringing down my body which he concealed from several inquirers but did not think of any real importance. I had almost forgotten butter as a delicacy. May I ask for another dish?'

He ate with concentration until a steak, a suet pudding and a camembert had vanished, nodding acknowledgement whilst Campion sketched the history of the search as described by the Press.

The picture, inhibited by the presence of Wykes, was incomplete but the little man did not ask for enlightenment.

'So, I am famous – infamous – notorious,' he said at last. 'A *veyoerr*, a criminal – a spy. It was to be expected.' He turned to Campion. 'I have wasted a great deal of time, but if Comrade Moryak has his way I have also wasted my life. Something remains to be done. You came to help me and not to hand me to your own Politburo?'

'I came because you asked me to help Lottie.'

'And now?'

'Now we must hide you again. That can be arranged, I hope. How long do you think you will need?'

'I must make a contact – a negotiation.' He glanced towards Wykes, who was watching curiously from behind a glass of cognac, and returned to his host.

'Even from you I wish to keep a secret. If I speak too soon then I have lost half my battle. Also what the good Grigor would call my soul. Where can I go?'

Mr Campion rose to his feet.

'To see an old friend,' he said. 'The hour is up.'

Outside the multi-shelved concrete cupboard in which ten thousand Londoners appeared to keep their cars Wykes halted the Lancia. He had not spoken during the journey. Kopeck, sitting beside him, his head only just above the dashboard, had been muffled by a balaclava helmet in the unlikely partisan colours of Club de Vitesse de Reims.

The driver turned to Campion as he paused for a moment at the head of the ramp. He was pleased with himself, glad to be finished with his passengers and exerting all his charm. 'I've a terrible memory,' he said. 'Infuriating at times – so convenient at others. I hope you suffer from the same complaint?'

'I remember bargains and I keep them. To seal this one, here's some advice before you go, a little something as a souvenir.'

'No ten bob towards the petrol?'

'I'm afraid not.' Mr Campion was prepared to be charming, too. 'It's about your mechanic friends, Parmilee and Smeaton. Don't inquire about their adventures last night – they wouldn't know what you were talking about. Bad for your image to look a chump in front of them, don't you think?'

Wykes frowned, took in the implication and reacted with uncharacteristic sluggishness.

'You invented that tale? I thought I worked for the biggest twister in creation, but you...'

Mr Campion eyed him affably from above his glasses.

'I made a logical inference. It's open to others to do the same if they get around to it, so don't push your luck too hard. Make sure that Denmark Holdings get the message – word for word, if your memory runs to it. You'll find quite a lot of it on your tape. Good-bye.'

They watched the tail lights of the Lancia vanish into the mist which was already swathing the city in opaque gloom.

Kopeck made a remarkable figure in his black cassock and woollen cap surmounted by a scarlet bobble, clasping the putty frog with both hands. He suggested a Russian toy, something from Noah's ark carved for a Tartar's child.

'Please, where now?'

'A taxi,' said Mr Campion. 'Just in case our friend hasn't learned his lesson. My own car doesn't live here. We'll pick it up at a garage down the road, where I can telephone to warn your host of our arrival.'

The journey across London and south to Sussex and the Downs was sedate after Wykes's professional wizardry in an open car, but infinitely more comfortable. Kopeck dozed, his breath filtering damply through beard and muffler.

Beyond Lewes they turned into lanes, climbing and twisting until a final curve through laurels and beech brought them to the gravelled forecourt of a white villa with a lighted porch.

L.C. Corkran was waiting in the doorway, his appearance, as ever, suggesting an officer who had momentarily donned a shooting jacket in place of a tunic.

Campion made formal introductions.

'Mr Kopeck joined me without the opportunity to pack. Perhaps tomorrow he could abandon his robes for something less conspicuous?'

'*Dobriy vyecher,*' Corkran made the words sound as if they were one of his habitual tags. 'I'm afraid that is almost the limit of my Russian.'

He led the way to the long room with the picture window, now curtained and firelit.

'There is cold beef, or a bird, and some respectable claret. A good host would have vodka to offer, but I have a few of the alternatives. As for kit–' He surveyed his guest speculatively. 'You present a problem. Perhaps my housekeeper, a man of resource,

272

can help us.'

'I am always a little ridiculous,' said Ko-peck. 'Please to forgive.'

Within the hour he was in bed and before midnight his gentle snores were assuring the guardian sitting in the passage outside his room that all was well. For the fourth time the man examined the mechanism of the snub-nosed pistol which had been given to him and settled to a vigil eked out with a flask of black coffee and the Sunday Press. After many weeks there was no mention of Kopeck. In Tchervignia the President of a state which was beginning to show signs of insurgence had locked himself in his bath-room and opened the veins in his wrists.

The view from the long window had become flat, an exercise by an eighteenth-century water-colourist in an austere mood. Gulls, wheeling like confetti caught up by a gust, showed that behind a belt of oak across the vale there was a ploughman on the weald. The lawn had grown its winter coat and was untidy with leaves and fallen twigs.

Corkran striding across it with a twelve-bore under his arm and a golden spaniel at his heels, left his trail as he bruised the grass in which the frost still lingered. He came briskly into the room to find Mr Campion watching Kopeck finish a considerable breakfast.

He had trimmed his beard to the proportions affected by British and Russian royalty at the turn of the century and was wearing a blue pullover several sizes too large, giving him a nautical air which was contradicted by the childlike *naïveté* of his eyes.

'No visitors during the night?' inquired Mr Campion.

'Not a trace. Complete security for the time being, though how long that will last is dubious. Now, Mr Kopeck, you must make some concessions if we are to help you. I have no official standing any longer but we must have some idea of what you are up to.'

He waited for his guest to empty his cup before continuing. 'Campion may have told you that we found parts of a message you seem to have been preparing when you were at Baxstable – some sort of broadcast – a warning which your conscience told you must be made. If you want publicity it can be arranged on a world-wide scale if the matter is truly important. Broadcasting, the Press, television, translations into every tongue. But before then we have to know what it is all about. I hope that is clear?'

Kopeck sighed. In his outsize garments he appeared shrunken and slightly pathetic.

'Oh, yes. It is a matter of saving many lives. You are thoughtful for me – and very kind. But first I must make my contact. Would like to do that – how to say? –

privately. Without embarrassment?'

'With Farthing Enterprises?' suggested Mr Campion.

The eyes became round with surprise touched with regret.

'You know of them? Of him?'

'I intercepted a signal from him in *The Alembic*. He refused to speak to me. "Face to face or not at all" – that was his message.'

'It is not surprising. We had to be most careful. I impressed that upon him and I think he understood. There was some danger and he did not wish to he involved.'

Corkran looked at his watch.

'Ten o'clock. If he's anywhere in England we could have him here today. Would that suit?'

'It would be wonderful. He sent me that message, you know – a little code, so to say – between us, but I could not answer. I had to keep my freedom but found I could only do this by losing it – a small joke, but I could not smile at it. The good brothers took all I possessed and gave me my life in exchange. I did not want to carry my troubles into their house, to cause them danger. Please to understand.'

'We see your point,' said Corkran dryly. 'But the position has now changed. Who is this contact – the man you call Farthing Enterprises? His name? Address? Telephone number?'

Kopeck was not happy. He drooped in his chair, avoiding their eyes by looking out over the garden.

'He may not wish to come, to make himself known in front of witnesses. If I could speak to him...?'

'If he can be reached by telephone, of course you can talk to him. Tell him that we can bring him here quite unofficially and in complete secrecy. All you have to do is to make a rendezvous. But first we must have his name. You do appreciate that?'

Corkran was wrinkling his nose and raising alternate eyebrows, a sure indication that he was irritated. His voice had become colourless and even more pedantic than usual. 'You do appreciate that?' he repeated.

Kopeck sighed.

'He may not be pleased,' he said. 'He is not – how shall I say? – polished. But I have no choice. I am in your hands. Please to be very careful – tactful – with him.

'Name. Address. Telephone number.'

'His name is Lawn. Ronald Lawn. He lives at Thursby, which is so close to Birmingham and not very nice. At this hour he will be at work. The name of the business house is hard for me to remember, but I do not write anything down which could be found if it should happen that I have a misadventure.' He hesitated and closed his eyes. 'Mimms – yes, Mimms, Curfew and Jackson. The number I do not know. Please, when you find him, do not give my name until I can speak myself. I will ask him to come.'

Corkran stood up, straightening his back.

'Understood. It may take half an hour or so. If you want to stroll around, don't go too far. Albert, perhaps you'll show him the estate?'

By eleven o'clock the charms of a November garden were beginning to pall, in Mr Campion's opinion. It is the unhappiest season of the year in England, not yet lusty winter, but chilly with decay which offers no promise of rebirth. He admired giant chrysanthemums on disbudded stems in a miniature conservatory, helped himself to an apple from an outhouse store and ruined the appearance of his shoes in damp grass. Far below them smoke from a bonfire carpeted the valley and the gulls continued their clamour.

Kopeck had become shy, withdrawing himself as a companion by devoting his attention to the spaniel who had accompanied them out of the courtesy which he felt should be extended to guests. The dog was delighted and clearly surprised to find someone prepared to take an interest. He retrieved sticks, sought out better examples to improve the proceedings and professed himself to be astounded when his new friend made interesting objects disappear by simple conjuring.

'Elevenses?' suggested Mr Campion. 'There will be coffee and biscuits, if I know Elsie, and possibly a *fino*.'

Kopeck flung a piece of wood into the shrubbery. 'At last I have eaten enough. I am a free man and not on my knees or peeling potatoes as I have been at this hour for many weeks. And I have a new friend. For the moment this is enough.'

The thin man returned to the house to find the living-room empty. Coffee was on the table and he drank in silence only broken by happy canine applause from the far end of the garden. A clock dawdled towards noon and he wandered into the hall to find his host standing in the doorway of his study, one eyebrow contracted in a frown. He jerked his head towards the garden.

'He's happy, is he? It's more than I am.'

'A little local difficulty?'

'Come in here.' Corkran indicated the inner room and sat down. 'I don't like this at all. This chap has been carrying his *sancta simplicitas* to the point of childishness ever since he arrived. He's either obstinate or stupid or both – it remains to be discovered. You never know with Russians. That is not the point. I've been investigating his friend Lawn and the information is disturbing.' He glanced at some notes.

'Ronald Chester Lawn. 31. A PhD in chemistry. Redbrick. Married, two children.

Separated but not divorced. Works for these people Mimms, Curfew and so on, who are a research division of J.B.D., who in turn are part of the United World Group – taken over last year.'

He looked up. 'I got all this stuff so quickly because he's a known security risk – on the list. This explains why he didn't get a better job with his qualifications, which seem to be good. As a student he was a ticket-holding party member, though he doesn't appear to have paid his dues since he married, eight years ago. Not active in politics now, but several of his friends are. The infection may be latent. Our people – Simpson remembers him – say he's an uncertain-tempered fellow with a chip on his shoulder, as most of them are. He's reported to be a considerable womanizer with a succession of mistresses. He was screened when he applied for a job with J.B.D. and turned down because of their government contracts. They planted him where he could be useful but out of the danger zone. It puts a rather different complexion on the whole affair.'

Mr Campion digested the announcement.

'He's interested in money,' he said at last. 'That fact should go into the bag along with the others. He wants cash in return for a service and presumably he wants it in negotiable form handed to him under the counter. He also has a suspicious nature. Have we spoken to him?'

'We have not. And for an excellent reason. He has disappeared. On Friday night he paid his bill, rather a large one it seems, at the private hotel where he lives, packed a bag with a few things and said he might be gone some time. Mimms and Co. had the same message. They can't help us and they seem rather angry about the whole business. So am I.'

'Frustrating.'

'An understatement. But that is not all. Ten minutes ago I had a more significant caller, ringing, he said, from London. Moryak.'

Mr Campion sat down, took off his spectacles and began to polish them.

'That was pretty speedy. What does he want?'

'In point of fact, a word with you. I did not admit that either you or our guest were here but I offered to get a message to you. It was perfectly reasonable to suppose that we might be in touch.' The flicker of a memory which was not entirely amusing crossed his face. 'I happen to know Moryak rather well – that is to say, I know all there is to know in one respect and nothing in another. I would describe him as a computerized chess player, particularly strong in his use of pawns.'

'Is he enjoying this particular game?'

'It would appear so. He was behaving very

confidently, very correctly, rather as one plenipotentiary to another. He sounded pleased with himself and it's not hard to guess why. He makes an offer which is difficult to refuse. The position does not attract me. I must tell you at once that I have accepted it – subject to certain conditions.'

'He wants to talk?'

'He has a proposal. He would like a conversation with Kopeck – an hour, he suggested, would be enough. After that he guarantees to withdraw his forces, create no diplomatic fuss, and allow Kopeck to retire, if he wishes to, back to the U.S.S.R. or anywhere in the free world.'

'Does he, now? You said you made conditions?'

'Oh, yes. I was quite specific. We name the rendezvous and he comes alone. You and I are present and the conversation is in English. We will also have a man of our own with us as an interpreter in case there are any asides.'

'And he agreed? He must have a very strong card or be thinking of selling a pawn for a knight, if we keep to your metaphor.'

Corkran snorted, a wry sound which was nearly a laugh.

'That is patent. The pawn is probably this fellow Lawn, who sounds to me if he had defected or was thinking of it. The knight is Kopeck. Having seen him, I wonder if he is

281

worth taking – yet he must be the *spolio optima*.' He smiled. 'This is prejudice. I find him unattractive. Moryak thinks him worth it. He's been to a lot of trouble and risked his own diplomatic skin. He would be acting on instructions from very near the top.'

'Whatever Kopeck has to say it isn't likely to be some simple thought like "God is Love and Mind the Step".'

'For that reason I have committed ourselves and our guest,' said Corkran dryly. 'Your share of the business is to make sure that he cooperates. Assure him of his personal safety. By the way, we shall have a strong escort, so there will be no tricks. But we want a helpful Kopeck, not an obstinate mule who is pursuing some private ambition armed with good intentions.'

'He may take some persuading.'

'You think so?' Corkran rubbed his nose. 'I also formed that opinion. I shall be absolute, possibly a little brusque – you will be persuasive. Conquer by force and guile. Caesar should have said that but I fancy it was Machiavelli. An unsavoury method but the only one my profession has taught me.' He stood up. 'I'm in the mood for my driest sherry.'

From the picture window Kopeck was visible, sitting at the distant edge of the lawn on a teakwood bench in earnest discussion with the spaniel. Mr Campion sipped without true enjoyment: the *fino* was remarkably sharp.

'How much does the Department know of all this?' he inquired.

'Officially, nothing – unofficially, everything. For the time being I have a free hand. Big brother watches.'

'And the rendezvous?'

'Tomorrow at six. At the Turrets, by the way. There is still a security guard there – reinforced after an episode on Saturday night. It seemed appropriate and Charlotte Cambric will be gratified.' He scowled towards the garden, one eyebrow raised. 'One of the reasons why I dislike that little man is that he gets on so well with my dog.'

21

Conference

'That satanic creature,' said Miss Charlotte Cambric, 'can wait in the library. Albert, if you and Elsie keep him cooling his heels for less than an hour I shall regard you both as very bad tacticians.'

Her welcome had been as warm as the glow radiating from the fireplace of the Great Hall where they were standing. She was wearing her business tweeds and had recovered most of her vivacity. An elm log from the fallen giant which now lay dismembered in the forecourt sizzled and spat in the cavernous recess, throwing sparks into the updraught, making the scene as unreal as a Christmas card. She held Kopeck at arm's length, her eyes glistening.

'Vassily, dear man, I'm so delighted and relieved to see you – even in that ridiculous beard. You've lost weight – or is it that your clothes fit you for once?'

For the first time during a day of interminable embarrassments he smiled.

'They are very new. Perhaps not so good as Russian tailoring for a *toton* – a teetotum – like me. So, if you can laugh a little at my absurdity, I may be easier to forgive. So much trouble I bring you – yet it is not over. Moryak is not acceptable, which I comprehend. I asked that it should be differently arranged.'

Corkran's attempt at jocularity deceived no one. He spoke like an actor who did not believe in his lines. 'This is home ground, isn't it, Lottie? Better to offer an opponent the least possible advantage. We want to win with the minimum of risk.'

Kopeck took her hands, clasping them tightly in his. 'He does not understand,' he said. 'I do not want winners or losers. Comrade Moryak is a patriot in his own way. He

284

is like a machine which has no good manners and cold blood in the veins but in many things we agree. How could it be otherwise? We are both of the same world. I will listen to what he has to say and hope for a good arrangement.'

He looked towards Campion, his eyes imploring and unhappy. 'I hope so much that you will feel with me?'

Miss Cambric had not expected the tension which made the air heavy with impending storm. She braced herself to deal with the situation and gathered the three men in a single gesture.

'Felix is in the morning-room waiting to meet you. He is mixing something special for Vassily and you two will have to put up with whisky.'

'Our interpreter.' Corkran was unbending. 'He is fluent enough, I understand, and he has no great love for the emissary. Whatever Mr Kopeck feels my own view is that we may be glad of an ally.'

Campion was not at ease. In his opinion Corkran had been mishandling the situation all day and he was cold despite the second welcome of more blazing logs in the grate beneath one of Landseer's bleaker Scottish stag-haunted glens. A silence born of frayed nerves and permutated inhibitions settled on the room.

Kopeck walked to the window and pulled

back a curtain, his face averted; he had not touched Perdreau's offering. Corkran contracted an eyebrow and made clicking noises with his tongue. Campion looked at his watch.

'I think we should be foolish to delay the proceedings, Lottie. Stage fright is a catching complaint, don't you think? Is there still a Burbage in the house to tell us when he arrives?'

'The man Carpenter is lurking somewhere but he refuses to dress properly now that I have no guests. Since you don't really want your drinks you may as well go up and face the interview.' She turned her head. 'He's here, isn't he, Felix?'

He nodded. 'His car came round to the porch just as you walked into this room. Carpenter will take him to the library, which is infernally cold despite our efforts. We'll go to the master's study next door and send for him when we're ready. The scene is set and I thought that piece of stage management justified.'

His choice of setting could not be faulted, for the room was one of Sir Edwin's successes as a designer. The original owner, in the Solomon J. Solomon version of 1898, looked down arrogantly from above an Adam fireplace and the bookcases in walnut and glass were not overwhelming.

Corkran placed himself at the head of a

leather-covered Georgian table with Ko-peck on his right, Campion on his left. An armchair, low and immobile, squatted some distance away, awaiting the visitor.

Moryak came in from the double doors of the library, his appearance bringing, as it always did, a sense of chill formality, a bleak smile tightening his lips. He ignored Per-dreau's gesture and pulled a small chair to the table opposite Kopeck.

'If you please,' he said. He sat down, hav-ing established a position of authority, ap-parently without giving the matter a passing thought. He had been carrying a black briefcase which he placed before him.

'If you please, we will have no prelimin-aries. An interpreter is quite unwanted and I will speak only to Comrade Kopeck. He has made this discussion necessary by his own conduct and I ask for no conversation with any other person.'

He looked directly across the table.

'It is quite clear to me and to my Embassy that you have information about a step forward in human knowledge – a discovery made by Soviet scientists – and that you feel this information should be given to the less politically advanced section of the world. It is not a discovery in which you were in any way concerned, so the information has been passed to you by disruptive elements within our country, the so-called intellectuals, most of whom have the mentality of spoilt children. They are dangerous friends because they have no understanding of problems outside their own small circle. Their opinions are not important. They are not the voice of the Soviet but of a tiny clique without root or following. Yet you have listened to them.'

His fingers were touching the table and he tapped sharply on the surface.

'You accept this?'

Kopeck was looking beyond him, apparently concentrating on the books lining the farther wall.

'I hear you.'

'Very well. Consider now what will happen if this information gets into the wrong hands. Death – many deaths – can be the only result. If this secret, so you call it – this discovery – can be controlled, it can be used for the advancement of our people. It may be shared, perhaps, when the time is right but that is not today. If it is given to every capitalist with a profit motive, to every criminal who cares to make use of it, it could destroy a generation. You would be releasing a plague for which there is no remedy.

'Have you measured this against your own vanity?'

Again he tapped the table and waited.

'I have thought for a long time,' said Kopeck meekly. 'That is why I am here.'

Moryak continued, his voice as impersonal

as a prosecutor reading a summary of evidence.

'I now speak of the man Lawn, with whom you are known to have had contact. It is logic to suppose that he has been engaged in work for you which I think is the illicit manufacture of this product. This could be called criminal, for it is the result of theft, whatever the motive.

'Unfortunately for your vanity, your *petit bourgeois* idealism, your obstinacy, this man is not entirely a tradesman, a capitalist lackey, as you have assumed. He has now asked for my assistance as a comrade and you will be unable to reach him. He is a man of some brilliance. His skill has been frustrated by reactionary prejudice and he is no longer prepared to have any dealing with you. If you were counting upon him then I must tell you that you have been wasting your effort.'

For the first time he turned to Corkran.

'This is the fault of your counter intelligence system. The man has been degraded and his skill allowed to waste. He is now what you would call part of the brain drain for he is no longer in this country and unlikely to return. In the Soviet Union we honour our scientists – we do not suspect and insult them.'

Corkran ignored the thrust. 'Have you anything further to say?'

Moryak straightened his back, opened his

briefcase and took out a long white envelope with a cipher in one corner which he pushed towards Kopeck.

This is from Comrade Zhukovsky, who is known to you at least by name. If you will read it then you can pass it to the interpreter. In case his knowledge of our tongue is not so complete as he pretends, I have made my own translation.'

He produced a single sheet and began to read.

'If Comrade Vassily Kopeck is prepared to return immediately to his country and to continue his work in his own section, any errors of thought or conduct will be overlooked. He will be promoted in his own department and given control of all equipment for research into solar radiation, with authority to make such extensions and additions as he approves. His memorandum and recommendations dated January of this year will be accepted in full. As a Director of Projects he will be answerable only to the Praesidium.'

'It is signed Zhukovsky, Supreme Director of Science, U.S.S.R.

'Mr Interpreter, is that a correct translation?'

Perdreau took the document and read it slowly.

'It is perfectly accurate. I have no idea

whether it is genuine or written in your office. That seems a question for others to decide.

Kopeck shook his head, dismissing the suggestion.

'I know the signature. I have seen it many times before in my work.' His face was expressionless, his eyes fixed once more on the far wall.

'This is a terrible choice. There is so much that I could do.' He turned to Moryak. 'Did you know that I was taught to pray when I was in hiding? That is what I should be doing now – praying to a God in whom I do not wholly believe.'

Moryak contemplated the man in front of him as if he was a specimen due for dissection.

'You have an alternative. You can stay here with ignominy and rot until your name is only an unpleasant memory. But many people will die if you choose that course. Other traitors will pay for your bad faith. You will also be letting loose a peril which it will not be possible to contain. I can offer no further advice.'

He held out his hand to Perdreau, who was holding the letter, placed it directly in front of Kopeck and produced a passport, air line tickets and a sealed envelope from his briefcase, setting them out in sequence, one by one, like a winning hand of cards.

291

'I cannot give you more than five minutes for your prayers or the searchings of conscience. My instructions are to report within the hour. After that...'

He left the sentence unfinished. A long silence settled on the room, sharpening the ear for distant sounds within the house: footsteps, voices, insistent words that could not be defined.

A knock on the double door to the library made each man start and turn his head.

Carpenter, his face wooden but his eyes mutinous, came in and spoke in an audible whisper to Campion.

'A young man outside is asking to speak to you, sir. He insists it is very urgent indeed or I shouldn't have bothered you. Miss Cambric said if I didn't interrupt she'd do it herself. He says his name is Rupert.'

22

Decision

Miss Perdita Browning was standing in front of the Italian marble overmantel in the library, hand in hand with Rupert, as Campion came towards them, the young man's red hair bringing more warmth to the room than the oil stove which sulked ineffectively in the fireplace.

Very few traces remained of Charlotte Cambric's demure niece who had graced Victorian weekends and guided tourists from original manuscripts to sherry and seed cake. She had become a sophisticated minx who was thoroughly enjoying life, confident in her command of the situation in general and her companion in particular.

Rupert was less assured. He faced the older man anxiously, like a runner who has finished a race but is uncertain of the result.

'Very quickly now,' said Campion. 'This chap Lawn has apparently skipped the country. Did you catch him in time?'

'Oh, yes.' Perdita was delighted with herself. 'Rupert and I dogged him all the way from the bookstall at Liverpool Street that evening down to the dreariest hotel in a ghastly offshoot of Birmingham. You can't have guessed what you were letting us in for or you wouldn't have been so heartless. As for our Ron – Mr Lawn to you – he's a cross between a goat and an educated codfish. I should know – I've been practically sleeping with him ever since I picked him up over a hot coffee yoghurt.' She wrinkled her nose at the recollection. 'In fact, I should be meeting him in Geneva tomorrow morning. Waste of a perfectly good air ticket, but he's not really my type.'

'We had to do it that way,' said the young man ruefully. 'My hair, you know. I'm a bit obvious and there were a lot of characters watching Lawn down their gunsights. I sat around, kept out of the way, and gibbered. Perdita did all the real work – just straight seduction. You said to be damned cautious about keeping in touch but you've been so elusive yourself that I...'

Campion brushed him aside and turned to Perdita.

'Forget it for the moment. You got the parcel – the goods, whatever it is – from him before he went?'

'We did.'

'At a price,' said Rupert. 'That's the catch.'

'Tell me later. The sands are running out next door.'

'Oh, it wasn't my virtue.' Perdita was still on top of the world. 'Just a thousand pounds in spot cash. Ron may be God's gift as a lover-boy but it's the lolly he's really interested in – that and his own skin. *A whole thousand quid.* Lottie's tiara that she gave me for my twenty-first, my overdraft and Rupert's life savings. I hope it's worth it.'

The young man produced a crumpled envelope containing two sheets of paper.

'Not much to look at. Ron says it's a year's work all done on the side with the company's equipment and he nearly killed himself whilst he was at it. Too bad he didn't succeed. Does it mean anything to you? I hope to God we haven't boobed.'

The papers were covered with figures, formulae, instructions in the abbreviated jargon of science, set out boldly in modern handwritten script.

Campion scanned them but they were as meaningless to a layman as a crossword puzzle in Chinese.

'Worth every penny – I hope. I'll know when I see Kopeck's face. Run along and comfort Lottie – and keep out of sight until I give you the all clear. There's just one more fence to jump.'

He returned to the study, his pulse beating uncomfortably and his fingers clumsy as he fumbled at the elaborate brass handles of the doors. Apparently no one had moved an inch in his absence. Corkran sat, one elbow on the table, as if he were posing for a portrait. Moryak's hands were clasped above his briefcase: the ticket, the passport and the letter lay evenly spread before Kopeck, whose head was bowed as he slumped in his seat. Perdreau stood uneasily behind the table, supporting himself on the back of his own chair.

'No decision?'

'Mr Kopeck appears to have one more minute,' said Corkran dryly. 'We are awaiting his pleasure.'

Slowly the little man raised his head. His

eyes were red-rimmed and misery showed in every line of his face.

'Dear Bertie. I wish I could be stronger in my mind.'

Campion crossed to the table, taking a position immediately beside Moryak, almost blocking his view. He swept the documents aside and put down the sheets of paper in their place.

'From Ronald Lawn,' he said. 'A parting gift before he left for a holiday. I hope you understand it.'

There was a moment of absolute silence before the blunt splutter of a log in the fire broke the tension with the impact of a rifle. Kopeck swayed as if he were giddy, gripped the table and bent his head over the lines of figures and symbols. When he looked up he was blushing and his forehead was moist.

'A gift ... from Mr Lawn? It does not seem possible. It is not his *métier* – his style – to make presents. Was it paid for? A lot of money?'

'A fair price.'

He took a deep breath and released it in a sigh.

'Then this is right,' he said. 'Mr Lawn is not honest, I think, in many things, but he would not deceive – cheat – make false pretences – about his work.' He turned to Moryak, his voice no longer hesitant.

'I can give you now your answer. I must

stay here and make what life I can. You will report this defection and I shall be condemned. This I cannot escape.'

A sudden impish smile crossed his face until it became childlike despite his beard. 'For you, too, it will not be easy, *tovarich*.'

Moryak picked up the passport and held it upright at arm's length.

'I ask for the last time.'

'And I do not accept. *Niet*. You have Mr Lawn – perhaps – in exchange for me. It could be that you have made a bargain.'

Corkran intervened. He was utterly mystified and took refuge in seizing on the one aspect which he understood.

'You have had your answer, Mr Moryak. I see no point in prolonging this interview. Our agreement was quite specific. No hounding of Mr Kopeck – no diplomatic protest or unpleasantness on an official level. I think you should now withdraw. No doubt you will wish to make your report.'

He stood up, placing his chair squarely under the table to emphasize the end of the meeting. Moryak, his face as impassive as ivory, swept the documents and passport into his case, snapping the clasp home. Only Kopeck remained seated.

He placed the two sheets of paper side by side, smoothing the creases by rubbing a finger along the folds, and pushed them across the table. The smile was still on his lips, as if he had found the sensation he was creating wholly delightful.

'You have a camera, comrade Moryak? One of those little toys that look so innocent – like a *briquet* or a cigarette case?'

'*Ya nye panima yoo.*'

'He means,' said Perdreau from the background, 'that he does not understand. Nor do I.'

'But it is so simple.' Kopeck opened his hands over the papers, as if he were about to consult a fortune-teller, and turned to Moryak. 'Mr Lawn has not been making anything for me, as you supposed. I made an arrangement with him to do research for which he is qualified. It has been said that he is brilliant but not altogether wisely employed. Certainly he is not well paid. But he has fine equipment in his control and there is no one who can truly say if he is wasting his time or working on problems which are not really his affair.

'So now I have something from him – a formula, as you see – which I wish to be made known. It has been bought from a man who is – how did you say? – asking for your assistance. If he has sold a secret once, then he will certainly sell it again, if he has the chance, and feels himself safe. He has no conscience, I think, except perhaps to his work. If you too buy a copy of this paper from him, or make him reveal it, there will be delay. But if you send a photograph direct to your bureau, then you have an advantage of some hours – perhaps days.' He looked up, anxious now and appealing.

'Mr Moryak has done his best. For him I am a nothing – a failure. This is a small excuse, something for him to show in his defence. You can understand that?'

Corkran was still out of his depth, a condition which shortened his overstrained temper. His lifted eyebrow gave him the surly look of a dog who is suspicious of a command and uncertain of what is required of him. He glared from Campion to the seated figure, finally returning to Moryak with a long speculative stare as if he were trying to force his opponent to lower his eyes.

'The point escapes me,' he said at last. 'You deserve nothing. The meeting should be considered closed. But if Mr Kopeck wants to make you a present I see no point in objecting. His logic can't be faulted, much as I suspect it. I suppose you *do* carry one of those useful Japanese devices about with you? I suggest you get on with it.'

Moryak bowed formally to both men. If he, too, was mystified he concealed the fact. A fountain pen had been projecting from his waistcoat and he took it out, pointing the blunt end towards the papers on the table. He pressed the clip several times, repeating the performance at varying distances.

'This one was made in England,' he said. 'A most ingenious mechanism. It is not quite so good as our own but it has for me a sentimental value as a souvenir, a present. You also have your defectors.'

He bowed again. *'Drobriy vyecher.* I wish you good evening.'

23

The Gift of a Friend

Miss Charlotte Cambric had changed into a high-buttoned dress of grey moiré silk with leg o' mutton sleeves and the suggestion of a bustle. Her eyes were bright as jet and the froth of white hair over her forehead had recovered its natural *élan.*

She stood between the tall doors to the library, holding them apart, scanning her guests, reading their expressions.

'You've won,' she said. 'But you've had a battle. You look as if you've just been acquitted of barratry and you're free men again. My dears, I'm so happy I could dance a fandango. I came over as soon as I heard that Slavonic Mephistopheles leave. It's no good being apologetic, Vassily – the place is sweeter without him.'

Her force recharged the air, infusing vitality after minutes of uneasy reaction.

'Champagne first and then food. I told Perdita and Rupert to put some on ice just in case – I knew in my bones that we'd need it. Albert, if those two aren't engaged they certainly ought to be. I can see it in that young woman's eyes. Without a ring on her finger they're almost indecent.'

She turned to Corkran. 'Elsie, stop looking like the Chairman of the Board and come along.'

'There is some unfinished business, I'm afraid.'

'Then it can wait, Vassily, you've still got something on your mind?'

The shy smile returned, touched with embarrassment.

'It is a little thing. I wonder if I could borrow a book from that case? I know where the key is because I hid it there a long time ago. You permit me?'

He crossed the room, opened a drawer in a writing desk under a green reading lamp, picked out a key and unlocked one of the glass-fronted doors of the long bookcase. From a shelf which was only just within his reach he drew out an elaborately bound volume, displaying it hopefully to his hostess.

'If I could take this with me? Perhaps to the dinner table? Comrade Moryak is so strong as a personality. Whilst he was here I was afraid he could read my thoughts and would guess what I was staring at. Now I would like to keep this close at hand.'

Lottie read the title, her head on one side. *'Archdeacon Cawnthrope's Moral Principles for the Young.* What curious taste you have! He was the rector of Inglewood for many years and a friend of Edwin's. Very dull in the pulpit and most amusing in his cups, I believe. No one will ever read him again, if they're in their right mind, though it might give Perdita something to think about.

'My dear man, you're welcome to it. Tuck it under your arm and come and help me open a bottle.'

She bustled them towards the door, taking Corkran by the elbow. 'When I was a girl the French used to call it "Strangling a parrot". I got into such trouble once for using the phrase in front of their ambassador. I'd forgotten his name was Perroquet.'

Despite her efforts, dinner served by Mrs Faversham was an occasion of stilted silences broken by sorties into small talk which emphasized rather than eased the tension.

Perdita and Rupert were sharing a private world and Perdreau's professional skill was useless in a company absorbed in heavier thoughts. Prudently he made no effort.

Lottie battled against the tide. 'I've changed two pictures,' she announced, gesturing into the gloom beyond the candlelight. 'Frith's companion piece to "Derby Day" – "Oxford Street" has come in to replace one of old G.F. Watts's rather woolly allegories "Myopia with Ennui" and I've brought in Aumonier's "Café Royal". Edwin was very naughty to buy it because it shows several of his friends sitting with entirely the wrong ladies. He had to store it away whenever he had their wives to dine.'

She looked round the table. Mrs Faversham had disappeared, her guests had coffee and port by their places. She was a hostess again, controlling the situation, timing the moment of truth.

'And now,' she said. 'Vassily is going to tell us what this is all about.'

He had been sitting on her right, the volume of essays on the table beside him, taking no part in the conversation. Now he looked slowly from face to face before his eyes returned to the book.

'This I owe to you all,' he said. 'I have thought so much about how to tell what should be told that I am like a cat which chases its own tail. Please forgive. It is a bad matter, not easy to speak of.

'It begins in Kalinin, which is a dull town on the railway between Moscow and Leningrad. There are laboratories there used for research in bio-chemistry – the cure of diseases, and sometimes the creation of them. The scientists, the experts who are the best in the world, work as they are directed, not choosing their own subjects. For me this is sad.

'Like other nations we have a problem of old age. So many people live on when they have become useless and perhaps unhappy in themselves. In a few years the old will outnumber the young and become a burden. How to solve it without unhappiness – without cruelty? In this country there is a word "euthanasia' – peaceful death – which is not well thought of. In the Soviet Union this is differently regarded.

'In Kalinin the experiments were to make a drug which could produce a desire for death, to make the crazy state – euphoria is your name – when to move to a new plane is so attractive that it is not to be resisted. With such a drug death is not something which is accepted with regret or even with a shrug of the shoulders, but an idea which blots out every other desire. At Kalinin they have made such a drug.

'It is not, if you consider, a great wonder. There is already L.S.D. which creates strange illusions, the idea that you can fly or walk on water or think such great thoughts that you can solve the whole riddle of life. This is common to many drugs and the harm is that the riddle remains unsolved: in water one will still drown. The drug developed at Kalinin brings all these illusions, but overall there is a desire for death. A man who takes a sufficient quantity feels assuredly that he is God – he has only to rid himself of his body to command every force in nature, to visit the stars, to talk with Chekhov or Shakespeare or to put the world in the order he chooses. Such a little step to so much glory! Each man dies by the way that seems easiest to him. Like many discoveries, it was an accident when it was finally achieved.'

He paused, searching each face, making sure that he had been understood.

'An accident,' he repeated. 'It killed Kireyevski, one of our best scientists, and on the same night three of his students who were subjects – guinea pigs – for testing. After that time there followed other experiments which I do not speak of.'

A candle guttered smokily in the silence and Corkran leaned forward to pinch it out.

'It comes to this,' he said. 'You have a poison which puts a man in a frame of mind to commit suicide. That explains a great deal – though something of the sort had been envisaged. Obviously it has been tried out extensively. Over here, too, it would appear.'

'Oh, yes, it has been used.' Kopeck lifted the book, hesitated and replaced it. 'It has been used many, many times. It is an instrument for murder or for political execution, and in the Soviet such things are controlled by the state.

'That is inevitable. Germ warfare is studied by all nations, even if they do not admit it. With this one reservoirs could be infected, perhaps crops also.

'But there is another side. We know – for people under experiment have survived – that this drug is very attractive to the subject who takes it, just like simple poisons, strong spirits, opium, even tobacco. It makes a craving which becomes a torture if it is not satisfied. An addict who is caught – hooked, you say – on other drugs can find relief in it. Until he kills himself.

'Did you, perhaps, read a story by the English writer Wells called *"The Food of the Gods"*? He was a permitted author in my country, much read when I was a young man. In that fairy tale the accidents were made to happen by the careless handling of a new drug and the vanity of the men who made it. With us it has been much the same. Already there have been mischances, leakages, deaths which were not officially intended. Many students have died through folly. Also what are called intellectuals – some through curiosity, some by official design.

'I am not a chemist and I know only a very little of the subject, but I have many friends in that world. Perhaps that is why they chose me to give the warning to others. They felt that this new peril should be known by people everywhere, not kept as a weapon for the use of one nation. It is like poison gas or the atom bomb – if the secret is known to both sides then it is not likely to be used.

'I wanted to do this for myself and for my friends who gave me the task. Also I wished to speak as a free man, not a traitor to my country who is seeking favours and asking for refuge.'

He turned to Campion. 'You will understand that?'

'I do.'

Corkran had allowed his cigar to go out. He looked regretfully at the stub and abandoned it.

'The heart of the matter is this,' he said. 'You want to broadcast this dangerous information in the hope that by doing so you can invalidate a secret weapon? I – I – what shall I say? I respect the theory but I doubt the practice. In any case the matter would be out of our hands – cabinet level – international–'

His voice wavered and he hesitated, trying to marshal his thoughts, irritated by the difficulties of making himself clear.

'My dear Kopeck, you cannot appreciate what you are saying. You are approaching the problem like a child who thinks he has been given a magic wand. This sort of information will be classified as top secret. It cannot be broadcast like a recipe for cooking a pudding. The possibilities are far too dangerous.

Any bloody-minded government in the world could make use of it. You do see that?'

'I see,' said Kopeck placidly, 'that sooner or later every nation will have this knowledge. But at this time if a body is examined by post-mortem the poison cannot be analysed fully even by the process which is called "thin-layer chromomatography". Long words – I had to learn them by heart. But it is certain that one day an intelligence agent, a spy from your country or America will bring back the drug itself. The chemists will not be a great deal wiser because the process of manufacture is complicated. It is, so to say, compounded of a derivative of a derivative. This is not for me to describe, since it is beyond my education. A new element is created.'

He turned to the book in front of him and drew out a sheet of paper which had been hidden between the leaves.

'This is the key. It was written out for me by my friend Kropotkin, who is now dead. I wish you to take it but it must not be kept for this country alone. If your Politburo think that, then they must hold me in prison or send me back to my own country. I have made other copies, which have other hiding places. I am behaving – being awkward, you will say – for my conscience and for my friends.'

He passed the folios to Corkran, who

turned them over so slowly that the rustle of the paper lingered on the air. Rupert broke the silence. He had been listening intently, one arm round the girl at his side.

'If this is what all the trouble was about, what on earth were Perdita and I doing mucking around with Lawn? What did we get that we paid a thousand quid for?'

Kopeck spread his hands.

'It is so simple. If a good bio-chemist – and Mr Lawn is a very clever man indeed – has the right data to work on, and the modern equipment, then for a toxin he can produce an anti-toxin. For this he must know the process as well as the basic substances of the poison he is combating. Mr Lawn has done this, he says, and he is not a man who would deceive on such a matter. He has many strange ideas for an Englishman but he is top class with his work. He will be a great loss to your industry if Comrade Moryak has his will.

'I did not want to bring only a new way of death from my country. I wished also to offer a remedy.'

24

The Private Party

Mr Albert Campion was standing beside the office window of the Turrets, his attention wandering from the sheet of foolscap in his hand to the scene below.

Thick cables coiled like snakes across the courtyard and the foreshortened figures of men in boiler suits moved expertly among portable arc lamps, microphones, trailing wires, batteries and the whole mysterious paraphernalia of television equipment which was being unloaded from a pantechnicon too large for the gothic arch over the entrance. At the front of the house the last scars left by the fallen elm were being plastered into oblivion and the trunk had vanished.

Lottie found him still immersed in the typewritten phrases which covered the page when she appeared in the doorway some minutes later. She was wearing her unofficial tweeds and her hat was pushed slightly to the back of her head.

'Three days' notice they've had,' she exclaimed. 'Three whole days and they have to leave it until the last minute. *And* an army of men – nearly forty of them – to set up all their lights and camera machinery. Edwin never had anyone to help him except Burbage the First when he made his recordings and he was really very successful. You would think they'd have found out how to simplify matters after seventy years but you'd be quite wrong.'

She sat down, clearing a pile of letters from the blotter on her desk.

'Albert, you look worried. Nothing is going to spoil the broadcast, I hope?'

'Nothing of significance. Vassily may be a little surprised at the statement he's going to make. My job, according to Elsie, is to sell him the idea.'

'But he gets his wish? He'll be allowed to speak freely?'

Mr Campion adjusted his spectacles.

'He's going to have to read a long rigmarole and I hope he can get his tongue round the difficult words. There's a lot of jolly stuff about diethylamide tartrate derivatives and ergot alkaloid compounds acting by competitive inhibition. It doesn't make for light after-dinner chit-chat at the best of times.

'What it boils down to is quite simple though, if not quite what Vassily told us on Monday evening. The diplomatic version goes something like this:

'"Mr Kopeck, acting on his own volition, has decided to present certain scientific formulae to the free world. They are not of detailed interest to the public since they are designed to deal with forms of drug addiction which are not widespread. Mr Kopeck's information will be made available to any nation which may find such a form of addiction appearing amongst the population.

"'The Soviet Government, after due consideration, has approved the release of this information as a contribution to world peace and goodwill, but it does not consider it to be of great importance.

"'Mr Kopeck, also after due consideration, has decided to ask for British citizenship and proposes to make such an application at the first opportunity."

'I hope I'm making myself – and Vassily – clear?'

Lottie pulled off her hat, tossing it on to a filing cabinet. She ruffled her curls and laughed.

'I think it's splendid,' she said. 'I can see Elsie's handwriting all over it. No bones broken, no irritating fuss, no sinister Mr Moryak. And all given out to the world after what pretends to be a cosy little dinner party at my table. My dear, they won't mention the Turrets but I could hardly have better publicity if I'd paid a fortune for it.'

'It's a way of playing the situation down and keeping him out of London, where he'd be besieged. This place is still protected territory, so after Vassily has had his say and been discreetly questioned in the library by an official interviewer he'll be safe from the Press for a week or two at least. Then he can make his fortune from articles and memoirs. I hope so, because he owes me a thousand pounds.'

'Safe as houses.' A thought occurred to her and she rustled through the pile of paper on her desk. 'And that reminds me. Another rude letter from Clifford Denmark this morning. I say rude because his lack of manners gleams right through his typewriter. If he wrote "yours sincerely" one would know it to be an insolent lie. Still, it's wonderful news.'

She passed a sheet to Campion. Messrs Denmark Holdings begged to refer to their communication of 27th September last and to the offer contained therein. In view of the fact that there had been no reply they were assuming that it was not acceptable and it was therefore withdrawn.

'Do you think he means what he says?'

'I think you can count on it. He doesn't want the Public Prosecutor on his tail. The ogre very nearly burnt his fingers so he'll look for other castles to pillage. This one stays with Vassily's fairy godmother.'

The telephone's shrill intervention broke the thread and she lifted the receiver.

'The caviare is on its way? And the smoked

salmon? Thank heaven for that. Tell Mr Mason that if there isn't enough I'll never forgive him. It's a very special occasion ... yes ... very special indeed.'

She rang off and turned to Campion, her eyes bright. 'Very special indeed. When it's all over – the public part, I mean, with the cameras and the statement and the microphones and the interviewers and Freddie Hale from the Home Office to make it official – we'll have our own small private party.

'Coffee and brandy and cigars in the Music Room now that it's straight again. Just you and Vassily and Felix and Freddie Hale and Elsie and Tony Evelyn, who deserves a scoop, and Gerhardt Mond, who's the most discreet gossip in town and the two stars of his next film whose names I forget. And, of course, Rupert and Perdita. He's going to appear as Burbage for the last time, unless that minx can trap him into doing it for life.'

'Any music?' suggested Mr Campion. 'The massed bands of Brigade of Guards, perhaps?'

'Music?' She snapped her fingers. 'We ought to have something rather splendid for Vassily. The trouble is we have so little that is Russian and suitable in our collection. Except, perhaps ... now I come to think of it, there is one little curio he ought to hear. Edwin made the recording in the Winter Palace in St Petersburg when he went to shoot bears with the Czar in 1898 and took him a pair of gun dogs he'd bred.

'It was never allowed to be played in his day – I suspect he'd smuggled it out. It is of Nicholas II himself, who liked cameras and toys of that sort and was fascinated by any new gadget. He's singing a German song, but in Russian and some of the words aren't quite right. Not a good recording, but then he didn't sing very well, poor man.

'It's a song called *"O, Tannenbaum"*.'

'I think,' said Mr Campion, 'that Vassily really would enjoy that.'

The publishers hope that this book has given you enjoyable reading. Large Print Books are especially designed to be as easy to see and hold as possible. If you wish a complete list of our books please ask at your local library or write directly to:

Magna Large Print Books
Magna House, Long Preston,
Skipton, North Yorkshire.
BD23 4ND